OPERATION WIND STORM

Manifest Destiny meets the Green
Revolution

A Zilla Gillette novel

By Lori Townsend

To Emily,
Happy reading!
Love from your Alaska Sister
Lori

Jade Bear Press

PROLOGUE

The blindfold was tight. A spot on her cheek where the black silk bands wound twice around her head was really starting to hurt.

It was pissing her off.

"Really guys? Can you take this off now? It's been what, two hours of this rough, potholed goat path or whatever the hell we're traveling on. There's no way I'm going to know where we are. Just take the damn blindfold off, will ya? My kidneys are flopping around from the road ruts." Zilla Gillette's patience was gone.

The paranoid duo escorting her to the hidden bunker of the GDC followed orders to an exasperating level. Zilla had agreed to be blindfolded on the plane ride then led, clumsily, to a waiting off-road vehicle of some kind. And now a long, rough-ass ride had left her over the experience and wishing she hadn't allowed this.

Besides, she had to pee.

The squeaks and groans of the SUV as it labored over rocks, ruts and roots was the only answer she got. Over it, she reached up and pulled off the black band covering her face. There was a gasp in the cab.

"Ok. Look. Nature calls. Can we stop for a minute and let me out?" Zilla still had her eyes squeezed shut, now against the bright sunlight trying to stab through her eyelids more than a sense of duty to keep from seeing where they were. She rubbed her cheeks where deep red lines crisscrossed.

"What the hell, lady? You said you'd keep that blindfold on. Cook and Ally are going to blow a gasket if we roll up and you're looking around." The young dude's voice was in front of Zilla; she knew he was in the passenger seat. The driver hadn't uttered a word during the entire trip.

"Yeah, well, I gotta pee, buddy, and my face hurts from how damn tight that blindfold was – and look, I still got my eyes closed, ok?"

The Rover slowed to a stop, the labored whine of the transmission replaced by the ticking sounds of a hot engine and drive train. They'd been climbing nearly the entire trip. For the first time, the driver spoke. His voice was deep, much older than the bro tones of the guy in front of her.

"It's ok. We're only about 10 minutes out now. Go ahead, open your eyes and get out for a break. Five minutes and we're leaving again."

Zilla did so slowly, squinting at the bright sunshine streaming into the dusty interior. She rubbed her eyes, massaged her cheeks and looked out the side window, forgetting for a minute her need to step out and get behind a tree for some relief.

They were on the side of a mountain in an enormous and breathtaking valley. Wilderness stretched out as far as she could see. She grabbed the door handle and slid out onto the ground, hearing no other sound than the faint rushing of water from a river far below them. There was no way to tell if she was still in Alaska. They could be in Canada or the Colorado Rockies. She didn't think they'd flown long enough to be in the Lower 48, but being blindfolded had messed with her sense of time and she couldn't be sure.

The Green Defiance Coalition's compound was well hidden and a hell of a long way from any other civilization.

Chapter One

It bloomed on the screen like a big splash of ketchup.

Or blood.

4:40 a.m. - Duty officer Rita Tiegs bolted forward in her chair, shocked by an earthquake of such massive scale. Lukewarm coffee in a tooth-nibbled Styrofoam cup tipped over, narrowly missing her keyboard as it dribbled to the floor.

"Christ!" Tiegs ignored the dripping mess and stared wide-eyed at the system that registered earthquakes through a series of seismographs threaded across Alaska.

She didn't trust her eyes.

Working alone was usually preferable for her, but the quiet of her office in the Alaska Earthquake and Tsunami Warning Center was immediately unnerving. She reached for the phone with an unsteady hand.

Her commanding officer answered promptly. Tiegs suspected the man was nearly always awake.

"Sir? Sorry to bother you so early but we've got a major event registering in the Aleutian Islands."

"Define major," replied Commander Fairchild, typically acerbic.

"I... it's hard to believe, sir, but the monitor shows a quake in excess of 9.6."

"Aw, hell, where exactly?"

"It's a ways out the chain, sir. Amchitka. At least it's not inhabited."

"Tsunami?"

"I see nothing indicated yet. It was very shallow and right under the island."

"Alert the Homeland Security office in Anchorage immediately. I'm on my way in."

"Sir? I don't think a tsunami is imminent. Are you worried about Adak and Kiska residents?"

"No, Tiegs. I'm worried about contract workers on an isolated island staging to remove a shitload of radioactive material that's been in three test wells on Amchitka since the late '60s."

Commander Fairchild hung up without another word.

Rita Tiegs sat back in her chair, confused by the scant information. But orders were orders. She leaned forward and called Homeland Security first, then, after only a brief hesitation, reached again for the phone and called the office of *Anchorage Daily Standard* reporter Zilla Gillette. Rita didn't know Gillette personally but had sort of a crush on the razor-sharp news hawk and knew she would want to hear about this story as soon as she got to her office.

She was surprised and more than a little embarrassed when Zilla answered on the third ring. Her office line forwarded to her cell phone, which was never more than two feet away from her. Even at night, or, as it stood, early in the morning.

"This is Zilla."

There was no hint of sleep in her voice, just like Commander Fairchild. Tiegs stammered, her face red. Thinking of her wife and how she would answer her prying demands if she found out Rita had called another woman in what was essentially the middle of the night.

"Oh, um, hello. I didn't expect to actually talk to you."

"Who is this?" Zilla's voice was impatient.

"I'm... this is officer Rita Tiegs with the Earthquake and Tsunami Warning Center. We've just had an enormous quake under Amchitka Island," she stopped, hesitant, and a little confused about the information she'd just heard from the C.O. and how to share it, or if she should. She didn't need to worry. Gillette was way ahead of her.

"Amchitka? Damn. All that toxic waste."

##

Some would call it serendipity; others would call it spooky cosmic bullshit. Zilla found it both. Writing a lengthy series on Alaska's nuclear bomb history and then having a major earthquake where the radioactive waste was still located in the Bering Sea on a national wildlife refuge was beyond spooky or serendipitous, it was damn crazy.

But that was what happened, and there was no sense in trying to figure out why.

Zilla and her reporting partner Ray Walker were laboring over a deep-dive multi part series chronicling a recent U.S. Supreme Court case against the Department of Defense. This, decades after the Atomic Energy Commission had been abolished.

A coalition of environmental and conservation organizations led by Greenpeace sued the DOD to force clean up of the nuclear mess the feds left on Amchitka Island more than 50 years earlier.

And they'd won.

Zilla and Ray flew to D.C. to cover the trial. It was thrilling to sit high in the reporter gallery, furiously taking notes and listening to the chief justices, perched above the attorneys like wise elders on a mountain, peppering them with questions, barely letting them answer before pouncing again.

It was one of the times Zilla was glad she was a reporter, an observer of the human condition, and not a lawyer getting grilled by some of the smartest minds in the nation.

Greenpeace, once considered one of the more radical environmental groups, had changed track. Known for blocking oilrigs or surreptitiously unfurling protest banners in front of unsuspecting corporate bigwigs, the far-left group now found traction in the courts.

The '70s and '80s marked a divide in the environmental movement. The radicals stayed radical, while part of the movement broke off and retired from what was called monkey wrenching, dangerous direct action like tree spiking to protest old growth logging or valve damage on oil transport pipelines, sometimes resulting in injury or death.

Now, their combat uniform for Mother Earth was a trim suit. Greenpeace leaders wanted nothing to do with the mean-spirited and often violent campaigns of Marcus Peterson.

Peterson had been one of the original founders and was on the Canadian vessel F/V Phyllis Cormack when it made its way to the Aleutian Islands in 1971 to protest and raise international awareness about the nuclear tests the United States military was undertaking on Amchitka Island.

But Peterson had changed. Bitter and angry, he decided he couldn't take on all the injustice being perpetrated against the oceans, so he targeted one group: Native subsistence whalers.

He had been incredibly effective in drumming up financial support for a vicious campaign of hateful rhetoric directed toward small coastal village communities in the United States who continued to hunt for protein as they had for thousands of years. The 'Save the Whales' crowd hated that hunt, regardless of centuries of sustainable use by tribes. Their histrionics fervently backed Peterson's campaign of physical confrontation in the ocean and online harassment, threatening violence against any who exercised their long standing legal rights to hunt for bowhead whales in Alaska waters – or in the case of the Makah tribe in Washington state, gray whales.

Across the nation and the world, money came in to support his efforts to stop the yearly harvests of subsistence whalers. His ego grew with each check and crumpled wad of bills handed to him by people who didn't know about or understand the traditional cultures of coastal Native peoples. All they knew was that Marcus

Peterson was trying to save whales from brutal, senseless slaughter, and they wanted to help.

He was only too happy to take their money for what he saw as a righteous campaign to protect the enormous mammals of the sea. Peterson also despised commercial fishing, but there was too much money backing the fleet and the processors that bought their fish. It was easier for him to bully small communities of quiet, traditional people. They didn't have money to fund protection. Some of the big trawlers had their own security forces that had been known to fire water cannons at Peterson's vessel when media was present and real bullets when media was not. He left them alone.

His rampaging vessel, with bold red letters spelling Sea Goddess across the bow, was also his home. He didn't want it shot up. Marcus Peterson refused to acknowledge the other groups who had invested a lot of money and legal expertise in the fight for cleaning up Amchitka. He claimed the victory for himself and fundraised the hell out of the win. He planned a huge, expensive media event at Amchitka, alerting and inviting every major news outlet, knowing that when the video went viral, so would his bank account. He couldn't know how spectacular, and fatal, the event would be.

Chapter Two

Three months before the monster earthquake chewed Amchitka into rubble, Zilla and Ray were on the expansive steps of the U.S. Supreme Court building, waiting for the lawyers, their clients and accompanying entourage to arrive. It was early on a Tuesday morning, the final day of hearing the case titled Green Defiance Coalition, et al, versus the United States Government and Department of Defense.

The lawsuit had attracted international media and the *Anchorage Daily Standard* reporters had wisely decided if they didn't get to the courthouse early, they'd get smashed up in the scrum and pushed to the back behind cameras, big wooly shotgun mics on boom handles and aggressive cable television producers determined to get the best shot and willing to bulldoze anyone in their way to do it.

"We're like the two little pigs Ray. Way early." Zilla was smiling, holding a paper cup of coffee, steam drifted out of the top in the chilly early spring air.

"Were you up reading Little Golden books again last night Zee?" Ray smiled back over his own cup. They had already snapped a few photos of the Courthouse steps, the tall white columns, an enormous U.S. flag flapping above. Now they were restlessly waiting for the day's events to unfold. Trying not to get too keyed up too early since it was going to be a long day of court proceedings and follow up interviews.

"You know me too well sir. I was thinking we're here before the big bad wolves of syndicated television arrive and try to swallow us whole."

"That ain't happening." Ray sounded sure.

"Unless you're willing to start throwing punches, you can bet it will." Zilla sounded equally sure. "They're going to swarm in here like hornets and bite like fire ants. We're gonna get shoved to the back, but I've been thinking about that." She nodded to one of the numerous officers who strolled back and forth along the upper level and took another sip of her coffee. "I think rather than fight it, we should move to the back because the winners are going to come straight out the front doors but the losers are going to slip out the side and one of us can catch them while the other catches the winners as they work out of the scrum."

"Zee, the justices aren't going to decide today. Just hear the arguments. You know that."

Ray raised his eyebrows at her. A breeze snapped the big flag and clanged its chain against the galvanized pole it was attached to.

"Yeah, I know they won't *say* it today, but I've got a feeling we're still going to *know* today. I don't see how the greenies are going to lose this." Zilla eyed Ray over her cup. "You read the briefs just like I did. Are you telling me you see it going otherwise?"

Ray bent over, put his cup on the concrete step and then stretched his arms over his head. "Yes, I did read the briefs and yes, the case is certainly compelling and appears based on solid legal footing. The U.S. military had legal authority to conduct the tests on Amchitka based on one sentence within the Wilderness set aside legislation that created the refuge in the Aleutians," Ray adopted a lawyerly persona as he recited the back story on the case, "No one disputes that, even though those bringing the case objected to that sentence. They hated it then and they hate it now, but today their dispute is that just like any other Formerly Used Defense Site that the U.S. Government is responsible for, they need to clean that shit up, not rely on the wells to contain the nuclear radiation."

Zilla played along. They were restless. Waiting was familiar torture for reporters and they needed something to entertain themselves.

"Why can't they rely on the wells sir? They were built to last in perpetuity and independent tests of freshwater sources and the ocean waters around the island do show some low levels of radiation but not enough to say conclusively it's from the wells."

Ray opened his mouth to answer but Zilla pressed on, adopting a legal persona. "In fact! In fact good sir, quite the opposite! If the wells were in leaking, the test results would be alarmingly high. The material is encased in concrete. It is stable! And has been for more than 50 years! I rest my case your honors."

Ray took the bait. They were on the steps of the highest court in the country. It was easy to channel his inner attorney. "Objection!"

"You can't object when I rest, dork." Zilla laughed.

"Well, I object anyway! Your honors, the waste material is not stable! It is not secure into perpetuity!" Ray theatrically raised his voice and one of the court officers glanced toward them.

"The Aleutians Island chain is in one of the most seismically active places on earth your honors. A study in 2016 by seismologists determined that the Aleutian Islands face a significant risk of a major earthquake within the next 50 years!" Ray pointed both index fingers straight up to punctuate his final point.

"Ok, settle down Ironsides, this isn't Law and Order and you're going to get us tossed out of here." Zilla was smiling and shaking her head, but she couldn't quite let it go. "How do you determine 'significant' risk? What does that mean and how does it stack up against the risk of problems that could arise, if rather than leave the material where it has securely been for all these decades, it is instead disturbed, opened up and possibly spilled into the ocean in a shipping accident? Have you considered these factors in your calculations of risk?"

Ray picked up his coffee cup, took a sip and squinted through the steam at Zilla. "That's why we won't have an answer today sister."

"We'll know."

"No we won't. Hey, here comes Peterson and his crew.

Below them, down the dizzying number of white marble steps, a line of cars pulled up. The first was a sedate black town car, the others that followed were a photographer's dream of slogan covered Subarus, new electric Teslas and older road warrior type vehicles, including a 1982 Datsun pick up so rusted that its sides looked like pin hole lace. All held together by bumper stickers that adorned far more than the bumpers. Save the Whales! Stop the War! Bring our Troops Home! Build Schools not Bombs! Save the Planet! And a host of others covered all but the windshields and side windows of several of the cars.

Zilla and Ray recognized Marcus Peterson as soon as he emerged from the town car. Tall, thin and with a mass of curly brown hair, he looked like a lanky, aging college student. Others jumped out of the parade of conservation mobiles. Young people with organic cotton shirts and blonde dreadlocks surrounded him as disciples surrounded Moses.

They were the core group of his trusted environmental soldiers. Others were also arriving. Less malleable as green warriors, these were well-dressed citizens driving expensive cars. The case had drawn a lot of attention on both sides and was a gauntlet thrown down between American citizens who wanted to preserve pristine wild places and those who wanted to "drill baby drill."

Development supporters were also arriving. Citizen Hummers in bright obnoxious colors pulled in. Some with Confederate flags painted on the hoods, revved their engines to intimidate the conservation crowd. More than a few wore military themed clothing or other identifiers to let all who looked, know which side they were on. Others wore hard hats and a few carried shovels with signs taped to the handles that said, Don't Lock Up Resources! America First! Energy Dominance Starts Now! The resource extraction proponents saw this case as the tipping point. If a lawsuit brought under the premise that natural places had inherent rights to exist undisturbed or if compromised, had the right to be restored, was successful, their way of doing business was doomed.

This was a line in the sand for both sides.

It had less to do with the concern over nuclear waste than with the concern over the future of unlocking oil, gas, coal and other resources that the shovel crowd was eager to jump on. The conservationists saw it the same way. They were genuinely concerned about the potential for nuclear waste to be dumped into the Bering Sea if an earthquake hit the area, in their minds creating a U.S. version of Fukishima, but they also realized the larger implications. If natural systems could be considered something akin to humans with rights, as corporations now were, and if these systems could win legal and permanent protections against industrial development, it would be a new day for keeping wild places off limits to those who called such protection 'locking up' god given resources.

An enormous black Dodge Ram pick up arrived, chrome dual exhaust kicking bursts of fire with each punch on the gas pedal, Springsteen's Born in the U.S.A. blared out the windows. Flame patterned letters along the side spelled *Mine Drill Cut Kill* The pick axe and shovel crowd roared approval.

Gerald 'Jerry Justice' Hansen stuck his arm out the passenger side window, waving one of his familiar props, a petrified walrus oosik up and down with the beat. His dirty, sweat streaked white cowboy hat jammed on his head. He leaned out the window, tipped his head back and howled. The development crowd went nuts and howled back.

Zilla looked at Ray and rolled her eyes. Hansen knew how to make an entrance. "I wonder what The Boss would think of his signature tune being used for a Jerry Justice entrance."

##

The unusual second day of arguments in front of the Supreme Court justices was another reminder of the far-reaching implications the case portended. If the conservation side won, the precedent could seize up everything from wetlands development to fracking in North Dakota to the much coveted and hoped for natural gas pipeline that the Alaskan government wanted to build from the North Slope to ice-free tidewater. Dragging through court after court for years.

But if the extraction side won the day, there would be an immediate pounce. With a Trump administration focused on energy dominance for America, conservationists shuddered at the stakes in this case. If the Aleutian Refuge lost the right to be made whole and wild again, there would be no stopping the bulldozers, drill rigs and timber mills. It would amount to revenge development and the fear was they would burn down everything they could before they lost their friends in the Interior department, the EPA and of course in the White House.

It was on. The new Civil War in America was between fossil fuel devotees and off grid greenies.

Two grueling hours later, the hearing was over and Zilla and Ray rushed to their pre-planned stakeouts. Ray had been right- it was impossible to tell what the Justices would decide, but Zilla was still sure the conservation side was going to take this. It was a military toxin clean up issue at its heart and there was plenty of legal precedent for forcing action on these legacy sites. She waited for Jerry Justice and his entourage while Ray started toward the front to wait for Marcus Peterson and the lawyers representing the various other environmental groups.

They were both surprised by what happened next and quickly changed positions, coming together in front of the main doors.

When they emerged from the imposing and cathedral like Supreme Court chambers, the high ceilings echoing the chanting voices outside, there was a clear divide on the steps, now five and six deep on both sides and flowing down the wide steps.

"Holy cow Ray, look at this crowd." Zilla kept her voice low, although the racket built so quickly there was no need.

As the plaintiffs, defendants and various legal team members stepped out, many clutching their brief cases like talisman against the angry mobs, the chants, yells and singing rose quickly. Hand made signs were on both sides but with vastly different messages. Save the Planet! Leave it in the Ground! Renewable Now! Stop Killing our Mother! Green Defiance Coalition-GDC for Mother Earth!

Zilla rolled video on the bobbing signs, capturing the voices yelling "Shame on you! Shame for destroying our kids future!" Ray was doing the same, pointing his camera toward the other side where the resource crowd was red faced and screaming, "Fuck you! Quit killing *our* future! Stop supporting terrorist countries! American energy now! D.A.D.-Defend American Development!"

It was exciting and overwhelming. Zilla saw Marcus Peterson pushing through the lawyers toward his nemesis. Jerry Justice had a menacing sneer on his face, his wide leather belt with its oosik strapped on the left and an empty holster for his 357 that he'd had to stow before entering the courthouse on his right. Now outside, someone handed him his hand tooled bandoleers. He put them over his head, careful not to knock his hat off, never taking his eyes off Peterson, adjusting them as he too pushed through the crowd toward his adversary, the nickel cased bullets crisscrossed his chest, looking oddly similar to the confederate flag held by one of his crew and waving behind him.

Peterson started hollering above the fray.

"We're gonna win this thing Hansen! Make the U.S. military take responsibility for their mess and stop the likes of you from sucking the blood out of our mother planet!"

In the absence of his handgun, Hansen again grabbed the smooth, ivory colored oosik. Zilla winced as she always did at the grossness factor of anyone who wanted to hold a walrus penis bone, but kept her camera rolling.

"Fuck you! And fuck your wimp-ass whining group of backwoods, snowflake hippies, Peterson!" The two men were right in front of each other now. The crowd pressed in from both sides. Zilla ducked down and pointed her camera up toward the men's angry faces, now inches from each other.

"This shit ends today Peterson. Your attack on the U.S. military and development should be treason and if our glorious President decides to charge you as a traitor, America really will be great again!" The extraction crowd exploded, pumping their shovels and axes in the air above their heads.

"Your support of killing the planet is the real act of treason, you fossil fuel addicted prick!" Peterson leaned in, defiant. He was a greenie, but he was no wimp. He was a narcissist who relished a dirty fight just as much as Jerry Justice.

Maybe more.

Meanwhile staff and attorneys for Greenpeace, The Wilderness Society, The Sierra Club and a handful of others, quietly moved away from the rabid crowd and waited at the bottom of the Supreme Court steps. They clearly did not want to associate with the stunts of Marcus Peterson and didn't want to get caught up in arrests if the nervous Capitol police decided the angry group was moving from protected freedom of assembly status to out of control mob.

More officers appeared, apparently summoned through some quiet cop communication plan and began politely asking people to disperse.

Justice and Peterson exchanged a few more insults, both acting as if the other was lucky to avoid fisticuffs and began to retreat back into their respective supporters. Slaps on the back and hell yeahs, could be heard on both sides.

Zilla stood up; glad Peterson and Hansen were done pawing the ground and snorting at each other like two old bulls. She was also glad that the fleeting concern over an actual fistfight and her accompanying worry that she might catch an errant blow in her vulnerable crouched down position was over.

It was rare that Zilla Gillette allowed herself to not be ready to physically defend if needed, but hey, getting the best shot was part of the job for a reporter and she had just struck gold by capturing the angry exchange from her low spot between them. She and Ray locked eyes across the crowd, nodded to each other and turned in opposite directions.

Zilla went after Justice and his crew. Ray dogged Peterson and the mavens of mother earth's defense. The fun was over. Time to get to work and interview the main characters. Zilla first zipped down the steps to the cluster of attorneys for the national environmental organizations, gathering cards and asking about calls for follow up. They were subdued, irritated that reporters would talk to the fringe elements before talking to them, but they were used to it.

Ray caught up with the black suited feds, their eyes shrouded by mirrored sunglasses. He did the same, gathered contacts for follow up, then turned and sprinted back up the steps to the crowd still wrapped adorningly around Peterson. He noticed the smoky expressions of more than a couple of college-aged women who stared wantonly at Peterson.

Oh brother, Ray thought. Groupies clung to celebrity no matter how insufferable their paramour might be. Some things never changed.

The *Anchorage Daily Standard* reporters interviewed and took notes for the better part of half an hour. The crowd started to thin out. Subarus and Hummers alike left the parking lot, horn honking, bird flipping and insults were hurled back and forth, but for the most part, the emotion was spent. It was now a waiting game until the Supremes released their decision in the case.

Zilla stood a few feet away, courteous of her colleague as Ray finished up his interview with admirers of Peterson's cause. When he quit nodding and writing, smiled and shook the hand of his interview subject, she walked up. Ray flipped his notebook closed. They had planned to each focus on a side, but ended up catching as many as they could on both.

"What did you hear?" Zilla cocked her head at Ray. She again heard the clank of the flagpole chain in the new quiet.

"Mostly predictable bragging about a big win that will finally crush the...." he flipped his notebook open again, reading, "Idiots who would destroy life on our precious and only planet." He flipped it shut again and looked at his work partner. "But I also heard about a plan for a press avail at Amchitka. Peterson says he's going to arrange a flotilla junket for news media to actually travel to the island so he can brag on site about winning the clean up war. This assumes his side wins of course." He grinned at Zilla.

"Of course." She answered, flipping her own notebook open. "I have similar quotes, 'We will win because God is on our side and the resources he has provided are our right to develop as we see fit.' End quote. The God of resource extraction is apparently a man Ray, in case you were unclear about that." The chain clanked. Ray smiled.

"Oh no, I knew that Zee. All the heavy Gods are dudes."

"Geez. I need a beer. Even if it is only noon." Zilla shook her head. "Mr. Hansen, he of bullets and x rated walrus bones-gross-also, has a gathering planned when he wins."

"Oh?" Ray looked at his watch.

"Yeah, Kincaid park. A Rally for Resources and fund raiser for the D.A.D."

"Where the hell do these guys come up with acronyms?" He yawned as he watched an old truck exit the parking lot, its rear end sagging with the weight of protest signs and young people piled in the back.

"Defend American Development? D.A.D? Come on man, that's actually damn clever." Zilla grinned and punched him lightly on the arm.

"What are you so cheery about? This shit is going to blow up and split the country even more no matter which side wins this fight." Ray looked serious. They both heard another clang and looked up at the same time. As if punctuating his statement, the enormous American flag, flying above the U.S. Supreme Court had come loose from its top hook and now flew upside down; A nation in distress.

Chapter Three

Zilla and Ray spent the next four hours holed up, writing. This was the biggest story the two reporters had been on since they'd helped track a human trafficking ring from the arctic to leaders in New Jersey. The company Sapphire Import/Export had been in the business of buying young people from foreign coasts. Their vessels slipped through the arctic passage in late fall. Several kids snatched from Nome and young Rohingyans from Myanmar had been rescued when the astute reporters found them in the basement of the shipping company's warehouse.

It had been relatively quiet in the months that followed the harrowing events on the east coast, at least for the investigative reporters. Even though Zilla Gillette and Ray Walker were the powerhouse journalists of the *Anchorage Daily Standard* newsroom, it wasn't the New York Times and when there wasn't big stuff shaking, they had to take assignments that were not as challenging to write about as a slavery ring operated by a wicked shipping baroness.

It had been a bit dry until the environmental suit: The Green Defiance Coalition et al versus the United States and the DOD. The lawsuit title was sexy in itself, journalistically speaking and the two news junkies had relished digging in to the back story of the history on Amchitka for a historical series in the lead up to the Supreme Court case.

And what a history it was.

When President William H. Taft signed executive order 1733 in March of 1913, just part of a single sentence of the order that set terms for a preserve for fur bearing mammals and fisheries development, left it vulnerable to other, less environmentally friendly uses:

'The establishment of this reservation shall not interfere with the use of the islands for lighthouse, military, or naval purposes, or with the extension of the work of the Bureau of Education on Unalaska and Atka Islands.'

That sentence, seeming almost an afterthought, as it was the last, save the final few words that stated the name as 'the Aleutian Islands Reservation,' preserved the option to use the islands for military purposes. Decades later when President Jimmy Carter signed the Alaska National Interest Lands Conservation Act or ANILCA, the Reservation title was amended to become the present day Alaska Maritime Wildlife Refuge.

But the century spanning the signing of the Presidential order in 1913 and the battle over clean up in 2019 was filled with an incredible history of military occupation, battles and eventual atomic bomb tests in one of the most remote, seismically active and wildest places in the North Pacific Ocean of the Bering Sea.

Zilla and Ray could scarcely believe what they read when they dug into the history of how nuclear bombs came to be tested in this ecologically sensitive and diverse place. As they researched the massive military infrastructure that was built up on the western islands in the chain during World War Two, more than a couple times they reminded each other, that one sentence had allowed this war time campaign build up, only to be followed by the more incredible testing of atomic weapons in the late 60s and early 70s.

As the United States fought Japanese soldiers who had garrisoned on Kiska and Attu Islands, the U.S. Army brought soldiers as well as thousands of construction workers, engineers and other civilian contractors to build their bases. By the middle of 1943, more than 83, 000 U.S. Troops and support personnel were stationed at six bases in the Western islands. Hundreds of thousands of tons of supplies and equipment built runways and infrastructure to house and feed the people stationed there. On Amchitka alone, nearly 15,000 people lived first in tent cities and eventually in Quonsets built by Army and Navy engineers. Steel for the Navy, wood for the Army.

Long years after World War Two was over, the scars of civilization left by large numbers of humans living on Amchitka and other islands were plainly visible. The runways, barracks, hospitals and myriad hangers, work shops, mess halls and other structures slowly moldered into the soil, reclaimed and disassembled by time, extreme weather and animals chewing through walls, burrowing in.

But after the horror of the bombs dropped on Hiroshima and Nagasaki, after hundreds of thousands of Japanese civilians were vaporized, when the world saw the awesome and terrible power of these weapons, the evil genie was out of the bottle. In 1949 the Soviet Union detonated an atomic bomb and the short-lived dominance by the west in atomic energy development was over. Like dominoes tipped and rippling away in a terrible sequence. That same year, Mao Tse-Tung declared success for the Communist People's Republic of China, wresting the nation from pro-western, pro-capitalism Nationalists. And a year later, in 1950, a top British atomic scientist was uncovered as a Soviet spy.

The United States felt vulnerable about its military nuclear secrets. This was capped by North Korea's invasion of South Korea that same year.

The rapid sequence of events sealed Amchitka's fate as a site for nuclear bomb testing. Military leaders pressed for tests beyond the airdrops, underwater or tower detonations that had come before. They wanted underground and flat surface testing.

President Truman agreed with General Kenneth Nichols that Amchitka with its remote location, rather than a few other Alaskan areas that had been considered, such as the interior, were deemed too difficult to reach and filled with miners and trappers. No concern seemed apparent for the Alaska Native people who were and had been in the area long before. Truman signed an order in October of 1950, authorizing a surface blast as well as underground tests.

Zilla and Ray named their investigative series Operation Wind Storm- the secret code name for the planned tests, led by Rear Admiral Thomas Settle.

Those early proposals were shelved after fears of leaked information regarding the secret plans came to fruition in March of 1951 and the Alaska press went with a story headlined: **Atom Bomb to be Tested on an Aleutian Island.**

Senators began to question how Russia would feel about fall out so close to their Siberian territory, and an admiral expressed doubt about the unstable soil composition tests on Amchitka, saying it could skew seismic results. Further military concerns over potential radiological problems stemming from surface and underground tests left the plans unpalatable and even the Atomic Energy Commission worried about the political consequences. The military took action, moving personnel, equipment and funds to Nevada to prepare for much smaller tests in the desert.

But the fight was still on for Wildlife Refuge managers who were trying to protect the sea otters on Amchitka. Manager Robert Jones complained bitterly about the war minded military leaders who wanted to test their weapons in what he referred to as a jewel of island ecology.

As Zilla and Ray read and wrote about the fascinating history, it became clear that the Refuge won a reprieve, in large part because of leaked information and national attention to the plight of the Aleutian area.

It was short lived.

When the 1960s arms race with the Soviet Union required increased and rapid testing on new weaponry such as Intercontinental Ballistic Missiles or ICBMs, Amchitka once again became the target.

Project Rufus was the name given to the AEC and DOD search for an appropriate test area. Most of the state of Alaska was under consideration at one time, including the southeast, Kodiak, Chirikof, St. Lawrence Island, the North Slope, the Kuskokwim and Yukon regions, the Pribilofs and the Brooks and Alaska ranges.

DOD wanted to secure an area that could contain the blast and radiation fall out from a detonation of one million tons or more of explosive material to gauge the electromagnetic and seismic affect of Minuteman missile systems.

After fights with environmental advocates, Alaska Natives and other citizens over the vast Alaska mainland and island geography, military leaders prevailed.

The largest nuclear bombs ever detonated in the world would be exploded on Amchitka. The first, code named Project Long Shot was in October of 1965. It was the first nuclear bomb detonated in Alaska and consisted of an eighty thousand ton bomb set off at the bottom of a twenty three hundred foot shaft. The next came in October of 1969. The two reporters' research into the second detonation led to a rare bit of hilarity in what was otherwise solemn and disheartening reporting work into a dark part of history.

The second test, more than one million tons of TNT force had originally been code named Project Ganja. The test was re-named Shot Milerow when someone decided that 'ganja' was a Turkish word for pot. In a state that had legalized cannabis in 2014, it made for late night jokes between Walker and Gillette before they focused on the incredibly unfunny and sobering third and final test on Amchitka; Shot Cannikin.

Military big wigs prevailed, despite a fight with international leaders including China and Canada after the Milerow test and despite a threat from the mayor of Old Harbor on Kodiak Island who said he would sue the feds if earthquakes and tsunamis resulted from the test.

The case ended up in front of the U.S. Supreme Court, a strange historical mirror, now bookended by the current case before the high court. In 1971, the Supreme Court justices met on a Saturday morning, November 6th, their split four to three ruling in favor of the AEC meant the Cannikin blast could proceed.

It was detonated just after high noon on November 6th, 1971. The blast was five million tons of TNT power, measuring 7.0 on the Richter scale.

The bizarre irony was not lost on the two astute journalists.

The same court, albeit with different justices, that had allowed the largest test to be carried out on Amchitka would now decide if the military that had pressed for permission, would be ordered to remove the mess they'd left there 48 years earlier.

You couldn't make this stuff up.

##

In the three months between the hearing at the high court and the justices' looming decision in the case, the hysteria over what the ruling would mean, ramped up on the develop and conserve sides. Both focused on the negative. For the GDC, a decision against the refuge meant certain death for the planet. To hear their alarming speeches, it appeared the world would end within weeks from the increase in fossil fuel and coal development. For the drill crowd, the rhetoric was equally frightening. If the greenies won, the U.S. economy would crash, every good paying job in the nation would be exported to China, (although why an oil field worker's job would go to China was never explained) and terrorists would be rolling, leaping and trapeze flying across the border from every possible direction to take over the government and make everyone wear a turban and read the Koran. The President tweeted incessantly that the high court must do the right thing and preserve American jobs and American energy security and dominance. It was the only way to truly make America great again!

Zilla's prediction was spot on. The ruling was announced on a cool June morning. It contained an interesting divide. The Supreme

Court justices had indeed found that the U.S. military must follow its own rules and clean up and restore Amchitka Island just as it had been mandated to do at Formerly Used Defense Sites, known as FUDS, across the country. Many of these sites, including in Alaska, were in various states of long term clean up and monitoring.

It wasn't exactly a big priority for military leaders to go back and sweep up after the party was over, but toxic materials that had affected ground water and hazardous particulate in dirt and sand had resulted in lawsuits over high PCB and lead blood levels, asthma and a host of nasty cancers. Lawsuits brought attention and reluctant, often horrendously expensive clean ups.

But the ruling was split on the decision regarding personhood for the Refuge and the high court remanded that part of the suit back to the 9th circuit for re-consideration. It meant a continuation of the intense campaign by the proponents of fossil fuel development and their foes, the environmentalists.

The clean up of Amchitka was a clear victory for the conservation crowd, but the big win would only come if they won on the right for the Refuge to exist undisturbed and unexploited. Until natural systems that supported all life were protected and treated with the respect allotted for human life, the battle was far from over. It was an ad revenue boost for every media outlet that could claim eyeballs and ears from small town papers to cable news. The 9th circuit would seat an en banc panel to hear the case. It was scheduled for July.

The battle for America's soul was under way.

##

As soon as the Supremes handed down their decision, Marcus Peterson got to work and wasted no time in setting up his grand scheme for media attention and the funds that would flow to him because of it.

Peterson offered 12 coveted spots on his very own vessel, Sea Goddess, to only the biggest outlets, the networks of course and cable such as CNN and MSNBC, even FOX got an invite. NPR and PBS were on the list. He also had his underlings contact The New York Times, The LA Times, The Washington Post, Time and People magazines and international outlets like The Guardian and the BBC. Local news organizations like the *Anchorage Daily Standard* and the state radio network would have to find their own way out there. Peterson didn't give a flip about small time operators. He wanted money and the bigger the coverage splash, the more the dollars would pour in.

Zilla and Ray's boss at the Daily Standard, Ed Brooks wasn't happy about the ding his meager newsroom budget took when he had to spring for plane tickets for Zilla and Ray to fly to Adak. From there they would board a chartered vessel to get to Amchitka, but hideous expense aside, there was no getting around it. They simply had to be there. The plane tickets and chartered boat could have paid for a luxury vacation but instead bought a bumpy plane ride and passage on a drafty, smelly diesel troller repurposed as a charter vessel for tourists after the owner sold his fishing permits to pay back taxes.

The event was scheduled for June 15th.

Marcus Peterson used the time between the Supreme Court decision and his planned departure to cram in as many interviews as possible. He worked hard to make this his victory and promised that the 9th circuit would do 'the right thing' and protect 'our sacred mother's amniotic fluid that is the oceans'. He used that line a lot. Mother Earth bore all life through the salty waters of her placental womb. It made sense to his followers, who would nod their heads, eyes enraptured as he spoke, especially women who fantasized about using their own wombs to birth his children.

With only three days until Peterson's media blitz at Amchitka, he'd raised close to two hundred thousand dollars. Once the story hit the papers, front page photos of him with his arms spread wide on the deck of his vessel, the Amchitka refuge behind him, the 200K would be pocket change compared to what would come pouring in from across the world.

Jerry Justice was also planning a rally, but he was smart enough not to compete with Peterson's event. He wanted to fund raise too and that meant making sure the big media outlets would be able to attend his gathering and splash his campaign of supporting the D.A.D and America First Energy Dominance across the pages of newspapers, websites and broadcast news outlets around the country. He decided a remote location was not a good idea since the Amchitka trip was going to be a big expense for newsrooms. He would make them travel to Alaska, but only to Anchorage, deciding the downtown park strip with the backdrop of the snow capped Chugach mountains and the city skyline of large oil company high rise headquarters was the perfect combination. He could tout the amazing wilderness so close to the city and point out the oil industry's might as a testimonial to the ability of both to co-exist. Soon he would change his rally plan and move it to Kincaid Park, southwest of downtown. The former missile base site was a better fit for rallying the resource extraction troops.

"Jobs and pristine wilderness can both be had!" he often bellowed to his followers. "The largest oil patch in North America is on Prudhoe Bay and when was the last time you heard of air pollution or a spill there? Huh? When?" He'd look around, waving his nickel plated revolver or his oosik, his dingy, battered cowboy hat pushed back so he could widen his eyes and lean forward to stare defiantly at the crowd, daring someone to challenge him. "You haven't, cuz it don't happen. That's why. You can live in a beautiful place, shoot yourselves a grizz or a moose, eat all the dang salmon you want and still have a great paying job on the slope ladies and gents. Woo-eee! I swear to the Lord above that's the truth!"

Jerry Justice knew how to whip up a crowd just as well as Marcus Peterson. They despised each other but they were more alike than either would admit. They both loved money, easy women and making a cushy, cashy living by shooting off their mouths. They were evangelists on two sides of the same issue and both were preaching their personal gospel of money and lots of it.

Chapter Four

Zilla and Ray flew to Adak on Sunday, June 12th. They went a few days early to gather stories of the people who lived in this extremely remote place and to better understand how the big military clean up may affect this community. It was an eerie full circle kind of event. The military had built up Adak during World War Two and faded signs of the thriving outpost it had been five decades earlier were still apparent. An old movie theater, military style housing, mess hall, commissary, hospital, mechanic shops were all still there, in various states of disrepair. The fish processing plant was in operation and a small population lived on the island, but it had been a quiet, mostly forgotten place since the United States had fought back the Japanese advance during the war and the incredible build up of military personnel and infrastructure had vanished almost overnight.

Now the prospect of another large build up loomed over the area and people who worked at the processor and lived low key lives were bracing for the influx of military contractors, inspectors and curious tourists. Some of the locals were thrilled at the prospect and some dreaded the thought. All knew it was inevitable and like good American capitalists, figured out how to charge a boatload of money for spare bedrooms and converted Quonset huts.

##

In Anchorage, long time editor Ed Brooks and longer time reporter Stuart Murphy were heading up local coverage of the Supreme Court's cliffhanger decision. There was definite excitement among Alaska construction executives and in the boardrooms of Alaska Native Corporations who had numerous contracts with the department of defense. Everything from security services for military bases to catering to sewing uniforms to building and maintaining facilities with clean rooms where highly specific components for missile guidance systems were built.

The Amchitka clean up work would take heavy equipment operators, excavation and explosives experts and an enormous team of radiation detection technicians who would crawl all over the island to test for nuclides. There would be underwater tests conducted from vessels circling the island and deep-water samples from a two-mile radius would also be gathered.

It was a bit over the top since any underwater caves that may have originated under Amchitka and were currently spitting toxic materials deep under the sea surface would be impossible to do anything about. But the conservation crowd's massive team of attorneys had demanded comprehensive testing to 'understand the scope of possible unmitigated damage that may have been emitted through the decades.' This was code language for more monetary damages that could be claimed later.

There was a buzz in Alaska's largest city and Brooks and Murphy were working their corporate and military contacts to better understand and report on the potential windfall for local contractors. Alaska had been in a moribund financial state because of low oil prices and a big deficit. State lawmakers had cut government services to the bone and the governor had even dared to cut in half the permanent fund dividend that is paid to every man, woman and child in the state each year. It is the holy grail of Alaska residency, the third rail of state politics and a more sacred cow could not be found. Now, just as other big events in the past had helped rescue the state's fiscal bacon like the Prudhoe Bay discovery, the 1964 earthquake and even the horrible Exxon Valdez oil spill, the Amchitka clean up project would take months, likely at least two summer seasons if not three and hundreds of millions of dollars.

There would be jobs and they would pay well. Brooks and Murphy scheduled an editorial meeting with the mayor, the president of the state chamber of commerce and the base Commanding Officer. The plan was to release a comprehensive, special edition of the *Anchorage Daily Standard* on the day of the media event at Amchitka. It would lead into live, online coverage and a big spread the next day in the print version of the paper. This was a big deal and the city was vibrating with excitement.

Ray's mom Ruby still owned her namesake Café in downtown Anchorage, but she was now the state's sole U.S. Congresswoman too. Ruby won a special election after the bizarre murder of Hank Emerson, the former congressman. Ruby visited Anchorage and her family business whenever she could, but her father in law, Ray Senior ran the café, bar and dance hall now. Reporter Ray, the third in the Ray Walker line helped out when he could with big weekend events. His fiancée, Mo Scott continued her bartending job for Ruby, even though she was now a syndicated columnist and a star attraction for the *Daily Standard*.

Representative Ruby Walker, still getting accustomed to the title, was scheduled to be in Anchorage in the days following Marcus Peterson's planned media blitz in the Bering Sea.

She would meet with some of the same business leaders that Brooks and Murphy were building stories around. Ruby saw this court decision as nothing but good news for the economic and environmental health of Alaska.

Whether or not the 9th circuit decided in favor of personhood status for the Refuge, a decision that would likely lead back to the Supreme Court again, the congresswoman saw the enforcement of the clean up as leverage for other FUDS in Alaska and across the nation. She was an independent who leaned a bit left in social policy and a bit right in fiscal policy.

Ruby Walker had little tolerance for the constant twitter hyperbole from President Trump, but she knew that touting the clean up of the military's toxic legacy across the country would mean jobs and this president loved to tweet about creating American jobs. If she could convince him this was a path to that goal, she didn't care if he took the credit; she only cared that it would get done. She wanted the communities closest to the toxins, usually occupied by poor people, immigrants or near reservations, to have safe drinking water, crop areas and playgrounds free from high levels of PCB, lead and other nasty stuff in the soil. It was also a path to good local training and employment in the clean up effort.

It would be astronomically expensive, but Ruby Walker could think of no better way to spend taxpayer money than improving air, water and soil quality while providing training and jobs for U.S. citizens.

Stuart 'Murph' Murphy was surprised to see a message on his phone when he hit the newsroom on Tuesday morning. It was June 14th, the day before Peterson's planned event. Murph had worked late Monday night. He left just after 10 pm and walked back through the door by seven on Tuesday morning. *Who the hell called that late the night before or so early this morning?* Murph didn't waste time pondering as he punched in the code for voicemail. The number the caller had used was blocked and the message was short. *"The new manager of The Slip is weird man. Something's going on there dude. Better check it out."*

Murph listened to the message twice, trying to decide if he knew the caller's voice. He decided he didn't but he knew what the quiet voice was referring to when he'd said The Slip, it was the local nickname for The Silver Slipper, a basement bar and well known gangster hang out dating back to the early sixties.

The Slip was so dubbed because of the passageways that ran under 4th avenue in downtown. The damp corridor had provided convenient escape routes for bad guys who were evading cops and the FBI. One passage allegedly opened up below 3rd avenue facing Ship Creek, conveniently near the railroad, although no one who claimed it existed had ever been able to take Murphy to the actual exit point. Another passage supposedly led to a secret door in the basement of tower three of the Captain Cook hotel.

Murphy didn't think much of the odd message, a paranoid citizen who saw suspicious characters at every turn perhaps, or someone with a grudge against the new manager, maybe after being eighty sixed from the bar. But Murphy always followed up on tips, regardless of how doubtful they might seem. He decided to visit the Silver Slipper at lunchtime for a beer and some bar food. If something weird were going on at The Slip, he'd likely pick up on it. Murph had highly tuned news antennae honed over decades.

##

As Murphy made his lunch time plans, the Silver Slipper's new manager was having his weekly meeting with his new boss. Malcolm 'MC' Ames could scarcely believe his recent good luck. Ames had been working as a flight attendant for Alaska Airlines, flying from Anchorage to Moscow and other Russian cities when he met Nakita Volkov on a trip back to the state from

Kamchatka. Volkov struck up a conversation with Malcolm, asking him where good places to eat and drink would be in Anchorage, claiming he was a first time visitor to Alaska, checking out recently purchased investment property, and was eager to know all he could about the largest state in the nation and, he teased MC, that had once belonged to Nakita's country!

MC liked Mr. Volkov's exotic accent, although he spoke excellent English, and when Volkov asked to buy the flight attendant dinner for being so helpful, Ames impulsively agreed. What else would he do on a weeknight after his flight duties ended? He had no girlfriend, no family in Anchorage and few friends.

Volkov was pleased and knew his boss, the universally feared Vladimir Putin, would be even happier. Although gauging when the Russian leader was happy was a tough call. He was not a man of mirth.

But Volkov's confidence in his bosses' plan for causing dissent by infiltrating disgruntled Alaskan organizations got a boost when MC Ames agreed to a dinner meeting.

Volkov could read people well and he knew a desperate man when he saw one.

Some people are impulsive, some are opportunistic and some are mean. A few are all three. They're the most dangerous and easy to hook. Volkov was not such a man. He was careful, methodical and didn't leave loose ends.

He was not given to impulse or greed, but he hired people who were. Before the dinner plates were cleared from Volkov and Ame's lavish meal at the Crow's Nest restaurant, high atop the Captain Cook hotel, MC was offered and accepted the job as bar manager for the Silver Slipper. MC had only been in his cushy new position for two weeks when Murphy got the anonymous call about suspicious happenings at 'The Slip.'

As often happens in newsrooms everywhere, Murphy's lunchtime plans were foiled by a late morning news event. The Anchorage Police Department's SWAT team was dispatched to an apartment building in midtown where a late night party had devolved into a knife fight, followed by a man who barricaded himself in a bedroom. APD cleared the other apartments and blocked the street while SWAT members deployed tear gas and finally talked the drunken lout into surrendering peacefully.

Murphy did the responsible thing and stayed on top of the story, posting real time updates as law enforcement moved in. His write-ups let local residents know why they couldn't get to their home or leave their home to get to work. It took about 90 minutes to get resolved, but it ate up the window that Murphy had allotted for a visit to the Silver Slipper. Instead of a burger, a tap beer and some reconnaissance,

Murphy ate a stale bagel he found in the lunchroom and a beef stick from the vending machine. He figured he could check out the new manager at The Slip the next day after the media event scheduled for Amchitka. Once he finished posting updates from his remote colleagues Zilla and Ray who were already on site near the Aleutian island that was now the focus of the nation and the world.

Environmentalists had won a victory that they characterized as landmark. Murphy reserved judgment about how big this decision was. The clean up was of note, but if the greenies won on the bigger issue of personhood status for natural systems, well that would be legally earth shattering in Murphy's estimation.

He wouldn't make it to the Silver Slipper the next day either and the term 'earth shattering' would float back into his mind more than a few times over the course of the next few days. Even though the much anticipated court decision was weeks away.

Chapter Five

Zilla and Ray were bundled up and standing on the deck of the fishing vessel turned charter for hire that had brought them from Adak to the Bering sea swells off the coast of Amchitka. It was calm but cold. A breeze flowed across the surface of the frigid waters, chilling all who lined the decks of the several boats that bobbed and rolled on the near shore currents. Zilla was amazed at how many news outlets had made the expensive trip.

Marcus Peterson was a master at self-promotion and Zilla and Ray counted six vessels with crews from CNN, NBC, ABC, a cable show called Whale Defenders and the BBC. A few other foreign news programs populated a small ship that had a satellite connection for a pool feed to other stations across the globe. Peterson would broadcast his self-serving message to the world and he could almost hear the flutter of cash flowing into his account.

The plan had been written into a colorful press release that had been emailed a few days before the event and handed out in a press packet from the deck of the Sea Goddess on the day of. Peterson would give remarks through a bullhorn on the deck of the Sea Goddess precisely at 11 am.

There would be time for questions from the press, plenty of photo and video opportunities both during the speech while they were on the water and then again in a planned shore lunch event organized by Peterson's minions. They had numerous vegan dishes to share with the media while Peterson was photographed showing reporters the area of the nuclear bomb test wells. He would brag about how the clean up would keep the Aleutians pristine into the future and how modern adults realized vegan was the answer because eating any meat was not only barbaric and cruel, it was extremely unhealthy!

Zilla and Ray snapped photos and shot video from nine thirty till 10:45, uploading them as fast as they could on their satellite phone connection back to the Anchorage newsroom where Murphy, their editor Ed Brooks and three young hotshot web producers hustled to crop, caption and post the material as quickly as they could.

"My camera trigger finger is numb Ray." Zilla rubbed her hand on her coat sleeve and blew steamy breath on her fingers. "Damn, it's cold out here." She shook her hand, steadied her camera and took more shots of Peterson on the deck of the Sea Goddess plus a few quick snaps of a CNN reporter clinging to the rails of the charter and the arm of another reporter as they tried to stay on their feet, unaccustomed to the roll of the ocean.

Ray snorted. "Guess they don't have their sea legs Zee."

"Don't be mean partner. Those city folks can't help it that the North Pacific Ocean doesn't sit still like the streets of DC."

"Well, we're 'city folks' and we can roll with it." Ray swayed back and forth in a semi silly, exaggerated way, grinning. He was excited about this cool reporting trip. They'd had a six month dry spell after the crazy story they broke when they found missing Nome teenagers and uncovered a human trafficking operation in New Jersey in the process. The Amchitka assignment was a fun story to be on, even if Peterson was an insufferable egomaniac.

"No, we live in a big town called Anchorage. Those poor fools live in a real city Ray. DC is big city in every way and Anchorage has moose, bears, ravens, eagles and salmon streams running right through the heart of it. That ain't city, brother."

"Is so." Ray teased and swayed again with the waves, partially mocking the landlubbers who looked increasingly green aboard their rented charters, wishing Peterson would hurry it up so they could get their final shots and head to land.

At 10:55 am, Peterson stepped to the very front of the bow of Sea Goddess and raised his bullhorn.

"My friends." His voiced boomed over the water, rising above the idling diesel engines of the nearby vessels. All eyes on the decks of the surrounding boats were on him. Fuzzy covered shotgun mics on long boom handles were aimed at him from every direction. One by one, the skippers of the anchored vessels killed their engines. Peterson was in his element. Zilla gave Ray a look, bracing for the boasting that would come next. He didn't disappoint.

"This marks a new day for peace and respect. For far too long, the U.S military has treated our beloved planet like their own personal playground to disrupt, toxify and destroy in any manner they chose." He paused for dramatic effect. "But no more! NO MORE!" Faint cheers from his devoted followers could be hear both from behind him on the Sea Goddess as well as from shore where the vegan lunch was being arranged on folding tables.

"I am here to not only claim victory for the planet and ourselves, but also to announce my new initiative." Another pause, this one met only by wave splash on vessels as the assembled press and Peterson fans leaned in for the message.

"Now that this terrible fight is over and I've won......I will be able to focus all my attention and resources on the desperate need to protect the Arctic Ocean from pirates. Yes! You heard me correctly"

It would have been hard not to hear him correctly or otherwise since the speaker his bullhorn was connected to was blaring his words.

"I said pirates! But I am not talking about the pirates who steal from cruise ships and cargo vessel captains. I am not talking about those who rob from other transients navigating on these precious waters. No, I'm talking about the need to protect the rightful inhabitants of these waterways from the ruthless pirates who would murder the peaceful beings in cold blood! Those who would murder our sentient cousins, our beautiful sea babies, the whales!" He was really revved up now. "These pirates claim they have a right. A right to murder? A right to take the life of another because of barbaric and foolish old beliefs? That's a license to kill? NO! It is NOT!"

He lifted the bullhorn above his head for a moment. There was a small splash off the port side of the Sea Goddess, and then another. Peterson cocked his head at the sound then railed on.

"I know the ridiculous worship of Alaska's indigenous people has become it's own religion, as if no one can dare criticize their archaic beliefs.

But I reject that thinking! These people are killers! They spread propaganda about how the whales 'give' themselves to them." His voice was sarcastic mocking now. "They spread this lie at every opportunity to continue perpetrating their horrific blood sport! Cruelly harpooning and shooting these magnificent denizens of the deep sea. Native pirates have perpetrated these untenable and outdated traditions for decades. Claiming it is their right! Their right to senseless slaughter? Should we also allow girls to be given to chiefs when they are 12 years old? Should we allow those deemed possessed of evil spirits to be driven out or killed by a Shaman? Should we allow the burning of witches? No we should not and we should not allow one species to kill another, claiming the animals give themselves to keep the people alive. We will speak truth to these lies and stop this senseless murder."

He stalks back and forth pointing the bullhorn toward the vessels with the biggest media outlets to make sure they catch every word.

Another splash off the portside of Peterson's vessel is quickly followed by two more. Camera operators turn their lenses toward the curious swirls. Then a large, black tail emerges from the water. A bowhead! Peterson can scarcely believe his luck. The whales are coming to greet him! He is their Pied Piper leading them away from the harm of the terrible, backward thinking of Native traditionalists who cling to the foolish notion that they are connected to the whales and the whales offer their flesh to the hunters.

Peterson brings the bullhorn to his lips again. "Yes. They are here! They want us to know they need help! They need protection from savagery!"

The camera crews are freaking out. Reporters can't believe what they're seeing. Zilla and Ray are also standing, eyes wide as they spot an enormous bowhead whale, then another and another, a writhing mass of whale bodies roils the water around the Sea Goddess. Peterson cheers and yells, waving his arms in the air in triumph. It appears he is not only right but also somehow part of a miracle, as if the whales heard and approve and are clamoring for his defense of them.

It is an incredible moment and even more so because national and international news outlets are capturing this miraculous event live! A huge splash sprays water over the bow of the Sea Goddess. Peterson's laugh, hoarse from shouting is loud as he is drenched by frigid seawater. After the splash, a leap, then another and another.

The bowheads are performing like a Sea World act and everyone watching on vessels, shore and on the deck of the Sea Goddess is in awe.

Peterson drops the bullhorn and clasps his hands like a preacher who just watched a man in a wheelchair stand and walk. There is another leap, this one much higher than the others. Peterson slowly raises his arms, spreading them wide, palms up. He turns his face skyward, a new age Moses.

The massive head of a whale rises higher than the wheelhouse. It seems to hang in the air for a brief second, then twists and begins to descend. The head turns toward the water, the tail flashes over the rails of the Sea Goddess like a giant fleshy club and Marcus Peterson is swatted off like a bad Vaudeville act gets the hook that yanks them from the stage. In less than a full heartbeat, he is gone.

Reporters, camera operators and vessel crew stand in stunned silence for a second. Shocked screams, *oh my gods!* and *Holy shits!* Could be heard as water streamed off the deck where Peterson had stood just a second before. The bullhorn was still on the deck, rolling back and forth in a half circle in full view of the shocked audience.

No one would ever know what Peterson saw or learned in that split second before he was flung off the deck. His perspective was of course completely different than what every other human being witnessed that day, although a couple of the Sea Goddess crew on deck with him heard his voice and saw the odd way in which the whale seemed to look directly at him before propelling the powerful tail in Peterson's direction.

Peterson final seconds were a rapid seesaw of enlightenment. He couldn't believe this celestial event, knowing in an instant that he was right. Had always been right. The whales needed him to rescue them. They had been waiting for *him*, the white human savior to deliver them from the barbaric fools who clung to their ridiculous old ways. He'd felt the full measure of his righteous certainty. He suddenly realized this was truly spiritual, so much more important than money. He was chosen.

And then he saw the eye.

The bowhead was well over 30 feet long, meaning it weighed more than 30 tons, 60 thousand pounds of muscle and bone that could be a century old. As its city bus sized head rose above the deck rails, Peterson felt a sudden heavy, stillness in the air. There was a complete absence of sound.

As if the barometric pressure had dropped all at once.

The bowhead's eye was the size of a coffee cup, the white coloring surrounding it, a contrast from its sleek black skin. The outer eye was blood red and the iris as black as oil. It locked onto Peterson's eyes and he felt a psychic jolt as it transmitted its message.

The whales are the people and the people are the whales. Those who hunt them are supposed to use their flesh as sustenance to survive the arctic human life they are destined to live until they can return to the sea.

The whales give themselves to help their descendant humans live and thrive.

In an instant Peterson went from his self-righteous assumptions to a humbling crush of realization about how ill conceived that was. He understood how wrong he had been and was filled with deep sadness and regret.

"Oh. I see." His only words before the tail swept him from the deck.

The Coast Guard and Samaritan vessels, (many with opportunistic camera crews hoping for the floating body money shot), searched the waters around Amchitka and the shoreline.

His body was not found.

Without Peterson's newly discovered, but brief lived perspective, no one knew of his revelation about the whales connection to the Indigenous people who hunted them. In the seesawing world of social media, the live video footage of Peterson's final moment flooded media outlets across the planet and outrage erupted like acid reflux after a night of heavy drinking and spicy food.

The effect rippled worldwide but Americans were particularly roused to action. Donations poured in to the late Peterson's organization to save the whales, since it was clear! Everyone saw it! The whales need our help! They are afraid of the cruel, Stone Age hunters who would not give up killing the poor sentient darlings of the deep. The posts online were horrific, threatening violence against entire tribes of Alaska Native and American Indian people, whether they were whaling communities or not.

Learn to shop at the supermarket you idiots or we'll harpoon you!

Stop hurting my precious sea babies!

Learn to live like civilized people and eat hamburger!

Go Vegan you heartless bastards!

Fuck you savages!

It was relentless. The zealous development crowd, whipped up as they'd been over the divided court decision, clinged in confusion and uncertainty to the President's Twitter promises:

'The courts will do the right thing. They were bad and liberal under Obama. Sad! But we're cleaning them up and appointing the right judges

to make America Great Again! We'll beat the failing fake news media!

Even the pickaxe and shovel-wielding group was subdued, privately wondering if there was something going on with these greenies that they didn't understand. Could it be that the Green Defiance Coalition bliss ninnies that wanted to protect every blade of grass and give it a name and legal protections were actually right? Murmured testimonies of confusion and uncertainty filled the confession booths of Catholic churches and the private offices of preachers, ministers, pastors and rabbis. The bosses of enormous multi national energy development corporations did some private soul searching.

For about a hot second.

As work ramped up at Amchitka, as C-130s delivered equipment and crews begin disassembling the infrastructure around the aging nuclear test wells, the message began to twist. Trump took full Tweeted credit for *'bringing jobs back to America.'* The military would *'do the right thing and clean up Amchitka and other sites, but the courts will be reasonable and continue to allow responsible development for even more American jobs!'*

But within three weeks of Peterson's dramatic end, after millions of video views of the spread armed conservationist being batted off his own vessel and the oft-repeated words of the crew who had watched it happen, everything zagged in the other direction.

An enormous earthquake hit Amchitka, killing crew and destroying much of the island. The quake ground up and spit out pulverized granite, iron, thick plate steel and concrete as if it were eggshells.

There was nothing recognizable left of the build up that was underway for the work designed to remove the toxic mess and remediate the island. And this reality caused more pain and fear for Americans than the deaths of the military workers who had been caught on Amchitka when the massive quake struck.

It caused national concern because there was no longer any proof of what was being undertaken at Amchitka and that was a credibility problem that scared more than just Americans.

Vladimir Putin did not believe the American military had been removing radioactive poison from the underground test wells. Putin raged that the Pentagon was instead building up to stage new missiles at Amchitka to aim at Russia.

He convinced North Korea's terrifying and U.S. despising leader that those missiles were also meant for Kim Jon's country. The squatty North Korean dictator was soon complaining to

Chinese officials that the three countries would need to stand together against American aggression.

In what passes for a moment in the nation's psyche, the fledging respect that even hard-core miners and drill rig roughnecks secretly held for their environmentalist enemies, evaporated.

Russia was doing what it did best, spreading propaganda, fear, dissention and paranoia. It was employing the best tools of divide and conquer. As the lies spread, the near honeymoon in the U.S. between developers and enviros swiftly turned to resentment and then anger as questions about the U.S. intentions on Amchitka permeated back room government meetings in countries large and small.

What the hell was America and Trump with his 'America First' rhetoric trying to do? Start World War Three?

Within days of the destructive quake, an ugly attitude rekindled toward what resource development proponents considered the whining, libtards who wanted to sing lullabies to the trees.

A Trump Twitter post railed against the *'soft minded protectionists that forced us to clean up harmless material on a completely remote island, causing needless fear and suspicion for our friends in Russia! Lies spread by the fake news enemy of the people media. UnAmerican!*

It was the catalyst that evaporated any common ground the development crowd may have seen with the other side and swallowed whole the budding respect that had briefly lived in their coal loving hearts.

Chapter Six

It was Nakita's idea.

Even when you work for a President that other world leaders consider vindictive and dangerous, the universe occasionally sends you gifts.

Mother Nature had certainly delivered one to Volkov. His current position as special advisor to the Kremlin was likely to get an upgrade.

Not long after the large circle had pinged on Rita Tiegs' computer screen, Volkov got a text alert about the enormous earthquake in the Aleutian Islands and a brilliant idea rose in his mind. They would use this information to claim the U.S. was conducting underground nuke tests. North Korea would certainly believe it since they'd recently done the same and it would not take much convincing to bring China along as well.

Volkov knew his President. Putin would relish this new rumor campaign against the U.S.

Divide and conquer was still the most effective way to defeat an enemy. Spread misinformation, point accusing fingers at prominent figures. Like a snowball rolling downhill, it required no work after the initial push, growing larger as it smashed everything in its path.

When the American FBI was caught using such tactics during the 1970s, Volkov had nothing but contempt for the way the U.S. domestic law enforcement agency had handled it. After the deaths of members of the Black Panthers and American Indian Movement supporters who were caught up in counterintelligence programs, the FBI said they would no longer use cointelpro.

Volkov was certain it was a lie. He was convinced FBI agents were still employing the tactics of planting false narratives about certain people to create suspicion about them with other members of their groups. But they had to appear publicly remorseful about the harm and death these tactics had caused. That weakness in front of the people of America was what infuriated Volkov and his boss. Leaders and their top henchmen should never admit and especially never apologize for covert operations, they should instead work to foster intimidation and strike fear in the hearts of citizens.

That was how you controlled the electorate. That was how you stayed in power.

Americans were undisciplined, ignorant fools who read next to nothing important but believed anything insipid they saw on a social media feed. It was a simple exercise to stoke paranoid conspiracy theories about the Deep State and the belief that 'liberal snowflakes' were trying to tax them to death, force them to buy health care insurance, take their guns, crush their religion and force them to share bathrooms with transgender, disease ridden illegal aliens from countries where they were taught how to steal, rape, murder and sell drugs in grade school. It was just as easy to flip the message and convince liberals that their ultra conservative foes would destroy all places of natural beauty, poison the water, air and land and use their hidden arsenals of assault rifles, hand grenades and dynamite to kill anyone who didn't want to cut, kill, mine, drill. Disinformation and hysteria reigned on both sides.

Volkov's new shill, MC Ames would help in this effort, sharing documents and dossiers with certain people who came in for bourbon and conversation. Material that Volkov would supply filled with propaganda about America's plan to sneak start the build up for the next World War. As the fake, classified documents were slipped to self-important paranoids, Volkov, through MC, would finance hiring thugs and provocateurs to help crumble the frustrating cohesion that had existed for so many decades in America: The cohesion that had kept the country strong, smart and militarily dominant.

No longer.

Now, many Americans were addicted, weak in the body and in the mind. Those who were not addicted did not educate themselves, believed what they were told by their liar leaders or the dark web. Worshipping anything their incompetent, petulant child president told them. He had been a bigger gift than the Kremlin had first imagined. Putin wanted Donald Trump to win because his ego was insatiable and swallowed everything in the name of self-glory and Putin was a master of manipulation. The Russian leader calculated that the scent of future money for the family empire would make the real estate tycoon president easy to sway to create confusion and dissention among U.S. citizens.

But Trump was much better than a malleable shill. He was like a laboratory creation, dreamed up by a diabolical madman intent on world domination.

Hello Vladimir.

##

Zilla and Ray were in the newsroom, working on what had become an endless and fast moving set of stories, swirling around and starting with the Supreme Court's split ruling. They were waiting for the lower court finding on the rights of natural systems. They wrote about the rapid build up on Amchitka to start the process of disassembling the underground test wells and the support infrastructure surrounding it.

They'd witnessed the sensational and fatal end to Marcus Peterson at what was supposed to be his shining moment of fund raising fame, to the alarming turn around in national sentiment.

A handful of weeks of tacit benevolence and begrudging acknowledgement that if cleaning up old military sites resulted in good paying American jobs, then by god, even the hardest core development proponents could accept it. But a massive earthquake, an uptick in fake news spin by Russia about the real intentions of the United States and a shift in sentiment across the nation turned into an ugly tone of blame. It was muscle memory for the anti-conservation crowd to quickly reflex back to hating on environmental organizations.

It was much more aggressive than in the past. It was an outright public campaign of blame and open threats of violence and assassination. Fueled by an endless string of hate stoking tweets from the very man who was supposed to represent, respect, honor and protect all Americans, regardless of their politics; The U.S. President.

It was exhausting. Zilla and Ray hadn't put in this much overtime since they'd finally quit being asked for interviews about their human trafficking reports.

It was just past noon and Zilla had returned from a quick trip to grab a salad from the lunchroom fridge to find that most exasperating coincidence for a reporter; Wait by your phone until you're weak from hunger or your bladder is in serious alarm, only to leave for a few quick, desperate minutes to deal with these pesky details of being a living creature and return to see your phone light blinking in a mocking way. A missed call. Damn it!

"Ah hell!" Zilla wasn't loud, but Ray still looked up from his desk several feet away.

He knew why she was exasperated as she punched the code into her phone. "Um, yeah, sorry. I thought about hollering when your phone started ringing but...." He shrugged.

You couldn't wait by the phone every minute of the day. This frustration was inevitable for a reporter. Even a course in J school titled- How to handle the stress of waiting in call back purgatory- wouldn't have mattered. No kid in college understands until they're anxious at their desk, on a looming deadline and make the error of a casual stroll to get some coffee or get rid of some and neglect to forward calls to their cell.

That's how you learn the real agony of a missed call. No classroom lesson will imprint that in quite the same, gut wrenching way.

Zilla didn't respond. She listened intently to the message. So intently that Ray took notice.

'Zilla Gillette? This is a call from the Green Defiance Coalition. The GDC leadership has gone underground for obvious, personal safety reasons but we'd like a chance to get our message out and want to invite you to our compound for interviews. There will be certain protocols you must agree to in order to be taken to the site. A private message with more instructions will be sent to your twitter account today. If you accept the terms, we'd like this to happen later this week.'

The message ended. Zilla stood absorbing it, thinking it through as she reached for her cell phone to check her Twitter account. Nothing yet.

Certain protocols?

Ray couldn't help himself. "The look on your face tells me this wasn't a call back from the Anchorage Assembly chair. Spill it sister. What gives?"

"Not sure." Zilla frowned thoughtfully. "Supposedly it was a call from the GDC, inviting me to interview their leaders at their Hole in the Wall gang hide out." She tilted her head and looked at Ray. "Could be a hoax call, could be legit."

"Well that is damn intriguing Miss Zee. Yes it is. Why do you get all the sexy calls? I feel left out and cheated." Ray looked genuinely pained and Zilla laughed.

"Calm down, lonely hearts club. Let's see if anything comes of this before you register your outrage."

Chapter Seven

Jerry Justice could not believe his recent good fortune. Not only had the sentiment in the nation made a complete turn about toward the environmental crowd, something he couldn't have imagined in the days after Peterson's death, but he'd also met a new lady friend, an evil, and vindictive new lady friend.

His favorite kind.

Jamie Lynn Carter was a criminal celebrity in Alaska for killing her militia leader boyfriend. She'd almost been killed herself after a fight with her sister Bernadette. They had both gone to prison, Bernadette for shooting Zilla and for planting an axe in General Alex Burke's head, Jamie Lynn for attempted murder, inciting mob violence, illegal firearms dealing and possession of heroin.

Bernadette found healing and salvation in prison. She met other women who had also experienced sexual abuse as children. She sought out counseling. She sought out religious teachings and she fell in love.

Jamie Lynn, scarred as she was from a freak accident during a battle with her sister, took an opposing path during her stint behind bars.

She became more lethal. As scarred on the outside as her killer's soul on the inside, Jamie Lynn embraced the look of her hideous facial scars. She'd spent her six years in prison, not working to control and make peace with her past and her inner demons but instead nurturing her hatred.

When she met Jerry Justice at a pro development rally on the Anchorage park strip, they both immediately recognized the caustic mindset of the other.

A match made in hell.

It wasn't a physical attraction. Jamie Lynn had never found any man attractive. From an early age, men had taken advantage of her. Her stepfather had abused and traded her for booze and drugs, sometimes just for cigarettes. But it hadn't destroyed her. It taught her how to manipulate men. She hadn't loved her former boyfriend, the dead militia leader General Alex Burke, but she wanted what he could provide, so she'd gone along with his stupid ideas and lured a lot of other stupid people to their planned coup of the federal government. She could smell money.

Jamie Lynn had been sniffing around for it then and she was back at it now. Staying on the couch of a militia sympathizer who saw her as the General's young widow and a victim of heavy-handed government law enforcement, she was able to survive, but Jamie Lynn wanted to be on top and she didn't care who she crawled over or killed to get there.

Enter Jerry Justice and the promise of being a movement leader again. She was instantly all in. She'd work this oosik toting fool like she'd always worked men and take his money like she'd planned to take the Generals' before she and her sister killed him and went to prison.

Thinking about that time upset her. Not because she'd almost been killed and had to stab her lover in self defense. No, that was not cause for remorse or regret or some sort of PTSD anxiety. It was upsetting because she didn't get rich and she'd gotten caught.

Jamie Lynn had bided her time until she could get released and get revenge. She refused any prison counseling or group therapy. She was so uncooperative and combative in lock up that she spent a lot of time in isolation and served an extra 14 months because of her disruptive behavior.

Bernadette had found peace in attending church services in prison. She took all the counseling that was offered.

And she found a life partner. Bernadette became a minister and she married her love, Krystal Wright. After release, Bernadette and Krystal settled in a quiet neighborhood in Anchorage. They ran a ministerial counseling service for recently released inmates and worked part time in modest retail jobs. It was a humble life but a happy one. Bernadette tried to connect with her sister but Jamie Lynn would have nothing to do with her. She despised Bernadette's new attitude of compassion and kindness. Jamie Lynn saw it as weakness and stupidity. Besides, Bernadette was a loser. She couldn't even kill one damn reporter.

Jamie Lynn was back. And once again she was going for broke. Jerry Justice's fundraising largess was her first target.

Zilla Gillette was her second. She was determined to finish what her hapless sister had been unable to. She was going to kill Gillette and relish every second of it. She planned to get away with it and Jerry's money.

But the most dangerous thing about Jamie Lynn was that it didn't matter if she did.

As long as Gillette was dead, even if she had to go back to prison, she'd consider it a success.

##

Zilla finally got the string of direct twitter messages the GDC had promised. It had only been two hours between the time of the call and the time they appeared, but it seemed longer for the impatient reporter.

Miss Gillette. On Friday, if you agree to our conditions, you are invited to travel to the GDC wilderness retreat to interview leadership. As you are aware, the Green Defiance Coalition's leaders have gone into hiding because of the extreme number of death threats against them and their families. Because of this risk to their safety, we must ensure that you do not know our location. This is for your safety as well. The federal government under the traitor in chief is charging many of us with treason. It is ridiculous but we cannot be arrested. The potential to be imprisoned for life or killed is far too high. Therefore, it is necessary for us to take extra precautions. Here are the requirements for you to accompany supporters to the GDC compound:

1.   *You must meet our team at 9 am on Friday morning at the bus stop on the corner of Muldoon and Northern Lights Boulevard. If you are not clearly alone, no one will approach you.*

2.   *You will enter a vehicle with the team and be immediately blindfolded.*

3.   *You must agree to keep the blindfold over your eyes until you reach the GDC's encampment. YOU MUST NOT REMOVE IT!*

4.   *These are not unreasonable demands but they are non-negotiable. Your safety will at all times be insured. We must insure ours also. If you agree to our requirements, reply Yes to this message.*

That was it. Zilla read it a few times, then sat back in her desk chair, realizing that she had been sitting bolt upright while reading. She didn't reply right away, wanted to think it through before agreeing to the GDC's terms, but she knew there was no way in hell she was going to miss out on this.

"What's it gonna be pal?" MC Ames wiped the bar top with irritating vigor. The Silver Slipper had always attracted an odd collection of under the legal radar mutts, but the guy who'd just walked in was particularly odd. MC couldn't help his fidgety behavior. The dude was freaking him out.

"I have package for you." His heavy Russian accent didn't help relieve any of Ames's anxiety. "Mr. Volkov sends it. Mr. Hansen will pick up. He will come today. He will ask for it. You will give to him. You will not look at it or ask questions." His eyes were piercing blue, guarded. Ames felt him bore into his thoughts with his penetrating stare, yet offered no hint of his own.

Without taking his eyes off Ames, he pulled a package from his jacket pocket. Wrapped in folded manila and covered with clear packing tape, it had the shape of a large bundle of bills.

Money? Ames didn't know what to do. He stood, staring at the package held in front of him. The stranger's intent was clear. *Here, take this.*

Volkov hadn't told him anything about deliveries from intimidating strangers. He hadn't been instructed to pass along such deliveries, no questions asked, to other people he didn't know. What the hell was this? Drug money? Some kind of pay off? He had a feeling it was a bad idea to accept it and a worse idea not to. He reached for it, barely able to keep the shakiness out of his hand.

"I, um, ok. I didn't hear about any delivery or pick up. How will I know..."

The stranger cut him off. "No questions! Mr. Hansen will ask for his goods. He will come alone. He will wait till no one is here. You will give it to him." As if to drive home the point of his demand for silence, the man, eyes never leaving Ames's face, unbuttoned his jacket and slowly, as if relishing the affect, pulled it back far enough to reveal a large gun.

MC took the package, feeling helpless and scared. Knowing that whoever this Hansen character was would come in and wait till there were no other customers didn't help him feel less afraid. It freaked him out all the more. What the hell was going on? He had loved his new gig, thinking he'd really gotten lucky for the first time in his miserable life, but now he wondered what he'd gotten himself into. If there was an illegal commerce pipeline running through The Silver Slipper, he didn't want to get caught up in it.

The stranger abruptly turned without another word, as soon as Ames grasped the proffered package. He went up the steps toward the street. Ames listened to his receding footsteps on the concrete stairs. He hefted the package up and down a couple of times. It was heavy. It could be a lot of money or it could be a lot of something else. Cocaine? Heroin? Jesus. What should he do?

He briefly heard traffic and street noise as the strange man opened the door to the sidewalk along 4th avenue. MC stood in the quiet, still holding the package outstretched, over the bar. He slowly brought his arm back and lowered it under the bar, sliding the package on top of the cooler beneath it.

He absently picked up the bar towel he'd been using to polish the wood top before the weird encounter. In a daze he resumed swirling the towel across the surface, as if he could recapture the blithe feeling of enjoying his new management position.

He wondered if he'd made a grave mistake. He hadn't asked questions when he was so rapidly offered what seemed like a dream gig. And now he'd been told, quite aggressively and clearly, that he could not. He'd taken the package! Whatever was going on, he was now part of it. His stupid ego, thinking he'd gotten the job because he was so charming and had wowed Volkov mocked him now. He'd been duped and now it might be too late to do anything but what he was ordered to do. The man with the piercing eyes who had just left made MC sure of only one thing.

He was expendable. He was a low level cog in whatever covert machine was operating through The Slip. And he would likely no longer be able to simply refuse future requests, be fired and draw unemployment.

MC was sure that he would disappear if he didn't cooperate and do as told.

Expendable meant dead.

Jerry Justice had developed his showman's style over long years of performance. First on local public access TV in rural Arkansas when he was a kid and later through his lucrative evangelizing routine.

He also had a knack for ferreting out those that could open doors to money and influence. He knew what it took to build a movement, funding and dangerous people willing to do anything to win.

Nakita Volkov was his greatest connection yet.

When he'd worked on developing his shtick on local cable as the star of Jerry's Fitness Club! A sort of low budget PeeWee's Playhouse for chubby rural Arkansas kids, he'd figured out what worked and what didn't. He never gave a rat's ass about the actual children who the program was designed for. He wanted to woo the moms who came with them. Kids didn't have money. Moms did. Jerry wanted money and working his celebrity to get it proved smart.

It was no wonder he and Jamie Lynn Carter took to each other immediately. She had worked over lecherous men for cash and drugs when she was a young teenager and Jerry Justice had worked over attention hungry moms who hoped providing sexual favors and money to young Jerry would somehow secure a spot in Hollywood for their pudgy farm kids.

Jerry and Jamie Lynn were a perfect team of ruthless hucksters.

When Jerry Justice met Nakita Volkov, another piece clicked into place. Neither man liked the other. Justice was an isolationist. He wanted American dominance in every sense of the word and would have loved to kick everyone except the whitest among the masses and the ones who spoke the best English, over borders east, west, north and south. He didn't care where they came from or where they went, he just wanted them gone.

He didn't like Rooskies either, but he had a finely tuned nose for money and Volkov smelled like he was loaded with it.

Volkov despised ill educated American rednecks, but they were useful tools.

Justice started hanging around the Silver Slipper not long after MC Ames took over as bar manager. Jerry heard there was a guy looking to hire some 'information specialists' for a campaign to push for development of Alaska's resources.

He didn't know, but likely wouldn't have cared, that the same guy was hiring 'information specialists' for a campaign to stop resource extraction. Nakita Volkov was working both sides of the divide, because widening that divide, disrupting what had for decades been an impermeable wall of solidarity in America, was at the heart of his work.

Volkov had been dispatched to Alaska to disrupt, cause suspicion, paranoia and divide. Divide. Divide.

Chapter Eight

"Hurry up and get this shit loaded. We gotta get ready to leave." Ralph Sims tossed a third, 50-pound bag of basmati rice to his low-key co-worker. Mook Davis wasn't known for moving fast or working hard and Ralph despised being teamed up with him. Ralph unlike Mook did not fit the stereotype of an environmental activist. He was a burly man who had spent the first 20 years of his professional life supporting the resource extraction side of the political divide.

A brick mason, Sims' oversized, Popeye arms and chest made apparent that he hefted concrete block for a living. He loved his work and never would have dreamed he'd end up supporting the causes of conservation. He'd thought of environmentalists as pale vegans who tended to be emotional and prone to hysterics. People who worked at natural food stores and juice bars.

People who didn't understand the work of real Americans.

But when his little sister died of cancer linked to PCBs in the well water of their neighborhood, his viewpoint evolved. Ralph Sims began to pay attention. Rather than skim the union hall board for the next notice of another project to treat the earth like a giant sandbox, shoving, digging, drilling, re-routing, moving, he read reports on drill rig lubricants, industrial pollutants and most painful to the Army veteran, military toxins sites. Sims educated himself, quietly. It wasn't the kind of thing you enlightened your fellow tradesmen with over beers.

Such talk would be considered treasonous and make you suspicious in the eyes of your hard working brethren.

Make you sound like one of those greenie lilies that kept suing to stop every goddamn good project that came along. He heard the talk daily.

Ralph kept his growing skepticism and anger to himself, but one day he simply couldn't tolerate being quiet any longer and he quit his local association and joined the Green Defiance Coalition.

Now the GDC leadership was in big trouble and being a recognized member didn't merely make you the target of ridicule by roustabouts and extraction proponents.

It could mean your life.

Ralph grabbed the last two sacks of rice, effortlessly tucking a 50-pound bag under each arm to stack near the front of the cab. He ignored Mook who was messing around with his ever-present cell phone. Ralph opened the driver's side door and pulled a blue tarp from behind the seat. The ubiquitous all purpose tool so common in Alaska. Used for temporary shelter, protecting woodpiles from snow, covering roofs, even finding their way into satirical fashion as gowns and tuxedoes for fundraisers in Anchorage.

Ralph was employing it for a more traditional purpose today, covering the staples of rice, beans and of course lots of vegetables, in the back of the pick up. They would transfer the goods to a plane later today but right now they needed to keep the food dry and clean.

"Come on man! Put that shit away for five minutes and help me secure this load. He tossed two bungee cords to Mook before he was ready ignoring that Mook was also ignoring him. They hit Mook's chest and fell, one of the hooks clanking on his precious cell screen.

"Hey! What the hell man? I'm trying to do some work here."

"On your Facebook page? Cut the bullshit and get this covered so we can get the hell out of here." Ralph had a hard time with undisciplined jerks like Mook who were better at standing by as work was being done than pitching in to help accomplish it. That was the biggest problem with this movement in Ralph's mind. It was full of soft people who didn't know how to work, who didn't understand that sometimes you needed to get up in someone's grill and make them see your point to get things done. Ralph felt like if he could convince the union boys, (that he secretly missed) to shore up this effort, they would change things over night from the slow progress of the ninnies who thought they could stop bulldozers through songs and linked arms to the head busters Ralph had worked with for decades.

That would speed things up. They would charge the line, throw the drivers off those bulldozers and turn them around.

But Ralph didn't know what he didn't know. And what he didn't know was that he was purposely placed with the Mooks of the movement to see how he would do. The GDC leadership was not at all like his current work mate. They were as tough, and work savvy as Ralph.

They were also a lot more dangerous than he would have ever guessed. He would learn about this higher level of the organization if he proved to be trustworthy. The GDC group had always been suspicious of those who came around wanting to join, especially former construction workers or brick masons, but they needed the help now and hard workers like Ralph especially so. He was being closely observed and quietly researched. Right now he was tasked with loading food, not firearms.

If he didn't prove to be a mole for the resource extraction group Defend American Development, they'd quickly elevate him.

He would also need to be found clean of any connections to the FBI. His careful vetting process wasn't complete so he would not be one of the staff making the trip to the wilderness compound. Only the highest level of security cleared GDC members knew where it was or even knew of its existence.

Zilla was invited to travel to the compound, (under a stringent list of demands) and though she would no more know the actual location than Ralph, she'd certainly go.

Jamie Lynn Carter was tired of men. An amusing consideration for woman who was not yet 40, but some human lives contain enough trauma and shock to be equal to dog years and Jamie Lynn had experienced bad, times seven.

She longed for money and a beautiful home with columns like regal sentinels along the front porch. She'd seen pictures of southern mansions in an old book among the few possessions her mother had left behind when she ran out on Jamie Lynn and her sister Bernadette. Leaving them vulnerable to the weaknesses of their drunken lout of a stepfather and his vagrant drinking pals.

A mansion on a hill somewhere and enough money to insulate her from the shit the world had thrown at her from the time she was a little girl. She closed her eyes and dreamed of men working on her expansive yard and gardens, men who would serve her drinks on the veranda and attend to her every demand, but none who would share her bed.

She wanted enough money to never have to put out for it again.

She opened her eyes, shook her head to clear the daydreams and exhaled a long sigh, the deep reddish purple scars that crisscrossed her face shining as if they were bright trails to her new future. She still had to work over Jerry Justice to take the money he was bringing in for the DAD, but she was smarter than when she'd fought with the General and almost died. She was smarter and more deadly than when she'd killed an old man at 12 and two women in her twenties. She considered her sister crazy and worthy only of contempt, with her new life as a lesbian preacher. It meant Jamie Lynn had not a single person she gave a rat's ass about.

And no one is more dangerous than that.

"Are you really going on this blindfolded escapade *by yourself?*" Ray pointed his open hands toward Zilla, like a man offering assistance. Assistance he suspected was not wanted, or if he really thought about it, likely wasn't needed by a martial arts master as he knew his humble co-worker was. But on top of his instincts as a man to protect and his instincts as a reporter to be in on a big story, he couldn't help himself. She was his friend and he cared about her. Zilla smiled and cocked her head at him.

"Escapade? Nice choice of words bud. Yes, I am going alone. Not because I'm thrilled about it, but because that's their mandate. Not mine. I'd welcome your help with what will likely be a lot of interviews, and hopefully they won't be so paranoid that they'll bar me from taking pictures."

"But you could push back!" Ray saw a possible opening. "Tell them exactly that, you need help and I'd be willing to be blindfolded too, hell, I'll blindfold myself if that helps! If they really want this story told, they might bend their rules."

"Maybe. Let me think about it. I appreciate your point but I don't want to spook or piss them off and have them give the offer to another reporter." Zilla crossed her arms and looked thoughtfully at Ray. She knew he wasn't trying to just horn in on a big investigative piece. They always worked in tandem on complex stories. It had become a comfortable, professional rhythm between them and it never felt like competition. Zilla knew that was rare in a job where getting it first and with your byline was the drug of choice for journalists.

"I better run all this by Brooks right now. And I promise I'll tell him your idea, see what he thinks. Ok?"

"Ok." Ray sounded disappointed and Zilla couldn't help but laugh.

"Ray, don't play poker. You won't win. You're way too easy to read."

"Only for you Miss laser vision, only for you." He smiled back at her.

"Quit trying to flatter me Mister. That's a skill you definitely have mastered but you need to save it for Mo. She likes it. I don't!" She gave Ray's shoulder a gentle shove and turned to walk across the newsroom to her editor, Ed Brook's office.

Zilla was fairly certain what the gruff oldster would say: Go Alone. And she knew Ray would be fairly certain of the same conclusion, that's why he was bummed when she assured him she'd run his suggestion past Brooks.

Ed Brooks had been a journalist for decades. A former war correspondent, he had reported from some of the most dangerous conflicts in the world. He'd almost died a dozen times. He knew how dicey visiting the compounds of paranoid people with complete devotion to a certain cause could be. But he also had a lot of faith in the people he hired and didn't approve assignments based on whether or not they had more testosterone than estrogen.

Brooks was a stand up guy in a profession dominated by chauvinistic leaders who ran newsrooms where the plum assignments too often went to other men. He assigned based on competence and that is never gender specific, just too often treated that way.

In light of the recent spate of purges that had happened in newsrooms across the nation where men who had used their top positions to harass women or demand some type of sexual exchange for the best reporting gigs, Ed Brooks was a breath of fresh equality air. Grumpy, often abrupt and someone who did not suffer fools, but when it counted, he was the best. He would not tolerate any nonsense in his newsroom between reporters based on ethnicity or whether they were men, women, gay, straight, trans or anything else.

Brooks was an equal opportunity believer and it showed in his work. If he heard personally or was told of any untoward action of one reporter to another, he dealt with it, immediately and decisively. The egomaniacs or harassers were quickly shown the door.

Brooks ran a tight ship and the reporters who were in his newsroom respected him and worked their ass off because of it. The smart ones knew what a good gig it was. There's always stress in newsrooms, it goes with a job where you're often reporting on people at their worst or in their worst crisis and you have to balance the need to treat them respectfully against your need to push for answers to serve the public's right and need to know. It's never easy but working in a healthy, professional environment certainly helps.

Zilla knocked on his door, making eye contact through the glass first to make sure he wasn't on a conference call or otherwise busy. As she rapped her knuckle on the dark wood frame, he motioned her in.

"Hi boss. Got a minute?" Brooks pointed toward a chair, indicating that he did.

"You know the GDC has been in touch with me about going to their compound to talk to the leaders there, right?"

"Right. They want to show you their digs and make their concerns public."

"Well, I hope they also want to clarify what they think is acceptable development and what they'll fight going forward. It seems a lot of where that line is, has been lost in the current hysteria over the Colorado River case." Zilla leaned forward as she spoke.

"I share your hope, but this might be a lot of complaining about how unfair, unreasonable and dangerous the development crowd is. And there are reasons for some of that thinking, but I agree, substantive discussion about what they want for the planet would be helpful. So, what do you need?"

"They've been back in touch with instructions. They're actually mandates. I can go in, but I have to be blindfolded, can't take it off till they say, I can't record or take photos until we're all the way to the compound, although I don't know how I would take pictures before that if my eyes are covered.... but they also insist I go alone. Say it's a deal breaker if it's not just me."

"Well, aren't you special." He grinned, a rare commodity from the serious editor. "So, what's the question? Do you think this is a bad idea? Are you worried for your safety? Your red flag warning pop up?"

Zilla smiled back at Brook's reference to her father's old expression. She'd told Brooks years earlier that her dad had called her particular spidey sense about dangerous situations, her red flag warning system. Brooks hadn't forgotten it. He had seen numerous times when she'd saved her own bacon and that of others, because of it.

"I'm not scared about it. I think it will be fine, but of course it's always helpful to have another set of eyes and ears, after the blindfold comes off I mean, to help out on such an important story. After all, every news organization in the country will want a piece of this story. It will be tough for me to handle alone." She paused for a split second, "Not that I can't! And I will, but Ray's eager of course and well, I promised I'd run the idea by you."

"Could put them off their feed and they'll tell you to shove off, give the story to someone else." Ed, always spot on.

"Exactly. I said as much to Ray, but he raised the point, and it's probably valid, that if they want their story to get out there, they might allow it."

"That's a big might for such a big story." He leaned back in his chair, contemplating. Outside of his office, they could both hear Murph and a couple of the copy editors hollering good-naturedly across the sweep of the newsroom about some rewrites. For as unruly and raucous as newsrooms could be out of the public's eye, the disciplined work was all the more impressive to those who witnessed the bawdry goofiness, understanding it was a useful and harmless pressure relief valve.

"I trust your instinct on this Zilla. If you have any hint of a red flag, go with your gut and try to push for Ray to go along. If you feel you can go safely, do it and enlist his help with national requests when you get back. I can pitch in too." He added, making Zilla think he didn't want to say out loud that he really thought she should just go alone. She admired his tact and was proud of his faith in her.

"Hm, you're not helping me here boss. I wanted to be able to tell Ray that you said not only no but hell no. Now I'll have to be the heavy myself!" She smiled as she said it. "I'll go alone. He'll be disappointed but he'll also get it. He'd likely do the same if the situation were reversed."

"I think that's a safe bet. Anything else?" He was already turning back to an edit he'd set aside when she entered.

"Nope. I'll get back in touch with them right now and let you know when I'll be leaving. Thanks Ed."

"Yur otta yur mind guuuurl." Jerry Justice exaggerated his southern drawl in an effort to tease and charm Jamie Lynn. He playfully squeezed her arm. She pulled away, repelled his cutesy efforts. They were walking on the coastal trail on the edge of downtown Anchorage. Jerry desperately wanted a drink, or eight, but he was trying to convince Jamie Lynn of something he thought was the best plan for their cause and being in a bar wouldn't fit the idea.

"It's the perfect set up hon."

"Don't hon me. I'm not your fucking hon." She growled the words without looking at him, her eyes cast toward the graceful, long sweep of mountain across the water that was called Sleeping Lady by locals.

"Ok, sorry, woo eee, you are cranky today darlin'.... I mean..shit, sorry. Just listen to me for a minute though, ok?" Justice turned toward her as they walked, even though she wouldn't look at him, her face turned toward the salty breeze flowing off Cook Inlet waters. The grotesque scars on her face shiny in the sunlight like neon lines on a backlit map.

"If you played up the religious angle, maybe start going to your dyke sister's church services and...."

"That shit ain't happening!" She spat the words, turning to look at him briefly, her one eye blazing, the dark patch over the other one seemed to also glare.

"Ok, ok, well, just play it up during the meetings then. Say you found god and salvation and all that shit while you were in prison. That you realized there was a bigger plan and that's why the General and you were together to lead people but Satan got involved through those fucking nosy reporters and cops and killed him! Think of how well that would land with this crowd we're working with!" He paused. She didn't swear or give him an evil stare.

He took that as a hopeful sign that she was listening and would buy it. He needed her engaged on this plan. Needed her to help rev up the restless militia that had lost momentum after the general was killed and Jamie Lynn spent six years in prison. Justice saw a big opportunity to combine the still bitter, still outraged and rudderless militia members with the Defend American Development group and channel that anger and aggression into a lucrative fundraising campaign to support their fight against the snowflake tree loving idiots they were up against.

He just had to convince Jamie Lynn to tweak her past performance as a pious, devoted champion of patriot causes to an even more pious woman of god and country who would once again help lead the disenfranchised to glory.

They walked in silence for longer than he would have liked. Jerry found quiet unsettling. He preferred to fill up all available spaces with the sound of his own voice, confident that he was an amazing orator and people were always eager to hear what he had to say.

Finally Jamie Lynn spoke. Jerry didn't realize until she spoke that he'd been holding his breath in an effort to keep from saying something.

"I get it. I know what you're thinking, and you're probably even right as much as I hate saying so. But I despise the idea of going back to pretending I'm a sweet, innocent fucking flower fighting against the government. I'm sick of acting! I like looking like a scary bitch. I AM a scary bitch and I don't want to fake otherwise." She started walking a little faster. "Besides, I ain't pretty no more, who's gonna want to look at me on stage now much less listen to anything I say?" The anger in her voice didn't completely cover the pain of her self-pity.

"Are you kiddin? Honey, oh shit, sorry. Jamie Lynn, you are a legend and a rock star! You had to fight with your man because the cops and the press had so lied and misled him that he thought YOU were the enemy! Guuurlll, Woo eee! You can work this like the golden goose, sugar!" He was so proud of his proclamation that he didn't apologize this time for his smarmy reference.

Jamie Lynn didn't answer, but she shot him a look, her one eye narrowed, that told him she was listening and that was good. He was clever enough to leave it there for the time being. Besides, the sooner he could get back to the parking lot, make an excuse about having to meet with some of the DAD members and get rid of her, the sooner he could head to The Silver Slipper and down a few shots.

Chapter Nine

The President was not helpful. Provocative tweets from his official POTUS account ramped up tensions at a time when decorum was called for.

Russia, North Korea and China were all making noise and raising alerts about Amchitka. Official statements from all three, expressed concern for the American lives that were lost when the massive earthquake pulverized the island, but the missives from the upper reaches of their leadership were thinly veiled threats. The CIA and NSA understood the actual message that was between the lines of the statements. The Communist and authoritarian leaders wanted more information about what had happened on the island in the lead up to 'what was proclaimed an earthquake.' Russia was most direct. Demanding an open, international investigation into what had gone wrong there that could have contributed to the deaths. The Kremlin demanded the release of work orders and materials to better understand the scope of the disaster.

This demand was laughable since no sovereign country would ever release such documents, classified or not. The demand was a positioning statement. Russia was casting doubt on the earthquake as a supposed natural event; planting seeds of suspicion that it was in fact, more underground nuke tests that had gone wrong.

It was the beginning of a hyper spin campaign by the massive network of foreign backed trolls that had proven so effective in creating misinformation and mistrust between Americans. All coming at a time when there was a sentiment that the nation was at the brink of civil war and all it would take is one troll message too many for things to pop off.

Jerry Justice tried not to be too blatant in his rushed goodbye to Jamie Lynn. They had not spoken on the quick walk back to the parking lot. She got in a borrowed car to head back to the home of her current benefactor, hating the lack of privacy and the indignation of sleeping on the couch in a crappy four-plex, but she had no other option beyond reaching out to her sister Bernadette. Jamie Lynn would sleep in the woods in one of Anchorage's many parks before she'd do that.

Jerry also hopped in his truck, oosik rattling at his left side in the double holster that held a sleek handgun on the right. He was shaky for a drink and drove straight into downtown in search of a parking spot near The Slip. Whiskey was calling his name.

Besides, he expected to pick up a package from the Silver Slipper's bartender.

And he wasn't disappointed.

##

Stuart Murphy, in his newshound Murph antennae way, knew Zilla was going to leave for the GDC compound soon and that Ray was bummed about not getting the nod to accompany her. Murph had confidence in Zilla and wasn't worried about her safety. Well, maybe a little, but he had as much faith in her ability as he would if Ray were the one taking off and Zilla was destined to be stuck in the newsroom.

Murph had his own plan for that afternoon.

He was circling back to visiting the Silver Slipper to see if he picked up any weird vibe there. He hadn't forgotten the call to his newsroom phone and although he'd received no others, he still thought he should check it out and besides, he was hungry and a guy's gotta eat lunch somewhere. Might as well be a place that had cold beer too. Normally that would be Ruby's and a pleasant conversation with Ray Walker's articulate grandfather. Ray Senior was running Ruby's Café along with Mo now that Ruby was a member of the U.S. Congress.

Murph enjoyed time spent with the elder Walker, a retired Air Force veteran who was a masterful saxophone player and always up on current events.

But today Murph was going to The Slip. As he drove downtown, he thought about the history of The Sliver Slipper. How it had been a renowned after hours club where great musicians would show up after their regular gigs in other venues and play until dawn. It was also a place legendary for international deal making, money laundering and a not so secretive underground pipeline of contraband or people at odds with the law.

Murphy had covered the trials of the Alaska politicians who had been recorded by the FBI while the hapless fools were eating the food and drinking the booze of a corrupt oil industry service contractor in a Juneau hotel called The Baranof, mere blocks from the state capital. One of Murph's sources had explained that a near constant poker game in that room was a handy way for industry flacks to give bribe money to lawmakers.

The source said, "The oilies bet big and curiously lost every hand. The politicians always won."

Murph had heard the FBI's tape at the trials. He was incredulous at what low amounts some of the politicians took. Ruin your life and career and maybe go to jail for accepting bribes of a thousand dollars? And they were quite proud of themselves, co-opting a slur that had been leveled at them, they had ball caps made with 'Corrupt Bastards Club' printed on the brim.

As he walked down the steps to the bar under the south side of 4th avenue, Murph heard the echoes of one Representative in particular who whined around almost constantly about being broke, while an underling of a corporate king maker dug in his pocket for a few hundred dollar bills to stuff in the buffoon's sweaty palm. He was then considered a sure vote on oil tax legislation that favored the multi-billion dollar industry. For the walking around cash in an executive's pocket, he sold his vote. Murph grinned and shook his head as he pushed open the bar door at the bottom of the dank, concrete stairwell. Even after all the decades he'd been a reporter, people could still surprise him with what he called ISDs-Inexplicable Stupid Decisions.

It was perfect timing for Murph. Not so hot for Jerry Justice and MC Ames. As Murph stepped through the door and cast his eyes toward the bar, he immediately noted two things; Gerald 'Jerry Justice' Hansen was the only patron at the bar and MC had just handed him an extremely interesting bundle. It was made more interesting by the resulting scramble by Jerry Justice to stuff it in his open jacket and the look of surprise and shock on both of their faces. Murph quickly registered that this was not someone returning a novel they'd borrowed and this type of hand off was not something MC had much experience with.

Murph focused on Jerry Justice.

"Mr. Hansen. How goes the fight against the conservationists?"

Justice recovered from his guilty expression of being caught and grinned broadly. "Woo ee, Murphy the reporter! It's going fine buddy. Finer than a set of double Ds. But we gotta keep up the fight. Let those hippy greenies win one battle and it's like the camel's nose under the tent. Pretty damn soon you won't be able to walk on the grass without paying each blade for pain and suffering. Woo ee, it's some crazy shit."

Murph laughed. "Well that sounds a might extreme but you don't mince words about where you stand, that's for sure." He paused for a beat. "Can't say I've ever seen anyone stick carryout inside their jacket. Aren't you worried about mustard on your shirt? Or was that not a chicken sandwich the bartender just handed you?" Murph kept his eyes steady on Jerry Justice but across the bar, MC took a step back. Murph saw him move almost out of his peripheral vision. He tried not to worry that he might be reaching for a weapon, like the handy baseball bat Murph's mom had kept under the bar at his family's tavern. He wanted to gauge Jerry Justice's reaction and he figured MC, inexperienced bar manager, was probably just a little scared.

The emotional shift was dramatic. The smile vanished off Jerry Justice's face and his eyes narrowed. The mirth left his voice and he spoke in a low, flat tone. "Well now Mr. Reporter man, I don't see how that's any of your concern or business. Best not to ask questions."

Murph as always, was undeterred. "Oh, but that's how I make my living. Asking questions. Being curious. And that package sure looked interesting. Not chicken sandwich interesting, but interesting. What's in it?"

"Now I told you once not to poke into my business. You don't want to piss me off boy." Jerry zipped his jacket, making clear he had no intention of showing what was inside it. He downed his shot, glaring eyes never leaving Murph's face. MC was stone silent behind the bar.

"I'm not a boy Hansen. And I don't give a damn if you're pissed off. If you've got nothing to hide, you shouldn't act like you do." Murph moved closer to the bar and sat on a stool.

Jerry Justice ignored Murph and turned toward MC. "Keep it locked down, kid." Then he turned and went out the door that led up to the street.

"Oosik toting asshole." Murph looked at MC and smiled. "Do you always let customers tell you what to do? Why don't you tell me what he just got, maybe I want that instead of looking at the menu."

MC blanched and stammered. "I, I don't know what you're talking about mister."

"You do know selling drugs will get this place shut down faster than you can yell 'Last Call,' yes?"

MC's eyes went wide. "I am NOT selling any drugs here! I would never do that! That was just something Mr. Volkov needed to get to......." He stopped, realizing he should have kept his mouth shut. That's what Jerry Justice meant when he said *keep it locked down, kid.* MC picked up the bar towel and started scrubbing the wooden top furiously. "So, do you want a drink or what?" MC didn't look at Murph as he spoke, but he felt sick at the older man's response.

"Sure. I'd like a tap beer and a menu. I'll take my lunch to go. Very curious to see how you wrap up your carry out here."

**

Zilla had a massive headache. The plane she'd ridden in was small, loud and either had exhaust issues or they were carrying jugs of gasoline. She could smell fuel the entire trip. She had no sense of how long they'd flown.

Being blindfolded made it worse.

Now after what seemed an interminable amount of time jostling along a rutted trail, she'd finally yanked the blindfold off, to the protests of one of her escorts. After a quick pee break, she was bouncing up the mountain road again the blindfold off and the two men in the front of the four-wheel drive vehicle were silent as they made their way up the final mile to the GDC compound.

The sun was brutally brilliant and it had taken Zilla more than a couple of minutes to get used to the hot glare. She rolled down the window next to her, not asking permission now that her eyes were uncovered and inhaled deeply, trying to clear the ache behind her eyes with clean air. A few minutes later, she forgot about her throbbing head as the trail leveled out and the trees opened to a clearing on a shelf of land that jutted from the mountainside. Buildings and people were visible in front of them. They had arrived at the secret compound of the Green Defiance Coalition.

Chapter Ten

The destruction on Amchitka Island had nearly blasted the island in two. Now a huge, sloshing maw where above ground infrastructure and the infamous test wells had formerly stood was evidence of an extreme event. Twisted chunks of metal, splintered, exploded pieces of wooden supports that looked like they'd been chewed on by monsters, jagged chunks of concrete, rebar bristling from what had been heavily reinforced walls of the test wells rose and fell with the surf like the respirator of a bomb victim on life support.

But if that had been the case it would have been a family in denial leaving the machine on. There appeared to be nothing left of the original build up from all those decades ago.

The signs of newer human activity were evident. Pallets of materials, three backhoes, several large dump trucks and other signs of a burgeoning construction, or in this case, de-construction, were there, farther away from the main test well site and the incredible power that had caused the earthquake destruction.

The years of fighting and the enormous expense of those fighting for full clean up and remediation, the resulting win, the beginnings of what would be a difficult and costly clean up, all vanished in the course of a very few minutes of grinding, heaving power generated from massive, tectonic movement far below the seafloor.

One of the engineers who, by luck of the draw, happened to be away from Amchitka when the earthquake struck, was in awe of the strength of the quake. After a helicopter flight over the destruction, MIT educated engineer Claude Sampson's comments to reporters reflected his amazement.

"I've been an engineer for 24 years. Never before have I seen such massive destructive. The core facility was completely destroyed. The devastation is incredible." Pressed for reaction to Russia and now China's suspicions about it, Sampson was emphatic.

"Speculation about this being a human caused event is ridiculous and dangerous for the global community. The American military did not cause this earthquake. The earth moved on it's own volition. Period."

But his clear, unequivocal statement did not matter to the bots that were busy pumping out negative propaganda at a breathtaking pace. The U.S. Government had lied in the past about Amchitka, why wouldn't they now? Because the destruction had been so massive and so complete, there was no way for the U.S. to prove there hadn't been an attempt at building a top secret, underground missile site at Amchitka.

The U.S. government would never release work orders, materials lists or other documents that would show the Amchitka work was absolutely the result of a Supreme Court decision ordering the clean up. Declaring the site there a FUDS-Formerly Used Defense Site that needed full clean up and remediation had been seen as the right and proper action by most of America's citizens, even at the enormous expense of restoring the island to the pristine state that a wildlife refuge designation demanded. But now the political fall out resulting from the uncanny timing of a mega thrust earthquake was causing division and dissent in a country already suffering a division not seen since the Civil War.

The Trump administration was in a precarious situation. Releasing Amchitka related documents would look like weakness to hard line isolationist Americans who didn't give a damn what Russia and China thought. There was also speculation that Russia, China and North Korean detractors would call the documents fake regardless. An easy bet would wager the release would be seen as manufactured propaganda to shore up the U.S. claims of a supposed earthquake.

Those suggestions were already starting to filter out through the effective network of paranoids who slurp up unsourced, unverified proclamations on YouTube channels and dark net sites, but wouldn't believe a congressional investigation no matter who led it or what the results were. The dangerous cracks and fissures in America's democracy where the growing stream of misinformation was pushing, constantly pushing, building force as more and more was fed into the larger online flow.

Small tributaries of hatred, bigotry, racism, sexism, homophobia, suspicion of Democrats, suspicion of Republicans, fear of Russia, dismissal of Russian threats, fear of environmental devastation, protests over 'snowflakes' who wanted to lock up natural resources, all trickled into the larger river that was building behind the dam of what had for more than 200 years, been a solid democracy. Even with the partisan yelling that has always gone on, the open criticism and ridicule of the occupants of the highest elected offices on U.S. soil was a testimony for decades, that a true democracy existed here, where you could publicly make those critical statements and not be hauled off in the night at the order of government backed military forces.

But the fractures were deep and the River of Hateful Rhetoric was relentless and rising.

If the dam gives way, the once again dubiously 'elected' leader of Russia and the recently installed, possibly for life leader of China would be well situated to take advantage of a weakened America. North Korea would gleefully come along for the ride for a chance to forcefully slap the American leader that Kim Jong-un had called an "old lunatic" a "mentally deranged dotard" a "frightened dog."

This was an extremely delicate time in great need of international diplomacy. Germany, Italy and France were drawing a hard line with Russia over the poisoning of a former KGB spy on

UK soil, but none of those countries nor Canada or Mexico was exactly thrilled with American leadership right now. Tariffs, immigration, the President's constant harassment about other world leaders and his calls for Mexico to build a wall had all worn thin the strong fabric that had been the UN and NATO alliance after World War Two.

The America First crowd continued their primal scream that we didn't need any foreigners to help us. *American Might will Rule!* was the common battle cry, but even the most prepper heavy, fight ready hoarder of guns and ammo, regardless of their numbers, which were admittedly impressive and growing across the country, would be no match for the military swagger of Russian and Chinese forces if America had to take on the fight alone.

It would be holding a handgun to a howitzer.

If America fell into a constitutional crisis and impeachment proceedings started at such a time, all bets would be off. One CIA cyber security agent who was watching the stream of misinformation about Amchitka grow into a torrent told his colleagues that it might be a good time to either 'move to Switzerland or learn Russian and Chinese.'

##

Jerry Justice was a happy camper. It took everything he had not to run out of The Silver Slipper after taking the so very intriguing taped up bundle from MC Ames. A casual response after the embarrassed surprise of having a well-known, sharp eyed reporter see the hand off between Ames and himself was important for at least trying to save face. Justice figured he wasn't fooling Murph but he knew he should try, resisting the urge to bolt out the door so he could dash to his truck and tear open the brown envelope to count the cash that was inside.

Beautiful, untraceable cash.

Jerry Justice had been dealing with Russian confidence men long enough to be sure that the money they offered would not be linked to anything. When he left The Slip, he forced himself to walk in his southern casual way that he was known for. His ridiculous and ever present oosik dangling from one side of his Howdy Dowdy leather holster, the other side snugly held a loaded handgun. Open carry was one of the things Jerry Justice adored about Alaska. It was one of the best states in the nation to be a gun lover. No matter the whining youngsters across the country that yammered for gun control. America was a violent place. Was founded on violence and used violence to control not only its poor and dark skinned residents but also other poor and dark skinned countries across the globe.

Nobody was taking any fucking guns from Americans. Jerry Justice was as sure of that as he was that his much loved oosik was the penile symbol of male dominance and his gun was the final arbiter of any disputes about it.

He unlocked and slid into the cab of his truck, finally able to dislodge the package from his inside jacket pocket. Jerry looked up the sidewalk and glanced in his rearview mirror to see who may be strolling by on the downtown sidewalk. It was fall so the summer tourist flow had tapered off.   This afternoon there was only the perennial crop of homeless inebriates sitting in the grass of the small Elizabeth Peratrovich Park on 4th avenue. They thought they were clever and possibly invisible as they snuck sips straight out of a clear plastic bottle of cheap vodka. Being drunk in public was not a crime in Anchorage, but sipping from an open container was. Jerry shook his head as he tore open the brown paper.

And there it was: three neatly bundled stacks of hundred dollar bills. Thirty thousand dollars.

It was just a down payment, but still an impressive symbol of serious intent. Jerry Justice knew what he was supposed to do with the funds and he would spend the rest of the day working his contacts to deploy assistants in neighborhoods across the city and in communities across the state. It was a phone tree on steroids. Every call Jerry Justice made would triple within an hour, and keep building across Alaska and the nation.

School kids seeking gun control would be no match for adults with guns and an unhealthy mindset of paranoia and suspicion. The cash 'donated' for gas, ammo and Justice suspected, lots of weed and heroin, made his cohorts even more passionate about their rights. Unlike the young people who believed in solidarity and the potential for change, the crowd that listened to the Jerry Justices and Jamie Lynn Carters of the world trusted only those they could see in front of them at meetings and rallies. They believed only part of the information on one cable news channel and got all the rest of their information from a handful of underground websites that churned out their particular flavor of conspiracy, misrepresentation of facts and outright lies.

They would never believe the nonsense that the 'lamestream' media kept trying to force down their throat. To believe in isolationism meant not believing that Russian bots were crawling across the cyber border trying to pollute their mind and persuade them with foreign propaganda. No true American patriot could believe that. The liberal media perpetrated that lie to try to confuse them. It was preposterous to think some Russian hacker could snooker good Americans.

They believed Pizzagate; the story about Hillary Clinton kidnapping children through an east coast pizza restaurant was true. Just like they knew Barack Obama was a secret Muslim who was born in Africa. The idiot snowflake liberals could swallow all the horseshit propaganda they wanted and hopefully choke to death on it, true Americans knew the score and you wouldn't find that truth in the 'failing' New York Times or on the whiny NPR stations that employed lots of dark skinned people with weird names, who were probably all transgender predators trying to spy on your kids in the bathroom.

The former Arkansas child cable star understood these Americans and a little cash, a lively revival style meeting with beer and salmon was all the Trumpinistas needed to be ready to kick ass and take names. Mostly for the purposes of deporting anyone not named Smith or Jones.

Jerry Justice whistled a cheery little song as he drove to his cramped apartment in east Anchorage. There was nothing he loved better than a good fight. Well, that wasn't exactly true. The cash resting against his leg on the seat of his truck was his true love, but spreading dissent and confusion, supplying a fat stream of misinformation that led to chaos and fighting, was a close second place.

Today's lesson boys and girls, centered on teachings related to hating thy neighbor. Especially if they drove an electric hybrid car and had a No Mines! Or Keep It In The Ground! Bumper sticker.

##

Zilla jumped out of the back seat of the SUV, glad to be over her gut-churning trip up the mountainside and rid of the irritating cover over her eyes. She blinked a few times to clear the haze from her vision and marveled at what lay in front of her. The Green Defiance Coalition clearly had deep pockets. This was no shabby 'repurposed' materials outfit. Zilla wasn't sure what she had expected but images of rusty fuel tanks and plywood shanties would have been wrong. This was a state of the art facility with every imaginable creature comfort. All of it off the grid.

Solar panels lined the perimeter of every natural opening. The panels featured specially designed camouflage coating to conceal its presence from the air. Buildings of no more than two stories were built in what initially appeared to be a haphazard manner, but Zilla would soon learn the meandering approach was purposeful and strategic. Above the buildings, more camouflaged panels covered the roofs, all of them secured six inches off the surface of the roofing. Zilla had her notebook out and was quickly writing notes on her first impressions. She'd decided not to take out her camera until she spoke to someone in charge. Best to start off on good footing with a group that suddenly found itself media wary.

"More solar panels?" She pointed to the curious coverings on every building, the six-inch airspace the same for all. She wasn't sure if the quiet driver would answer. He'd said only a handful of words on the trip up the mountain. She could see two men and a woman coming toward them after the younger man who had been her escort went to fetch the leaders. She waited, hoping for a quick answer, her pen held aloft above her narrow reporter notebook.

The driver shuffled his feet, seemed irritated at her expectation that he would answer. He was thin and tall with salt and pepper hair and a few days beard growth. He frowned, looked at the roofs and then at Zilla, his eyes though, were a soft brown, no malice lived there.

"They're heat shields. Someone flying over at night wouldn't see a heat signature from the buildings."

Zilla wrote while she responded. "Really? Is this a new addition since the trouble after Amchitka?"

He smiled. It was pleasant but a little sad. "No, the compound was designed five years ago to be as hidden as possible. We saw trouble coming. Every environmental court case that is decided in our favor, in the *earth's* favor raises the hate quotient by a factor of 20. As climate change and environmental causes have gained traction in other countries and here, the threats have grown more serious."

The three people, accompanied by the young man who had ridden shotgun up the mountain were almost to them. The brown-eyed man finished. "We knew we'd need a place to retreat to eventually. Just didn't think it would be this soon." He drew his lips into a tight line, looked out over the expansive valley to the north and said no more.

The trio of leaders was upon them now and a smiling woman with blonde dreadlocks held her hand out toward Zilla. "Miss Gillette? I'm Ally Sanders. Welcome to GDC's oasis." She shook Zilla's hand, her grasp dry and firm, palm rough with the calluses of one who does a lot of physical work. Zilla figured Ally was in her late 30s. "This is Frank Cook and Steve Wallace. We're GDC's counselors."

Zilla shook the hands of the two men. Both also had firm, callus-laden handshakes. Snowflakes indeed. These people were clearly tough and in the kind of physical shape that comes from years of manual labor.

"Counselors? As in camp counselors?" Zilla asked, only half kidding.

"Ha!" Ally laughed and the other men smiled. Zilla relaxed a bit. " No, we're legal counsel for GDC. We're the Green Defiance Coalition's staff attorneys."

Zilla was a little surprised, a little embarrassed. It was a good reminder to never judge a book by its cover. These three, as did her drivers, all looked like college dropouts. Longish hair, dusty clothes and scuffed up work boots. At a fast glance you would be tempted to see them as Timothy Leary followers. Tuned in, turned on and dropped out. But Zilla registered the intelligence and apparent health in their eyes. None of this first group of five looked like druggies or dropouts.

Their don't give a shit appearance was misleading. Zilla wondered if that was by design. She was eager to meet more of the workers here to see if this impression held. How many more would be well educated and unconcerned about the so-called social norms of dressing for success? Looking lawyerly didn't seem to be a priority for them. Even though they were in a remote location, Zilla had spent enough time around lawyers and top tier executives to know that even when they're on the beach, they still manage to look at least semi official.

Marcus Peterson had been a self centered egomaniac who came to a shocking and dramatic end but Zilla was now wondering if he was a rogue outlier, as she'd heard suggested from other green movement people.

"I imagine you're tired, it's a grueling trip to get here and I know you were blindfolded which adds to the stress. Are you hungry? Thirsty?" This was the man identified as Frank Cook. "Want to lie down for a while?" His concerned tones were unexpected and a little off-putting. Zilla was a reporter. She was here to work. She wasn't a delicate flower that needed care. As always with these types of superfluous questions, she wondered if Mr. Cook would ask the same things if Ray would have been here rather than her.

"I'm fine. Thanks. I'd like to get to work if that's finally allowed." Zilla already had her notepad in hand but she was itching to get her camera out and wanted to set up interviews immediately.

Ally spoke again. "Yes. You're free to take photos now if that's what you're referring to. And as far as interviews, you can speak with any of the three of us." Her smile had faded a bit and her tone was firm.

"Only the three of you or am I cleared to talk with others here?"

"Only the three of us. Although we may identify a few others who will also be able to answer some questions, once we know what you're hoping to learn." The young woman clearly wanted to control the message that would be leaving the compound in Zilla's notebook, camera and mind.

To say she was irritated would have been putting it mildly, but Zilla was also good at controlling the message she conveyed with words or body language. She kept her anger in check. "Why the tight sideboards? I was hoping to speak to a wide range of people. Would like to learn about their backgrounds, how they came to the movement and rose to a level that brought them here."

She swept her hand, gripping the notebook, in a wide arch. There were people working on various projects. Within her view she saw four people gardening, three others were feeding a large pen of chickens, or rather two were feeding, one was gathering eggs. Still others were doing carpentry work on what appeared to be a new housing unit. Zilla could hear voices, laughter and the sounds of kitchen work from a building off to the left of where she stood with the others. That's where she'd seen the tall driver and his younger companion walk off to when the lawyers had shown up.

Ally stuffed her hands in her back jean pockets and shrugged. "Well, that's a problem."

She leveled her gaze at Zilla, the intensity of it made Zilla glad she wasn't facing this young woman in court. She would clearly be a formidable adversary. Zilla had a brief thought about the casual-by-design attire the three attorneys were wearing. Suits and ties were the standard battle armor of most of the denizens of court appearances. Lawyers wore them to look imposing, impressive, intimidating- pick your descriptor, and it was meant to convey a sense of being in control, in charge. Maybe these attorneys employed a different tactic. One that let you assume they really were the granola crunching, hapless snowflakes that the hard right would want you to believe.

But in only her first five minutes on the ground, Zilla had already learned that these people were not bliss ninnies who zoned out on flowers and chirping birds all day. They were serious, smart and in charge. Ally continued.

"You don't know this yet, couldn't know it, but you will by the time you leave here Miss Gillette. Everyone on this GDC compound," she swept her arm toward the various buildings, people and activity going on behind them, "has either had numerous death threats, outright attacks, their homes and cars broken into and ransacked, their kids harassed at school, or all of these things combined. There are a number here who have also been injured by small explosive charges wired into their cars, garage door openers, mailboxes, even a few cases of lawnmowers and leaf blowers detonating and causing shrapnel damage to legs, arms, one man lost an eye." She pointed to a nondescript, long, single story brown building that looked like barracks. "That's an infirmary. We've got staff doctors and when people are hurt in these attacks, whenever possible, they're brought directly here rather than going to a local hospital."

"Why?" Zilla was close to speechless but asked the obvious question.

"For a lot of reasons. They're safer for one thing. We don't give the opposition the satisfaction of letting their attempts to intimidate and silence us get into the local press and more importantly, Miss Gillette, we take care of our own. We take care of our supporters. Their lives and identity are at risk and we won't let you talk to just anyone here. When they leave, the last thing they want is for their names and affiliation with us to be public. This is real."

"Why would you let me know this but not let me confirm those stories with facts and names? I'm sorry but what you're telling me sounds...a little crazy, paranoid. If it's true, why not let me confirm and legitimize this? It sounds like you have victims of domestic terrorism here."

Finally now the man identified as Steve Wallace spoke. His voice measured, cautious, Zilla could easily imagine him in court, wondered if he ever wore a suit and tie or if his brand of armor was always the sneak attack kind. His words cinched that thought for her.

"Because we trust that you will be able to tell this story in the right way without putting our members, our supporters at greater risk. We trust that you will be honest in your approach and follow the rules we've established for this visit. We trust you won't create a situation where someone who helps in our cause ends up dead, or one of their family members does. This is not paranoid conspiracy Miss Gillette. These attacks are real, they're coordinated and they will only get worse if descriptions of them make it into the press in the wrong way."

"The wrong way?" Zilla cocked her head and raised her eyebrows at him. Someone across the clearing shouted to a co-worker that more nails were needed. "If you're looking for public relations, you brought the wrong person up here. I don't shape my reporting one way or another to fit someone's idea of the right message. I observe, research, ask questions and repeat that process until I feel confident I have an accurate picture of the story I've been assigned. I take my work very seriously and I don't burn sources, but I also don't embellish or subtract to make the people in my reporting look better or worse." She looked all three of them in the eyes, tamping down her growing anger. "So, I need you to let me off the chain so I can do my job. The more you try to control your message, the fewer questions I can get answered, the more it looks like you're hiding something."

Wallace lashed out. "We've got nothing to hide! We're trying to protect people's lives! The United States has gone insane under Trump. He foments dissent, hatred and division. His supporters are rabid and love nothing better than a good ass kicking on a Friday night. Gays, Muslim, blacks, Hispanics, take your pick and now he's turned his ire on the conservation and environmental movement that is trying to save the planet. Save THEIR lives! And all they want to do is belittle, silence and destroy us, all with the blessing of a man who is functionally illiterate and shockingly the president of our nation. And all in the name of developing, burning and sucking up every drop of oil, cutting down every old growth tree, mining every mountainside, damming every river to stupidly water unsustainable luxury crops to feed massive, land poisoning lots full of antibiotic ridden cows and pigs and chickens." He blinked, his face red with rage. Zilla stayed quiet, as did his colleagues.

His tone softened and he smiled. "I realize that sounds like the flip side of the rant you'll hear from the supporters of the Defend American Development crowd. Those who say we don't want to walk on a blade of grass or eat a chicken wing. That we'd have us all living in caves in the dark, but look around you, Miss Gillette." he tipped his head toward the activity behind them. "Who do you think is closer to the truth for the future? I trust you believe in science and facts. Do *you* think we can keep burning fossil fuel at the rate we are? Do *you* think cutting down vast swaths of carbon sequestrating forests to plant acres of water guzzling almonds will help us achieve the goals of the Paris Climate Accord? Do *you* think we can keep ignoring the signs of our planet wobbling toward complete chaos?"

They were all silent for a moment. A Steller's Jay, that curious blue bird sporting a head tuff resembling a guy with bed head, swooped over them, squawking. It landing on a tree branch a few feet away, peering at them intently.

"You raise compelling points Mr. Wallace and I do believe in science and facts. I also believe in independent, clear eyed reporting that separates heat from light. I'll focus on the light and to do that well, I need access, as unfettered as possible."

He looked at her as if she hadn't heard a word he'd just said. His voice was bitter. "I'll keep focusing on the heat. From hysterical, misinformed people who would rather see us jailed or dead than listen to the truth and do the hard work of changing their behavior. I'll focus on the heat of the passion the people who support us have for doing what is right, whatever the personal cost. And I'll focus on the literal heat. Increasing degrees of it that the deniers scoff at. When their homes are destroyed by hurricanes, ocean storm surges, extreme cold or wild fires, mudslides and every other sort of climate disaster coming our way, maybe they'll stop scoffing. It will be too fucking late by then. I don't enjoy the idea of having the last laugh, Miss Gillette, because it will mean the end of a habitable earth for humans."

Zilla leaned in. "Then let me talk to people beyond the three of you. If you truly believe this apocalyptic vision of the future, then what the hell do you have to lose by letting one Alaska reporter tell your story?"

Chapter Eleven

It wasn't noticeable at first. Ray Walker Senior or Poppa Ray as he was known to his grandson, the astute reporter and third in the line of Raymonds, added it up to just a couple of bad weeks. Business ebbed and flowed and Ruby's Café maintained a healthy flow of clientele. Paying the bills and making payroll was never a problem.

But Poppa Ray knew something was off, there were faces that normally could be seen focused on a steaming bowl of gumbo, chomping on a halibut burger or dancing to the hot blues and jazz music that flowed off the stage from Joey 'Strings' Tagliano's deft guitar riffs, that were now absent from the bar.

They just were not there. Ray Senior had been in Anchorage for years; helping his daughter in law Ruby run the business after his son, Ray the second, died of a heart attack. Poppa Ray was retired from the Air Force and a second career as a Post Master in Louisiana but Alaska was where he would live out the rest of his days. His wife was also gone and he missed her every day. Being in Anchorage where his son's lovely widow and his only grandson lived was his salvation from a lonely old man's misery.

Here he was productive and needed. Ray senior loved to work and had happily taken on some of the daily chores that running a bar and café required. He also drew a great crowd on

Tuesday nights, his old saxophone like the Pied Piper's flute, drawing them in the door.

Maybe that was the distinction. The Pied Piper had lured rats and when Ray pondered his hunch about a change in the customer base, it occurred to him that rats were missing in the crowd. Ray knew rats. He was a black man who had grown up in the south. He knew the overt kind from his home state of Louisiana where blatant racism was too often tolerated and subtly encouraged, to the more covert kind that lived in northern cities. They had to be a little more careful about their hatred of dark skinned people, had to work a bit to hide their fear, their distain, their lack of education. Education that lessened fear of those who come from different backgrounds, that led to acceptance and the knowledge that diversity is good and healthy for any society. The cultural and ethnic values that make us different also make us interesting and skilled in ways that are worth knowing and respecting.

Ray knew well the expressions. The smile that faded when a Caucasian first time customer saw him emerge from the kitchen, crisp white bartender apron snugged around his waist. An old school tavern keeper with a radiant smile that never faltered on those occasions, when he realized this customer was suddenly wishing he hadn't walked in with his wife but now couldn't figure out an easy way to walk back out without looking like a racist dolt. Even racist dolts don't always want to look like bigots in public.

Usually Ray, or Ruby's legendary food, won them over. Ray didn't treat the men who had that veiled look of race contempt in their eyes any differently than he treated those who looked like him or those who didn't but respected who he was.

Taking the money from a man, who through small words and actions revealed his small mind but despite his wish that a white person was their server, couldn't resist the food and music, was a deep pleasure for the elder Ray. It tickled him immensely to consider how often the electric bill, the taxes, the food suppliers and booze distributors were paid with dollars of those who wished men like Ray didn't exist. He'd spent more than two decades in the military and he understood that greater good could be achieved with the resources of unwilling individuals. Sometimes those resources were bodies for cannon fodder, sometimes dollar bills.

He felt like he was seeing the answer to the puzzle of missing clients. The race rats that didn't like black or brown men but sure loved a well-cooked slab of salmon or a bowl of fragrant brown roux gumbo filled with fresh seafood. They had begrudgingly frequented Ruby's Café, like guilty philanderers sneaking around on their white friends, but now were no longer coming through the door.

Ruby was a U.S. Congresswoman now. After the bizarre poisoning death of former Alaska congressman Hank Emerson, Anchorage residents enlisted Ruby to run for the open seat. Ray senior and his grandson Ray the third were terrifically proud of her but the elder Ray knew it would affect their clientele.

Even men, who could tolerate a black man running a business where the food was too good to pass up, could not tolerate a Democrat, and Ruby was a D all the way. Both Rays had suggested she run as an independent since national politics on both sides of the political divide had become so untenable, but Ruby felt it was important to try to right the ship and she believed in many of the tenets the Democrats had traditionally espoused.

The current absences in customer flow were another layer of civic divide. It started soon after the Amchitka disaster and was more obvious in recent days. Poppa Ray was troubled by the widening gap between the pro industry supporters of groups like Defend American Development, the D.A.D. crowd of burly construction and heavy equipment workers and those who sent donations or at the very least had a bumper sticker championing the cause of the Green Defiance Coalition, the G.D.C. believers.

What had been the long running but generally non violent philosophical differences between those who wanted to drill baby drill and those who wanted to plant carbon absorbing trees had become more aggressive, more heated, more violent. Those who assumed that Ruby's D meant she fawned over tree huggers were not showing up for their weekly shot of hot music and cold beer. There was a growing tension in the city, as in the nation. Poppa Ray wasn't worried about paying the bills; he was worried about the erosion of those small things that keep a diverse community loosely knitted together in a harmony that kept at bay the worst interactions between those who hate and those who are the target of that ire.

He'd seen those ugly clashes too many times in the deep-south when he was a young man and his worry focused on his grandson, the reporter and especially on his daughter in law, the newly minted politician. Ruby's family reflected the growing reality of the nation. Ruby was white, her late husband, Ray the second was black, their son reflected the blended America of today.

This gnawed at Poppa Ray's peace of mind.

Fear, which is at the heart of racism, gets more erratic, unpredictable and dangerous as it is threatened with extinction. He knew those missing faces from the weekly crowds at Ruby's had not disappeared to some all white planet in another galaxy.

They were still around.

They were still gathering, now away from the blended crowds of a harmonious community. Now they were going underground to reinforce each other's hateful rhetoric and fan the flames of paranoia and disinformation.

Separation meant something and it was rarely good.

##

The intuition that was needling Ray senior was also the brooding focus of Mo Scott, long time evening bartender for Ruby, fiancée of Ray the Third and columnist for the Anchorage Daily Standard. Mo also understood the subtle and not so subtle race tensions that were part of daily life for people of color.   Mo's people had been centuries long in this country when white immigrants first showed up. Mo was Athabascan Indian from the beautiful and wild country northeast of Anchorage where her relatives still lived along the mighty Yukon River. Her cultural antennae had also been thrumming and she was working on a series of columns to delicately address the growing chasm in Anchorage, a city that had the dubious distinction of being one of the most dangerous in the nation for women, especially Alaska Native women.

She felt the current climate was a broader angst than one race imagining itself superior to another. This was rolled up in deeper politics, money and legal decisions that sought to change the power dynamic in America in a profound way.

Mo had seen environmentalists make assumptions about Native people. Thinking that because traditional people understood that clean water meant life and clean soil and air meant healthy physical beings, they must adhere to all of the same beliefs. But extremists of any stripe are always a concern.

Just as Mo knew the elders did not want mine waste in salmon rich rivers or oil development to drive off the bowhead whales that her Inupiaq cousins relied on for sustenance, she also knew they would never align themselves with supporters of men like the recently deceased Marcus Peterson. He would have stopped at nothing to prevent the whaling tribes from catching one of their most important yearly harvests of protein.   The elders were also not uniformly opposed to growth and development. They had adapted to modern ways of living and they understood that if cultural identity were to survive intact into the future, they must figure out how to keep young people connected to their villages, their language, their subsistence traditions. The practical answer was responsible development of some resources. Jobs were needed. There was no going back to heating and lighting homes with seal oil lamps. Young people were hungry for both worlds, that of their elders, and that of the Instagram generation.

To have that, you had to have cash. You could no longer barter with neighboring communities or tribes for all of your needs. You couldn't trade fish or hooligan oil or meat, hides and berries for the monthly electric bill. The local Internet provider wouldn't accept bear fat for unlimited data.

Too often well-intentioned people who thought they were saving Native people when they were fighting to protect a river or a mountain were as unwittingly paternalistic as the government they were railing against. Too many times had elders seen strangers show up offering to 'help' them address concerns over off shore oil development or massive gold mine prospects that threaten salmon, only to have those same helpers drown out local voices and muck it up for everyone. Dividing families and communities in ways that hadn't before existed in ten thousand years of rural life.

There had been skirmishes over territory and game resources, family disputes or disagreements about leadership, but those had largely been handled through traditional methods, like consultations with elders or other respected leaders. It was the way people of the north and the arctic had maintained vibrant cultures and thrived for thousands of years before paler skinned distant relatives showed up, elbowing in with a different way of viewing the world and an aggression that was at odds with the norms of the past.

Mo was too young to remember the broader civil rights struggles of the 50s and 60s, but she'd studied them, she'd heard stories of despair and triumph from her family members and friends from the lower 48.

She couldn't know exactly what that tension felt like from those turbulent days of struggle, but she figured it was a lot like what she was feeling now.

None of them had discussed their collective sense of unease. At least not yet, but Zilla's reporting partner Ray was experiencing the same anxiety that his granddad and his girlfriend were.

Ray was nervous about his mom's scheduled appearance at the annual Midnight Sun Midnight Run. It was a fundraiser for local organizations that helped people struggling with health problems, empty pantries or a lack of gas money. It was wide ranging assistance for neighbors in need and it was a very popular event. Alaskans can be cantankerous contrarians but they are top notch when it comes to helping each other when needed.

It was the 10th anniversary of the event and the number of pre-registrants had set a record at two thousand. Ruby was scheduled to speak before the first wave of runner/walkers took off from downtown. The various courses were all 5Ks so the plan was to have people filtering into the downtown area starting around 8 pm, where fourth avenue would be lined with food trucks, live music and performances in a festival atmosphere that would conclude around ten pm. All the registration fees and half of food and beer sales would get divvied up among the selected groups.

It was the kind of gathering that was normally all about the good will of good humans but the tension in the nation also rippled through Anchorage like a rogue electrical line seeking to ground. Ray felt like he was waiting for that nasty shock and he didn't want his mom around when it happened. It was the first time he felt she might be safer in the DC swamp than in her home city in Alaska.

Anchorage had become the staging ground for the two sides locked in a philosophical battle over resource development and the future. Other groups were also coalescing around those sides, like moths to a flame, drawn to the heat of dissent. Those who supported the right to develop, those who didn't, those who loved the military and thought forcing clean ups threatened resources to protect the nation in a conflict, those who thought that was deflection bullshit.

More and more fringe provocateurs were arriving in Anchorage and most of the dissenters loved to hear Jerry Justice speak. The green defiance supporters were less visible, less vocal than they had been in the past both because their leaders were in hiding somewhere and because being public about their belief in renewable energy and denouncing fossil fuel had become a dangerous gambit. There had always been conflict and confrontations between those who wanted to wean the world off oil and those who wanted to develop more of it, but since the Supreme Court case it had gotten worse and now it wasn't just threats of violence. There was violence.

Ray didn't want his mom to be caught up in a clash that could pop off between the angry factions. The Midnight Sun Midnight Run was supposed to be a fun family event and usually was exactly that. Ray had a hunch it could be co-opted by angry D.A.D supporters who wanted to make their case about the need to develop and the threat to jobs that the still to be determined lower court decisions could mean. They would want to plead that case in a very public place and the gathering before the run where a U.S.

Congresswoman would be speaking meant television cameras.

Ray had hoped for some legislative snafu that would require Ruby to stay in Washington, but none had surfaced and she was on a flight to Anchorage right now. He felt like he was trying to carry water in a leaky pail to a raging fire. Zilla was on assignment at some crazy remote compound with no ability to contact or be contacted. He figured she'd return but who could be sure? Ray wished she were back. Partially because he'd feel better once his friend and working partner was safely back in Anchorage and mostly because he appreciated her clarity in dicey situations.

Ray also knew from experience that if shit was going down, Zilla was who you wanted there to have your back. His reporter antennae was picking up the static that was building and he had a growing sense that it was directly related to Ruby's safety, although he had no idea why or what that meant.

For the hundredth time he wished Zilla were back as he drove toward the airport to pick up Ruby.

The rally the Congresswoman was this evening. Ray felt helpless. He couldn't stop his mom from addressing the crowd by telling her he had a bad feeling about it, but he couldn't make peace with the idea of simply letting it happen either. He left a message for August Platonovich, the Anchorage police head of homicide and possible amour of Zilla. August would know what the security at the race rally start would be. Ray wanted August to know about his concerns. August was a serious detective, but intuition and trusting your gut could save lives. He would listen to Ray and adjust his team's approach to securing the area if needed.

Ray's next call was to Mo. She answered on the first ring.

"Pick your mom up yet?"

"Heading to the airport now." There was a beat of silence.

"You ok?"

"Not sure. It will be great to see momma, but Mo, I...." he struggled to voice the sense of doom he was feeling.

"What is it? What's wrong?" The concern was evident in her voice. He felt a measure of comfort in hearing it.

"I'm just...worried I guess. There's so damn much angst and anger. I'm. I'm kind of worried about mom speaking tomorrow night." There, he'd said it out loud.

"At the run kick off thing? Seems pretty A political honey."

"Yeah, it should be. Normally I imagine it would be, but right now..." He went silent again.

Mo could hear the faint windy sounds of passing traffic and a plane overhead. She pictured him driving, his face serious, concerned. She didn't want to voice her own similar feelings. Like waiting for a foregone event that you wish wouldn't happen, but knew surely would. She closed her eyes and waited for him. Gave him time.

"Right now it just feels like everything could fly apart at the seams at any minute. The animosity keeps building. The vitriol that's being shouted around about what the court decision, whatever it is, will mean. It's got to give at some point, Mo. I'm afraid that when it does, bad things might happen. People could get hurt. I don't want Ruby to be one of them because she's in office and a target."

"I don't either Ray. We'll take extra precautions. I'll be there with you too." She knew that sounded weak, as if they could somehow stop a surging angry mob because they would be there, but at least they would be there.   What else could she say?

##

Jerry Justice was whistling an irritating shrill little song as he walked to his truck to start yet another run to a supporter's house. The money

Volkov was supplying was the most effective tool for convincing fence sitters that they should join up and help spread the propaganda that the Russian disseminated to them.

Justice thought Volkov's dark web manifestos created a very winning strategy of disinformation about the Green Defiance Coalition leadership, (they were all treasonous felons who hated America and supported smuggling illegal immigrants into the country so they could become terrorists) the lawyers who were fighting their court case, (they were all cannibal pedophiles who loved Hilary Clinton, also hated America and wanted to kill the jobs of the good people from coal country) and even the new congresswoman Ruby Walker, (she sold heroin out of her bar and restaurant that she got from terrorists and she slept with blacks and Jews and Muslims).

But Jerry Justice didn't know that Volkov was fomenting the x ray opposite campaign on the other side of the political divide. He'd wanted to recruit the burly brick mason, Ralph Sims to help infiltrate the GDC and spread propaganda about the DAD and other development hawks, but one of his Russian underlings had made a serious error in researching Sims' background.

The lazy young man had found out that Sims had worked in construction all of his life and assumed that he'd appeared to switch teams as a ruse to get close to the leaders of the GDC for ill intent. He'd lost interest in the boring middle-aged man's resume after that. Missed the life-changing event of the death of Ralph's little sister. He led Nakita Volkov to believe that Sims would be easy to roll, was no doubt sympathetic to the development cause as he'd been a life long union member who had built so many brick walls in his career that put together, would have satisfied the most paranoid fever dream of Trump supporters who thought a Mexican border wall would solve their crime, addiction and job worries.

It was a costly mistake.

Volkov had an awkward and fruitless encounter with Sims at the Silver Slipper. The young research assistant soon after disappeared, never to be seen or heard from again. Perhaps a cup of tea had not gone down well.

But the meeting at the Slip had not been a total loss. Volkov was surprised when Sims abruptly turned down his generous offer of a cash only reconnaissance job working for the DAD and had lumbered off to the can. The Russian operative's surprise was compounded when Mook Davis sidled up to him. He'd appeared so quickly after Sims stormed off to the bathroom that Volkov's hand instinctively moved toward the unseen pistol beneath his jacket. He stopped short of shooting the pale young man, but glared at him, wondering why he was suddenly standing near his elbow beside the bar.

"I need a job sir. And I'm damn sick of being pushed around by redneck pricks like that dude. Can I meet you somewhere else later? I don't want that jerk to see me talking to you. He'll probably drop a pallet on me or something."

Volkov had recovered from his surprise, but was a wary man. The CIA had people everywhere and most of them didn't look like government workers. He smiled thinly, relaxing his shooting hand back onto his leg.

"Perhaps, my young friend. What is your name? Give it to me and then meet me tomorrow night at Time Out Lounge. You know this place?"

Mook kept his eyes on the bathroom door across the bar, worried Ralph would emerge and see him, maybe give him a pounding later for talking to the Russian. "Yeah, yeah, I know the place. I'll see you there. My name is Maxwell Davis, but everybody calls me Mook." He turned and walked back down the bar, picked up his drink and drained the last of the beer in his glass, just as Ralph strode across the tile floor, shooting a jaundiced look in Nikita Volkov's direction. Ralph finished his scotch, glanced at his irritating co-worker Mook, and threw a twenty on the bar. Without a word to anyone, he turned and left. Volkov paid his tab, instructed the bartender to get Mook another beer, nodded at his new prospect and also took his leave. Mook drank his free beer, a little apprehensive, but a little excited too. He had a nose for easy money and that Russian guy reeked of it.

##

Poppa Ray, Mo and Ray the third shared the dread that flowed from both sides of the environmental rights case that the Supreme Court had remanded back to the 9th circuit. The entire nation seemed to be holding its breath and no where was it felt more keenly than in Alaska; a state where battles over resources and how they should be used was much older than the relatively new legal designation that made it the 49th state.

APD homicide chief detective August Platonovich felt it too. He recognized what it meant and prepared to deal with the fall out that would inevitably come.

Chapter Twelve

For as dirty as the Kremlin's hands were when it came to international espionage, shooting detractors in broad daylight, frequent poisoning of those who would dare cross Putin's dictates on Russian and other nation's soil, they were squeaky clean when it came to an evidence trail. It was a source of great frustration, anger and embarrassment to the domestic intelligence entities in America, Great Britain and Germany. Pinning his dirty deeds on him was like trying to pin smoke to the wall.

They couldn't get him, but increasingly he was getting them. Cyber war was so much cheaper, faster and easier and so wildly more effective than traditional warfare with its ground artillery, bombing runs and painstaking advance to gain physical and political control of territory. All took great sums of money, time, and engineering skill, not to mention human capital to feed the battle machine. It was also completely visible to the world and painfully slow.

The World Wide Web offered a constant battlefield that could span the planet in a matter of seconds, be fully operational both day and night and cost nothing compared to the price of nuclear weapons or a fleet of tanks. For a laughably small sum, Putin could command thousands of workers to spread confusion, dissent and disinformation on a scale that Tokyo Rose would have been in awe of. The casualties were not bodies blown to bloody bits on a battlefield, but instead deaths caused by virtual bombs that blasted paranoia, chaos and anger at ill educated, bitter Americans who were looking for a boogey man.

Putin was only too happy to oblige. As the fake news smoke screen was pumped into computers, Putin orchestrated a high level, very secret meeting with Chinese and North Korean military officials about the dangerous rogue nation that he claimed the United States had become. They had been building up a nuclear arsenal on Amchitka Island he insisted. The Americans were hoping to take Russia and China by surprise. Pretending to care about some nonsense fake court case that allegedly ordered their own government to clean up the twigs and beach pebbles on an uninhabited island. How stupid did they think the rest of the world was? What court could make the most powerful military in the world pick up trash, like a prisoner cleaning ditches on a chain gang? It was preposterous and clearly a lie. They were staging underground missiles. And clearly those missiles had been so powerful they would have devastated the infrastructure and people of Russia and China, but instead they had stupidly blown themselves up with their own weapons. The obliteration of the island was a clear testament to the size of the warheads they'd been staging.

His message was unequivocal. The Americans must be punished. They must not be allowed to continue on their reckless quest for world domination, especially under a leader who would cut off international commerce to line the pockets of his supporters. Trump was a ruthless fool who was greedy beyond comprehension. He was a threat to world order and must be stopped. There was nothing else to do.

##

Zilla wasn't upset at the lack of diversity of thought among the GDC compound members because she never went to a reporting assignment with a preconceived notion of what it should be. That nudged dangerously close to influencing her objectivity when she wrote her story, but she was surprised that none of the hard working people in the mountainside off grid village questioned the best course for advancing their mission of a cleaner, lower carbon future.

They all adhered to the guidance of the GDC leadership council and didn't express concern about death threats and being shut off from the rest of the country while the court case and public sentiment simmered along ideological lines.

Zilla was always troubled by lock step thinking of any ilk. Even during her polite, Midwest upbringing she had been taught to question authority. Always question authority. How did the people calling the shots get that power? What else have they done that qualified them to be in control? Who were they connected to and how might that influence their decision-making? It could be altruistic and pure but Zilla, through the years had found that the more concentrated master control was, the more susceptible to corruption and negative influence the organization became.

She wasn't a cynic, she was realistic but she'd learned frustratingly little from those she'd finally gotten access to. They all believed or at least insisted they did, that the way forward was to stop all efforts of the D.A.D. All oil development; tree cutting, fossil fuel based work of any kind must be stopped completely. Period.

It was a ridiculously Pollyanna mindset. Zilla had to bite her tongue a number of times when she heard these views expressed, adamantly, with a fist slapped into a hand for emphasis as the supporters again and again said, "'We've got to stop! We've got to draw a line in the sand and forego ALL future fossil fuel endeavors! If we've any chance of saving our planet, which means *ourselves*.....we have to take radical steps!'"

She maintained her professional decorum, didn't let sarcasm seep into her questions and she didn't point out that all of those assembled here at Green Defiance Coalition summer camp had flown in or taken jeeps up the mountainside. Electric planes and off road vehicles were coming of course, but they were a ways off. Moving toward a clean renewable future was important for everyone and every thing on the planet, but declarations that mandated an immediate end to the use of all fossil fuel was just silly and minimized the important message that the GDC brought to the conversation around climate change.

It reminded Zilla of PETA's rhetoric around animal rights. There were legitimate animal welfare concerns that needed and deserved to be addressed but when PETA targeted the boy scouts because they took kids fishing, they diffused their credibility for the big stuff like the woeful conditions of massive feed lots jammed full of cattle standing in muck, or animals that were chained up, neglected and forced to fight to the death for the enjoyment of gamblers. These were serious and needed to stop. Fishing for bluegills? Come on.

Most of those Zilla spoke with and asked questions of were smart, hardworking people who truly believed the planet was wobbling toward a point of no return where mass destruction brought by climate change would devastate coastal communities, forcing mass migrations of people, many of them with subsistence skills closely connected to a life in harmony with the sea. Living away from the oceans that had sustained them for generations would create a new wave of trouble. How will people survive and feed themselves? What level of extra pressure would be brought to bear on the resources of inland communities, many of which were already suffering from other effects of a warming climate?

Drought, floods, mudslides, increasing wildfires, bomb cyclones and wandering polar vortexes, sounded apocalyptic because it was and the GDC believers were mostly passive warriors, but some of them were older and had been involved in earlier clashes with resource extractors. The Cut, Drill, Mine, Kill crowd had run up against some of the more aggressive earth protectors. Men and women who had spiked trees in the Pacific Northwest or monkey wrenched with coal fired power grid infrastructure or broken locks on shut off valves for pipelines, turning off the flow that backed up oil and damaged pumps. These were the 'by any means necessary' adherents to the idea of cleaning up the act of those that damaged the environment that sustained their very life.

These radicals believed that thriving by destroying the water, air and soil in the name of cheap energy would result in a lot of money concentrated in the hands of very few but little else. Even if that money were shared equally, it wouldn't matter if there was no food or clean drinking water. You couldn't eat dollar bills. For many of those Zilla had talked to, it was simple math. World populations were multiplying at an unsustainable rate, food production was in decline, the oceans were acidifying, warming and becoming less productive and fresh water sources were not replenishing fast enough to keep up with birth rates.

The GDC hardliners adhered to an ideology that dictated action, forced if necessary, to protect resources that sustain life. That did not include oil or coal or harvesting more timber.

Leave It In The Ground was their mandate and if it meant civil war between the wealthy American extraction barons and those who would fight against locking up resources and polluting the earth and atmosphere, so be it. They would clash to protect the rights of human beings to eat before they would defend the rights of American Oligarchs to more fossil fuel wealth.

The younger members of the GDC had rarely engaged in acts of aggression or outright violence and property destruction to get their point across but they feared a world that was so polluted and so hot they would not be able to bring children into it. They were freaked out and scared.

One young woman gently gripped Zilla's arm as she described her worry. "I was raised with every possible advantage. We lived in a massive home with staff. My father gave us anything and everything we wanted. I went to the best schools and graduated from Stanford, but the irony is that the money that sent me there was dirty. My father made his fortune by selling coal! Coal! I got my education on coal money and when I finally woke up and realized how many people have died from asthma or poisoned water or starved because of crop devastation caused by climate change, I nearly killed myself. I am so ashamed. I can't undo what happened, but I can fight like hell to stop it from continuing."

Zilla asked if her father and her family agreed with or at least understood her new position on her family's legacy or if they were upset by it. "I wouldn't know." She answered coolly, "I haven't spoken to any of them for years." She paused for a beat, then continued. "And I have no intention of ever doing so again."

Zilla believed her.

It had been three days of interviews, observations and photographs. Now it was Saturday morning and they were preparing to leave the compound. Zilla was packed up and standing by the jeep that had brought her up the mountain when the same driver, he of little words, walked up with the keys in one hand and a blindfold in the other.

"Really? We're doing this again?" She looked exasperated and irritated.

"Yes. We are." He held it out in front of her. Zilla shook her head and plucked it from his outstretched hand.

Chapter Thirteen

Stuart Murphy had zeroed in on Jerry Justice since witnessing the clumsy hand off of what was likely a bundle of cash. Murph was relentless in digging to learn about Hansen's connections. What the hell was that southern televangelist transplant up to and why was a lot of cash involved?

Murphy had a hunch it wasn't drugs. He figured it would need to be bigger than simple narcotics trafficking to be of interest to the cowboy caricature. Justice was bloated up on self importance and Murph had studied and reported on a lot of men like him. They mostly wanted wealth, power and to be at the center of something big and influential. Justice wasn't a purist. He'd take money made from drugs with no moral qualms, but it would have to be at the level that was far above street sales in order to maintain his ego and self-image as a child star that still had important dealings through the years.

The reality of his life's work as a huckster and outright liar who preached a false gospel of whatever the wind told him would sell, would never permeate his carefully constructed belief that he was rising toward a destiny of greatness.

He thought it no coincidence that the president used the word 'great' in his MAGA slogan. Jerry Justice believed in Trump and soon he would be famous on a level that even the President would notice. The cash he'd been entrusted with proved he was an important player in the larger scheme of taking back control of American resources from the ninnies who would sing lullabies to every test lab rat and force the mighty American military to bow down to activist courts to spit shine every former defense site.

It was a stupid display of weakness to the rest of the world and by god, if Jerry Justice had anything to say about it, the hippy flower loving peacenik bullshit would be crushed, once and for all. If they couldn't rely on the courts to uphold humanity's destiny and right to develop the earth's resources for cash, then the D.A.D would fight alongside the nation's army to preserve that right.

Jerry Justice saw himself at the helm of this great movement. He would help the president Make America Great Again or kill a whole bunch of hippies trying. Woo ee, yes he would.

Murph intuitively understood a lot more about the motivations of Jerry Justice than the Arkansas child star would have liked, had he known. Murph figured Justice was angling for bigger things than heroin sales, but he couldn't put his finger on exactly what that would be. He decided to spread the itch for information to someone who would also dig.

He called Detective August Platonovich. Murph still preferred his old desk phone with its full sized handset that he could clamp between his shoulder and cheek while typing, but the long time homicide cop's cell number was one of his few speed dial options on his cell phone, so he used what he considered a woefully small, wireless device. Murph and Platonovich had a decades long working relationship based on trust and mutual respect. The detective answered on the second ring.

"Hello Mr. Murphy. I have not seen your number come up for some time. How can I help you?" Platonovich, ever the polite professional.

"Hello Sergeant. Do you have a few minutes to talk?"

"It is a busy day, preparing the security plan for the rallies that are planned for this afternoon, but please proceed."

Murph was intrigued. "You're working security detail for the rallies? Seems below your pay grade."

There was a moment's silence as the detective chose his words carefully. "It is possible there will be larger crowds than we're comfortably able to keep an eye on through the available number of officers on duty. There is also a concern that skirmishes could break out."

"Hm, skirmishes eh? As in, you're expecting riots?"

Platonovich could hear the rapid-fire fingers of Murphy taking notes on his computer.

He closed his eyes, wishing he'd said less. "I would not say 'expecting' riots. We are employing an abundance of caution. I would say we are being careful to insure we can maintain order while allowing the rallies to happen at the same time. It is a lot, logistically, to have two major gatherings of very passionate people in the city." The distinct rat-tat of fast typing could be heard over the phone line. The Sergeant waited, not saying anything else, the typing stopped.

"Well, I saw something odd yesterday Detective. Gerald Hansen, I'm sure you know of him, goes by the self imposed title Jerry Justice?"

"Yes, I am aware of him. He will be one of the rally leaders we'll keep an eye on."

"That's a good idea. I happened to walk into the Silver Slipper yesterday right when the bartender was handing a taped up bundle over the bar to him."

"Bundle?"

"Yeah. It wasn't a cheeseburger, that's for sure, but if my hunch about the size and shape of it is correct, it would buy a whole hell of a lot of them."

Platonovich exhaled a worried puff of air. "Bundles of cash are certainly always of interest. Especially handed over a bar top. Did they realize you'd seen this exchange?"

"Oh yes. Hansen tried to get tough but opportunistic bums don't scare me. They both looked guilty as sin and when Hansen left, he told the bartender, MC, to 'keep it locked down.' It would have been laughable if the nefarious nature of it were not legally concerning." Murph grabbed his too small cell from its hold between his shoulder and cheek and stretched his neck where a familiar muscle pain was throbbing. "In other words Detective Platonovich, Hansen is up to something that requires anonymous infusions of cash. He's probably not shopping for a new oosik."

Platonovich chuckled quietly. "No, likely not. I have not seen him connected to drug trafficking, but I'll check on connections to other illegal avenues."

Anxious or not, Ray was damn glad to see his mom when she came around the corner and stepped into view at the Anchorage airport. He hugged her fiercely and kissed her cheek repeatedly until she laughed out loud.

"Wow, did you really miss me or are you amused at the idea of kissing a member of Congress?" She held his face in her hands as she asked, her stunning blue eyes reflecting the joy she felt.

"A little of both." Ray gave her another loud smack on the cheek, hugged her again and then released her. They walked toward baggage claim, other travelers streaming around them toward the carousels that were not yet circling much less delivering a tumble of suitcases and other lumpy, duct taped boxes, coolers and long tubes of fishing gear. Watching the luggage carousel at the Ted Stevens International Airport was always entertaining as people traveled in and out of rural Alaska with all the supplies that would be delivered by truck or rail in other parts of the United States. In Alaska, if you couldn't fly it or barge it to remote communities, you wouldn't get it. Amazon Prime had become all the rage for rural residents. Jeff Bezos was taking a hit to his wallet with free shipping to remote regions of the state.

Ruby and Ray stood in silence for a moment, practicing that time-honored ritual of staring at the carousel, trying to will it to start moving. When it finally did, Ray spoke.

"So, the rally this afternoon, I guess the organizers are calling it the Rally for Peace and Respect, will likely draw as many detractors as supporters." His eyes were on the suitcases that were now sliding down and dropping onto the slowly rotating metal track while travelers watched. "I have to say I've been concerned about that momma. There's a tremendous amount of tension between the environmental and development factions and...."

"There's always been tension between these sides honey." Ruby waved a dismissive hand and stepped toward the carousel, spying one of her bags lumbering down the conveyer.

"Not like this momma. It's all wrapped up in the hyper sensitive politics of the Trump administration and the court decision that will ignite one side or the other based on what gets handed down from the 9th circuit." Ray grabbed Ruby's luggage, the first and second bag that emerged as he was speaking and she silently pointed at.

"Maybe I'm getting DC jaded already. Protests and tense gatherings are daily occurrences on the Hill, Ray. This is Alaska! We'll be fine this afternoon. I can handle a few naysayers yelling at me during my comments today." She offered him a brilliant smile and slipped her arm around his waist as they headed to the parking garage. "That's democracy honey. Everyone gets their say."

Ray was unconvinced. "Yes, democracy means people can spew whatever they want, whether it's based in fact or reality or not. I can tolerate that, but I don't like the tone of some of the extremists on both sides of this divide and that's what worries me about you speaking today." They walked in silence for a moment, their footsteps echoed off the damp concrete walls of the parking garage. "I'm just not used to having my own mom be part of the story I'm covering. Makes me nervous in a way I've never experienced before."

"I can appreciate your concern. This is new territory for both of us but I'm not worried," Ruby waved her hand in a dismissive way that wasn't convincing. Ray noticed but didn't say so. "Let's go see your granddad. That will make both of us feel better." She jumped in the passenger seat of Ray's car as he loaded her bags in the back seat. Ruby was serious about seeing Poppa Ray. He was the rock of the family now that her husband, his son, was gone. Ray the second had died after a heart attack more than 15 years earlier, but the hole he'd left in the lives of Ruby and his son, Ray the third, was still there. Poppa Ray was their anchor and a man with broad insight into human behavior. Ruby wanted to consult with him about the vibe in the community and what he may have been hearing or seeing. If Poppa Ray was nervous, then Ruby knew she should be too.

It's hard to carry worry on a beautiful Alaska spring morning. It was mid May now, weeks had passed since the U.S. Supreme Court justices had harangued lawyers on both sides of the natural systems rights case. The 9th circuit court was still deliberating the remanded portion, the most critical part of the decision that would come.

The country and especially Alaska waited with anticipation but focus is tough when the weather is a spring caress and the leaves are unfurling in the vibrant neon green that relays all systems are go. A feeling that anything good is possible fills the air along with the sound of returning birds.

Seagulls wheeled overhead, their excited cries reflecting the exuberance of a gentle spring morning. Ray and Ruby drove Minnesota Boulevard toward downtown and the café, sunlight streamed into the car as they made the curve along Westchester Lagoon and the incline that leveled out as it headed into downtown. Ruby loved the treat that came as they neared the intersection with 15th street.

The view of the Chugach that suddenly appeared to the east was a vista she never tired of. She was grateful that it still gave her joy. Today was no exception. The mountains were snowy but increasing patches of dark vegetation was visible and soon that color would turn from the monochrome of black and white to lush green as the Chugach range, like the trees in the city were awakened to the flourish of spring and the soon to be vibrant colors of the upper mountain valleys.

They pulled into the familiar gravel parking lot of their family business and Ruby felt like she'd never left. Washington DC seemed a surreal dream as she watched John, their long time handy man apply a fresh coat of urethane to the split rail cedar fence that outlined the parking lot alongside the bar. Almost on cue, like a Disney movie, a momma moose and her gangly legged calf ambled around the corner, looked at old John for a moment, ears perked forward, then lost interest and walked off toward the expensive homes in the trendy South Addition neighborhood.

She and Ray had fallen silent as they got out of the car and headed into the front door. John, an ever-present cigarette clamped between his lips, raised his brush and nodded to them both. Ruby gave him a smile as she stepped inside. The café and bar smelled of smoked salmon, gumbo and hash browns.

Poppa Ray had been busy, preparing a hearty breakfast for his grandson and daughter in law. It was too early for the regular kitchen crew to be working so it had to be Ruby's wonderful father in law rattling the pans for them. He proved her right as he emerged, radiant smile intact, expertly carrying three plates piled high with fresh made hash browns, bacon, eggs and toast. "My two favorite people in the world!

Let's eat." Poppa Ray put the plates on a table just off the end of the bar and scooped up Ruby in a hug. "Glad you're here Ruby. It's good to see you."

"It's good to see you too, Pops. And breakfast smells delicious!"

Ray grabbed cups and poured coffee from the ever-present pot behind the bar. It was fresh and added to the sweet family moment.

Even through their laughter, conversation and catching up on news from DC and news from Anchorage, there was a small sense of unease among them as if they all understood but didn't outright acknowledge that this might be the calm before the storm. Their peaceful breakfast seemed like something that should be carefully noted and remembered for the very ordinary scene it was. As if ordinary and simple pleasures such as breakfast with your family would be something that was in the 'before' category.

No one at the lively table was sure of what was coming, but something unstoppable loomed and this cherished family gathering was perhaps more important than it appeared.

The dueling rallies were happening later today. Ray finished off his hearty breakfast before Ruby and his grandfather. "Excuse me, I'm going to call Mo. I'll be glad to clean up the table and do the dishes after I get off the phone. Thanks for a great breakfast granddad."

Ruby watched her son's smiling face as he got up from his chair and fished his cell phone out of his pocket. She was struck by how much he looked like his father and a little jag of loneliness pained her heart for her much loved man. It took her by surprise. Ray the second had been dead for so many years and although she thought of him often, it was usually a simple fond remembrance, not a bolt of pain.

She let her mind wander for a moment as Ray walked toward the front door to step outside for his call to Mo and Poppa Ray lingered over his coffee and the last of his breakfast. She thought of her husband, his business savvy and intellect, his brilliant, heart-snatching smile, his easy laugh and sweet disposition. His kindness, his love for Ruby and little Ray. She missed so many things about him and was grateful that his father had stepped up to help the family. Her husband had been known for his business prowess, building the now prosperous bar and food plan for Ruby's Café from a modest sandwich and beer joint, into a thriving day and night operation that featured some of the best Alaska themed food and hottest music in the state and west coast.

Ruby thought of the future and her son's marriage to Mo Scott. She considered the delight of grandchildren and marveled at the beauty their varied ethnic mix would reflect in those kids. It was a fleeting joy almost immediately replaced by the small nagging worry that had nibbled at the edges of her happy homecoming since she got off the plane. Her face reflected the inner turmoil and intuitive granddad didn't miss it.

"Appears there's a lot on your mind, daughter." He had referred to her as his own since the early days of his son's courting of her. He had fallen for her too and was thrilled when they married. Poppa Ray knew a quality person when he met one.

He gently covered her hand with one of his big work worn ones. "You've got a lot on your plate, both right in front of you," he nodded his head toward her food, "and in your new position as an elected official." He couldn't stop his proud grin. "Congresswoman Walker. I do like the sound of that!" He gave her hand two quick little squeezes and released it. "I'll get us some more coffee and then why don't you tell me what's got you sitting in this chair, but 1000 miles away from this room."

"Thanks Pop. You know me too well."

The elder Walker got up from the table and Ruby noticed a slight slowing down as he stood, a sign of aging that she'd never witnessed before. It sent another quick jolt to her heart as she thought of Ray Senior getting on in years. Geez, why was she so emotional this morning?

"Not too well my dear, just well enough. I know you well enough to know you've got heavy considerations going on and if I can help share that load," he refilled their cups, "Well, that's what I want to do." He set the pot down on a bar towel, always careful not to mar a surface with a hot container. "Now talk to me Ruby before that nosy reporter gets done on the phone and comes back in here." His eyes crinkled with love and mischief as he tilted his head toward the door where his grandson could be seen standing on the front porch, talking earnestly into his cell.

Ruby relaxed back against her chair, realizing that she'd been sitting nearly bolt straight, she slid her fresh coffee closer and wrapped her hands around the warm cup. "I don't know. Maybe it's Ray's nerves that are rattling my own. He's worried about the rally today and I guess I hadn't been too concerned until he expressed his anxiety over the tensions here." She shrugged and looked at her father in law, taking a sip of her coffee and holding his eyes.

His lips clamped together and he furrowed his eyebrows in a look that mirrored his own concern. It wasn't the reassurance she was expecting. "Well, I haven't said much to my grandson about this mess that's been building around here because I see how worried he already is, but Ruby, something could pop off in this town soon." He shook his head and glanced at the door where Ray was now off the phone and stood talking to John while the older man took a break from re-sealing the parking lot fence. "I don't want to sound paranoid but I know this feeling all too well. I wish it wasn't true but the divide between people who want development and people who want protection is getting like the old divide of people who look like me," he pointed to the dark brown skin of his arm, "and people who look like you," nodding toward her still lovely, but very white, skin.

"The people who would just as soon see me on a boat bound for Africa but until now couldn't resist a bowl of gumbo or a halibut burger have simply quit coming in the door Ruby. This anger between drilling supporters and the leave it in the ground crowd increasingly feels like a race divide." Now it was his turn to shrug and sit back in his chair. "I don't know why it's happening in this way, but I know racial tension and there's a lot of it now."

Ruby was a widow but she'd lived for decades in a mixed race marriage. She was no stranger to the hard looks, the snide comments, and the outright hostility from white and black people when she and her husband had gone out together. "Come on Pop. Racial divide is as old as the hills. Why and how is it tangled up with fossil fuel?"

The first Ray Walker sighed and leaned forward again. She was a good woman and couldn't help that she didn't have the lifelong experience of being a person of color, always being watched with suspicion, always questioned, always needing to work a little harder, step a little quicker, smile a little bigger, just to fucking get along. He'd lived it every day of his life and Ruby had come into awareness about bigotry only after she'd fallen in love with his son, and even then, she was still white and could really never understand. It was not a resentment or anger he harbored about it, it was a simple fact.

"When people can't or won't contain their feelings of dislike or discomfort or bias. When they stop trying to overcome their angst, when they quit doing the small things like buying a burger and a beer from a black man that means they've stopped caring about community cohesive. They are getting affirmation from someone or some group that it's ok to hate, that they're right for feeling superior and for not wanting to fraternize with Blacks and Hispanics and Natives. That's when it's really dangerous Ruby and that's what I see and feel building in this city in a way that makes me worry."

"About what specifically Pop? Worry about what? Help me understand." They heard Ray junior open the front door and walk back in.

Her father in law looked tired and sad. "About us honey. I worry about all of us. Our family and our community. I worry about you going......" He stopped as the younger Ray reached their table. An awkward silence hung between them. He sat down and eyed them both.

"Guys, I'm not a kid, remember? Please don't stop talking when I walk up like I can't handle adult speak."

Ruby stood up and started stacking plates. "Come on, let's not ruin the intention of this lovely breakfast with heavy conversation. I'll help clean up and then I'd like to go home to organize my notes for this afternoon's speech." She avoided the eyes of both of the men in her family.

The younger Ray stood up also, grabbed the silverware and water glasses. "Ok. Leave me in the dark. I'm only your son AND a reporter." Ruby and the elder Walker stayed silent. Ray senior gripped his coffee cup with both hands, his eyes distant as he looked out the glass front door into the parking lot.

Son Ray and Ruby carried dishes to the kitchen and began to clean up. "I'll drop you off mom and then I'll pick up Mo and granddad before we come back to get you. We'll all go together this afternoon." His voice was resigned. Ruby didn't disagree.

"Ok honey. Sounds fine." They worked in silence, quickly cleaning the dishes, counters and stove in a well worn, years long routine, then headed back into the main room where Ray senior sat, the weary, pondering look still on his face.

"I'm taking mom home granddad. I'll be back to get you in a couple of hours."

His grandfather didn't answer, just raised his hand in a small farewell to them both. The jovial mood that had enveloped them all just a short time earlier had evaporated. Now a grim feeling of unhappy anticipation seeped in like a chill and there was nothing to do but wait.

Across town it was much the same for August Platonovich. He had helped develop the security plan for both rallies, an effort that was taxing the law enforcement staff in a way that he didn't like. Even though he and the Anchorage Police Chief had assurance that the state troopers would be in the mix because Congresswoman Ruby Walker was speaking today and extra officers were justified, the number of cops was still too thin to cover both events in the way he would have liked.

Alaska officials struggle perennially with how to fund proper numbers of law enforcement in a state that could swallow most of the Midwest. Troopers patrolled enormous sectors that could encompass thousands of miles of dicey travel conditions and often a complete lack of roads. Pulling officers from one area meant leaving citizens in that region vulnerable. It was always a gamble and a heavy responsibility.

August called the Chief. "Hello Sir. Do you think we should ask Glenallen to send officers this way? It's difficult to know how many will show up today but the weather is clear and there is a lot of static right now." August chose his words carefully, his accent still prevalent even after nearly three decades of life in Alaska and away from his Polish homeland. He knew the Chief would catch his meaning.

Chief Derrick Rogers was at City Hall in downtown, waiting to meet with the mayor. "Yes," he said quietly into the phone, "I understand your reasoning here detective but we've already requested back up from the Valley and the trooper post in Girdwood and Kenai. I don't think we can leave the rest of south-central with no officers because of two rallies in Anchorage."

There was a short silence. "Yes sir. Thank you. We'll deploy as strategically as we can and stay sharp."

"I know you will August. Thanks for your diligence. I'm confident in your leadership on this."

"I appreciate that sir. Goodbye." August hung up, wishing he felt the same confidence the Chief had expressed in him. But he didn't feel it any more than he'd suspected the Chief did.

There was nothing else to do but prepare, be on high alert and hope they could control whatever broke out.

Jerry Justice was employing the philosophy of the three little pigs, with his own modifications.

Get started early, get the development crowd revved up on self righteousness and get organized for the big showdown at the supposed family event which he figured was a front for the GDC and get done before the cops AKA the Big Bad Wolves started arresting the good people who comprised the DAD.

He was certain the GDC would have an unfair advantage today because everyone knew that cops were part of the liberal elite. They would go after the hard working men and women that believed in America and American energy dominance before they would put cuffs on those limp wristed bliss ninnies who dreamed of living in harmony with barn mice and cockroaches and wanted to protect cows from becoming a decent steak. Hell, everyone knew that cows were a big part of the so-called problem of so-called climate change! If those idiots really wanted to stop their fantasy boogey man in the atmosphere they should start by slaughtering more cows. The gas those enormous three-stomach bovine methane factories spurted into the air continuously was the true culprit if there really was a problem, but Justice knew it was all horseshit.

There was no fucking doomsday climate change happening. There was just one group of morons who wanted to pray to every daisy and protect every flea and another group of people who understood reality and the need for American jobs in the honored business sector of coal, oil, mineral mining and timber. It was as simple as that and it irritated the hell out of Jerry Justice that other people had such a hard time seeing the black and white of it all.

But he wasn't so angry this morning. This was going to be a great day! It would be a day to move toward the path the President had worked so hard to get the country back on. The path back to world domination and greatness! Before we started letting liberal whiners gain influence and work to derail the foundation of corporate money crafting government. Who the hell else should? Illegal aliens? Should we let them decide policy? Corporations have money and money greases all skids, changes frowns to smiles, the weak into the powerful.

It was simple logic. Those that have the money must be on the right side of history or they wouldn't have that kind of power. Even though everything was now forced through the rosy lens of political correctness, Jerry Justice was a history buff and he understood the proper historical order of things.   The plantation owners were right to make certain people of a certain skin color work to advance their industries of cotton in the south as were the federal plantation owners who made certain people work in the fur industry in the north, that was how the world operated.

That was manifest destiny baby, and it worked.

People of certain blood lines were meant to be the owners, the leaders, the commanders and others, well, they were meant to carry out the orders. And it wasn't like they weren't taken care of! Hell, even slaves had cabins and chitlins provided for them! They didn't have to worry about paying taxes or where their next meal would come from. All they had to do was work and do what they were told without question and everything was handed to them. Goddamn simple arrangement and it had worked for hundreds of years in the new country that was the United States. It was how the country became a world powerhouse. But now you couldn't force those who clearly lacked leadership ability to work the jobs you needed them to. Not even prisoners! What sense did that shit make?

All these troubling thoughts were bubbling through the over heated lava in the mind of Jerry Justice as he worked around his apartment, getting ready for what was going to be a big day and a big turning point. He was rubbing saddle oil into his leather gun holster and would next clean and polish his side iron and even shine up his oosik. Got to look the part if you're going to lead the people back to greatness. When his phone rang he was engrossed in working oil into the belt, polishing the brass buckles at the same time.

"Justice is my name, god, guns and jobs is my game." He was in a good mood when he answered, but wasn't joking.

"Hm, ok. Are you ready and do you need anything more from me before this afternoon?" Jamie Lynn didn't identify herself on the phone (or try to keep the irritation out of her voice) before speaking, even though he couldn't tell from the number who was on the other end. They were all using burner phones. She despised the creepy Arkansas cowboy but was willing to go along with his plans since she smelled money.

"Darlin, all you got to do is bring your sweet self over here and help me load up some signs and then we're set."

Jamie Lynn sounded doubtful. "Really? So, everything else is ready?"

Jerry Justice's chuckle was cold and even the hardcore Jamie Lynn shivered as she listened. "Everything and then some is ready sister. There's a surprise coming today that ya'all are gonna love and it's going to cinch the deal. Woo ee! It's gonna to be some big shit!"

Jamie Lynn rolled her eyes. She had come to expect that when men described things as 'big shit' it was usually bullshit, but whatever.

She would find out in a few hours that for once, a man's boast matched the event in a spectacular and lethally awesome way.

Chapter Fourteen

On Mount Olympus, the code name Zilla had given to the secret GDC compound, they were finally leaving. Zilla had given in to the irritating demand of once again being blindfolded and was sequestered in the back of an all terrain vehicle, ready to traverse back down the mountainside.

While she waited for their departure, she sat quietly listening and smelling all that had become familiar over the last few days. The early morning routines of a campsite, birds on tree limbs discussing the humans below them, the smell of coffee and food being prepared, people calling across open spaces to each other. These combined with the more rigorous sounds of permanency. Construction, the whine of a skill saw, already employed before breakfast, a hammer pounding nails, a truck being unloaded.

Zilla begrudgingly admitted to herself that this would be a good practice for any story. Not being blindfolded, but with her eyes closed, she was paying much closer attention to her other senses and those sounds, smells and vibrations were cementing the scene of this place in her mind in a way that went beyond the multiple photos she'd taken. It would help her write the stories she planned to report out about the compound, the long range plan for this and other similar places that were in development and the people who built, ran and lived at them. They would be separatists, like their antagonists but with a polar opposite worldview.

She was eager to get back to Anchorage and to work. It was hard to be disconnected from the world and her usual steady diet of news.

Zilla was surprised by how her feelings about being off line had changed over the course of the days she'd been without the Internet. At first she was anxious and had to remind herself not to check her phone for email or news alerts. There was simply nothing to check. It was strange and unnerving, as if something big would surely happen and she wouldn't know or be able to pitch in and help.

But after two days, that feeling started to subside and Zilla found her mind lingering on the songs of birds or watching the antics of two squirrels chase each other, showing off their skill as they leaped from limb to limb and scampered around tree trunks. There was an unaccustomed stillness that allowed her mind to focus in a way that she hadn't known she was lacking until she was able to do it. As if she was decompressing and purging the constant flow of ones and zeros that demands attention and devours so much time.

It made her ponder a change for the first time since arriving in Alaska. What would it be like to live like this for a few months or an entire year? How different would your thought process and your anxiety level be if all of your information came by hand written letter and week old newspapers? As she sat quietly thinking and listening, it was a preposterous notion to consider. It could either be incredibly relaxing and enlightening or incredibly boring and strange. It was hard to know which would emerge as   truth for a reporter who is usually hyper connected.

It appealed to Zilla in a way that it wouldn't have a decade earlier. Was she getting burned out?

##

Far away from Zilla's backseat contemplation, Nakita Volkov was considering a different type of life.

One that didn't involve insipid Americans.

Volkov was nervous about more aspects of the plans for the day's activities in Anchorage than he would have cared to admit. He was still a bit rattled, and he didn't rattle easily, over his encounter with Ralph Sims. How had they misread the man so badly? He seemed to fit the perfect mold for someone who would defend American enterprise and extreme development based on his life's work. He was also the size that could be useful when events went sideways and a muscled up roughneck was needed to crack a few heads and send the greenies scrambling away.

But much to Volkov's dismay, Ralph was not a head-bashing ally in this fight, not that Volkov really had sides here. He despised the Americans on both sides of this dispute over resources and cared not one iota about their silly beliefs. They were all weak fools who needed to be herded like the sheep they were.

And that was Volkov's plan. Herd them right off a cliff or scatter them to the winds. It had worked during the Presidential election and it should be working now. But his former assistant was too lazy to thoroughly research Ralph Sims and it had been a costly mistake. Not only had Sims abruptly turned Volkov's offer down, he was now likely a foe and someone who probably needed to disappear.

Just like the hapless assistant had.

Volkov's bigger concern on this morning was Jerry Justice. Justice had assured the Russian mobster that he had arranged for a large distraction for law enforcement during the downtown rally that was the precursor to the family run event.

Congresswoman Ruby Walker would be speaking there and she was the target. Volkov had no confidence in the southern cowboy's abilities to organize and pull off all that needed to work in tandem to get the job done, but he had little choice at this point and that was nerve wrecking. It was extremely important that this all came together.

Fomenting civil war in another country was familiar work for Volkov. The Kremlin had sent him on numerous successful missions through the years, but dealing with Americans was never simple. They had a long history of double-crossing former allies or even people they professed to want to help. Look at the plight of the Native peoples of the Americas. Robbed of their land, locked up and given disease-ridden supplies, starved, shot, hanged. Their children stolen from them and tortured in schools that sought to reprogram them all in the name of the lie of improving their lives.

Living in America was still a highly sought after prize for many global citizens. The country was beautiful, had resources and space and opportunity. But dealing with Americans was not as pleasurable. They were undisciplined and intellectually lazy, refusing to challenge themselves through education and credible sources of information. It made them easy to manipulate, politically malleable and ready to turn on any one of their neighbors.

Volkov marveled at the success of the country's propaganda machine that continued to convince others in the world that if they could get to America, they would be protected, welcomed and have a fresh start of incredible promise. Millions, perhaps billions did not realize how self centered and mean spirited U.S. citizens were and are. Isolationism was growing more popular under Trump. Volkov believed he understood the selfish mindset of most of the current inhabitants of this resource rich country.

Who was more cruel or unpredictable than Americans? He would often ask himself when arranging and paying for more chaos and division in the country? Who? No one.

Volkov's Kremlin boss was a cold eyed killer, yet a man of great intelligence and understanding of what was best for the world and the people in it, even if they did not. It was one of the many things that Volkov admired about his imposing leader. Putin took on the challenge and the great burden of steering the world toward the prosperity that would exist if he were at the top of a new world order.

Americans needed this leadership, even though they were too daft to understand what was best for them. They were bleating sheep that unwittingly allowed themselves to be herded and corralled. Calming as they were captured. Finding reassurance in being told what to do and in which direction to step. Flowing through the gate to be sheered and then, when it was far too late, struggling to escape, right before the bullet to the back of the head left them as so much meat for the supreme leader's table.

##

"Ok, I think we're finally ready to take off."

Zilla jumped at the sound of a voice, filtered through the closed door of the SUV and then it was open and a cool draft of fresh air made her wonder how long she had sat, silent and focused on the sounds around her, her eyes helpless to add to her intelligence gathering, covered as they were by the dusty black blindfold.

"Hey lady, do you need water or the bathroom before we leave outta here? It's gonna be about three hours before we hit Anchor town."

Zilla didn't recognize this voice, but appreciated the tidbit of information she was just given. "Three hours? Does that include......"

"Never mind. We'll be there when we're there." She recognized the voice that cut her question off; the same quiet driver from her trip to the compound days earlier. The GDC was apparently careful to match older, more seasoned members with younger ones who may not understand that anything you say to a reporter is examined for its information value and what it may help pry open for more.

"We're going to be traveling for a while. It's an hour, maybe even two, before we're down the mountain, then we'll fly back to Anchorage. That will take between two and three hours depending on weather and route."

She could tell he was turned in the front seat, to speak more directly toward her in the back.

"That should be enough information to let you know you're going to be back in your city somewhere between three to seven hours from now. We'll stop for a break here and there of course, but if you need something now, say so because I'm not stopping for a while."

Zilla wanted to smart off about his bullshit information, but she was tired of this paranoid game and simply wanted to get back to Anchorage, drop off her gear at the *Daily Standard's* office and see what was happening in town, so she stayed silent.

Today was the Midnight Fun Midnight Run event that Ruby Walker would help kick off. The D.A.D. planned an earlier rally to whip up their supporters in the lead up to the downtown event. It could mean just some sharp elbows and angry shouting or it could turn violent. It was hard to know after days away but she wanted desperately to be on time to help cover both events and help keep Ruby safe if called for.

The GDC leaders had every intention of being at the downtown rally to display their support in public. It was risky, but they were banking on strength in numbers. They had informants who were in Anchorage, feeding them encrypted information through satellite phones. The reports let them know there were growing numbers of people on both sides gathering in the city and an unspoken sentiment that this was a line in the sand.

The families who had signed up to jog along while pushing their expensive baby chariots had no idea that identity politics would be a bigger presence in the rally than the organizer's push to raise money for charity.

Jamie Lynn was eager for the storm that was brewing. Her sister Bernadette was praying for her city's safety and Jerry Justice was as gleeful as a pig in mud about the spectacular plan for the best distraction ever imagined.

As the SUV started its labored, creaking, bump riddled trip back down the mountain, Zilla told herself to be patient. She couldn't speed this trip up, hell; she still had no damn idea where she was. Even if she wasn't blindfolded, it was doubtful that she would recognize any landmarks and be able to find her way back to Anchorage faster than staying with the two silent yahoos in the front seat.

But it was hard to wait. Her Red Flag warning was up and on full alert and she felt an urgency to get to town and a nagging fear that she wouldn't be there in time.

In time for what she wasn't sure, but her built in warning system, something her dad had nurtured in her to help her protect herself, was turned up to high. Zilla had honed it to help others and right now it signaled a time issue.

It was going to be damn hard to wait the hours that she knew she must.

In the *Anchorage Daily Standard's* newsroom, Stuart Murphy and Ed Brooks were digging in on new information.

There was money, a lot of it, flowing through the city's crime underground. What Ed referred to as dirt bag back channels. They were hearing about it from reporters who covered the drug trade and the handful of illegal gaming rooms in Anchorage. When there was a new infusion of illicit funds, dealers of both the drug and card ilk had a field day. In this case, it had been weeks of big money floating around the city.

The curious part of the information was that Jerry Justice allegedly supplied the cash. Where was that small time, fake evangelizer getting this dough? And what was he up to with it?

Ed had been told by one source that he saw at least fifteen thousand dollars change hands at a meeting between Jerry Justice and one of the local heavyweights who wasn't a prize fighter but spent a lot of time moving stolen firearms and drugs along a prolific pipeline that rivaled the legendary Trans Alaska Pipeline System carrying crude oil from Prudhoe Bay to tankers at Valdez.

The pipeline the heavy weight dealer fed, moved less volume per day than TAPS, but the price wasn't nearly as volatile for drugs and weapons as it was for oil.

The payday was always big.

The back channel pipeline was older than TAPS. Through the years it had moved from an Arizona supply center in the earlier thug days of Anchorage when mob leaders ran the booze trade during the formation of the 49th state's largest city, to now somewhere in Mexico, where new supplies of drugs moved through California and up the coast on planes, on barges, on military and fishing vessels, picking up other interesting items along the way.

Automatic weapons and shocking amounts of ammunition were in that pipeline. Drugs always rounded out the lucrative purchase list. Other commodities rose and fell with market whims, but alcohol, tobacco, drugs and firearms had stood the test of time for providing a steady cash flow.

Evidence of how sure a bet these goods were can be found within the government's attempts to regulate them. The federal Alcohol, Tobacco and Firearms agency or ATF was transferred to the U.S. Treasury Department from the IRS in the 1970s. It had a name adjustment and moved again after the September 11th attacks of 2001. Now under the Department of Homeland Security, The Alcohol, Tobacco, Firearms and Explosives agency still goes by ATF but its mandate encompasses more than cigs, guns and booze.

The job of trying to keep illegal weapons out of the hands of the lawless has never been tougher. Even with more than a billion dollar federal budget, enforcement was stacked against the sentiments of a growing wave of Americans who believe they have a right to own nearly any type of fire power. The ATF was losing the proxy war with the NRA and citizens who screamed about the second amendment and bristled at any weapon control measures.

Never mind the fact that these same bristled Americans had no qualms about trampling the rights of other Americans who had different skin tones or spoke with a foreign accent. If you didn't reflect the Make America Great Again white, America First resident, then the hell with you. Go back to wherever you came from and who cares about your so-called rights as a new citizen under the constitution. It wasn't written for you. It was written for those who could claim white ancestry dating back a few generations.

Try to restrict a gun sale however and the constitution fanatics came out in full force, screaming from the rooftops about God Given Rights!

As if God was a white guy in a big chair in the sky, handing down rifles, pistols and grenades. *Here you go my dear children. Verily I say unto you, go forth and blow shit up.*

Rita Tiegs was a member of Bernadette Carter's church. It had been weeks since Rita's impulse call to Zilla after the massive earthquake on Amchitka had pinged her warning center computer screen. Rita and her wife were volunteers at the non-denominational Church of Open Hearts.

It was a diverse mix of gay and straight couples of multiple ethnicities, former convicts and recovering addicts. People who had grown weary of the side eyes they got at other churches because they were gay, or trans or an interracial couple or they made other pious church goers nervous because their hard drug lives of the past had taken a physical toll and they carried the scars of addiction in their haggard eyes and wrinkled complexions. As if the punishment of addiction wasn't cruel enough, the scarlet letter of it stayed publicly visible long after the cravings were brought under control.

They were people who simply wanted a place to worship without judgment. The Church of Open Hearts fit the bill and Bernadette was a popular preacher who brought her own truths of a violent past. She spoke honestly about the physical and sexual abuse that had been perpetrated by their stepfather against her and her sister, after their mother abandoned them. Bernadette was candid about her own history of violence and her stint in prison for attempted murder.

Bernadette, although still a large woman, no longer carried herself like a menacing figure. She didn't have to put on a front of serial ass kicker to protect the scared child inside.

For most of her life she had presented an aggressive persona to the public, but it was her little sister, Jamie Lynn, who was lethal. Jamie Lynn loved drugs and manipulation. She enjoyed killing others and toasting it with a syringe full of heroin. She relished being a ruthless killer.

Bernadette had never indulged in drugs and was abhorred and frightened by the violent acts of her sister. She was happier now than she'd ever been, in a loving nurturing relationship with another woman who treated her with respect and was also respectable.

Her time in prison had saved her life. It was there she found counseling and others who had suffered the same kinds of physical and sexual abuse that had consumed her young life and left her deeply wounded, shamed and angry. She'd been able to heal her heart, as much as anyone with a lot of psychological scarring can, develop an understanding of her own sexuality and embrace rather than despise it, and it led to a new way of seeing the world through calm, compassionate eyes and a peaceful heart.

Bernadette and her wife Krystal Wright, a recovering alcoholic who was in prison for a third DUI when Bernadette was thrown in, now dedicated themselves to each other and helping those who struggled with poverty or domestic violence or addiction. Both women wanted to polish up their karma after past mistakes, living a life of service and giving to others. Working to make Anchorage a better place for all.

Rita Tiegs appreciated their work and would never admit to anyone that she was morbidly fascinated by Bernadette's past attempt to kill Zilla Gillette. Rita admired the reporter, a bit more than she perhaps should, married as she was, but she wished to know Bernadette to understand how and why she'd tried to kill Gillette. She wanted to ask questions, but didn't dare.

Chapter Fifteen

Jerry Justice was sure everything was ready. Nakita Volkov wasn't so sure. Volkov didn't have the level of confidence in the bow legged man with the southern drawl that he would have had in another Russian. Americans were flaky enough when it came to proper planning for large events, but his dealings with the smiling Arkansas native who dressed like an extra in a cowboy movie had made him worry. The money he had so freely dispensed to Justice and the numerous other thugs who were supposed to help them was small in the grand scheme of the Kremlin becoming the dominant world leader, but it was enough to be noticed.

Volkov didn't like loose ends and wagging tongues rumoring about where all the cash was coming from, he didn't need.

"Don't worry about anything. We're set. Woo eee, this is going to be a wild ride this weekend!" Displaying his usual over confidence, Jerry Justice was hopping around on the trail near Earthquake Park like a kid at a birthday party. He had parked at the Point Woronzof parking lot as Volkov had instructed and walked the trail back toward downtown. Volkov met him in between the upper parking lot and the lower lot where he had parked. Best to meet on the trail where only a couple of people might remember seeing the two men together rather than risk a meeting in one of the parking lots where the steady stream of bikers, hikers, runners and dog walkers would be coming and going.

"I certainly hope so. We will not get a second chance." Volkov's tone was ominous and he didn't smile. Jerry Justice was used to working with nervous criminals. They were often worried about failure and the consequences that came with being caught. Jerry Justice worried about none of these things. As long as there was money, he was happy and the serious eyed Russian seemed to have unlimited supplies of cash.

"We are in a good place here." Volkov swept his hands in a circle indicating he was unconcerned about being seen in this wooded spot that looked out over the expanse of upper Cook Inlet, the city skyline to their right, the mountains of the Alaska Range and Denali to the left. Waves on the silty water glittered in the morning sun. "Run the plan through again."

Jerry Justice didn't mind. He was damn proud of his great idea. "Sure thing boss, woo eee, this is going to be big. The downtown rally starts around 4 pm. That woman politician is supposed to speak right near the start, so I figure since our event gets underway around 3 this afternoon, we'll have plenty of time to get everybody all hot and bothered and......"

"What is hot and bothered? What do you mean?" Volkov interrupted.

"It's just one of those expressions Americans use boss. Means getting' people pissed off and ready to do something. Something you tell em to do! So, we get them motivated to take action and then, right on cue, as we're piling in cars to go downtown and disrupt their little hippy love fest, our star attraction takes off from Merrill Field and it all goes down in one big bang! woo eee, yeah!"

His over simplified, short on details run down didn't reassure Volkov, but he had to trust that it would work. There was no time to double check or try to change it now.

It had to work.

"I'm glad you are so sure of these things Mr. Hansen. It is important that you are right." His voice was cold and Jerry Justice felt the chill, but he wasn't worried and he wasn't scared of Nakita Volkov. They were on American soil and a Russian guy trying to act intimidating was ridiculous to the Arkansas cowboy. He didn't understand the long reach of the Kremlin. People who bucked the leader of Russia didn't have to be in that country to end up on the wrong end of a gun or a lethal cup of tea.

"Don't worry! This will work and we'll have that woman hog-tied and stashed away before the cops have any idea what the hell is going on. Yessir, grabbing a U.S. Congresswoman is mighty fucking bold, but I love it. We'll have some real leverage then. Woo eee!"

"I need to take care of a few more matters. Please check that all parties to this plan are in place, ready to go and have everything they need. *Everything.*" Volkov stressed his final word. He turned and walked back up the trail without saying goodbye. Then turned to face Jerry Justice again. "I will see you at the Kincaid Park this afternoon. In approximately three hours. You will be near the west side of the building, this is correct?"

"I'll be there. Yes I will."

Volkov turned and walked off. Jerry Justice gazed over the inlet for a few seconds, thinking about the plane that would glide over those very waters later in the day and surprise the shit out of everybody in the city. Yes, it was going to work. He was sure of it. It was time to get Jamie Lynn and get ready.

Volkov was fairly certain that Jerry Justice didn't understand Russian, but still waited until he was well out of earshot before he made his call. Walking at a brisk clip toward the upper parking lot, passing walkers and bicycle riders as he spoke quietly into his phone. These calls were brief with no clear details given but a coded conversation laid out the current information.

If his new American contractor was capable, there should be good news coming later that day. Events would unfold quickly and Volkov in his relaying of the weather, the fishing and the great restaurants in downtown Anchorage was all the while detailing what would go down within a few hours. At the end he laughed and said he'd gotten lost on the trails, meaning communications would need to go dark for about 24 hours as they made their move on the U.S. lawmaker. He said he would call the next afternoon and signed off.

As he disconnected he knew his message was already being delivered to the highest office in Moscow. This had to go as he'd just said it would. Volkov was an important member of the Kremlin's international intelligence and control organization. Putin had people all over the world gathering data and removing those who would cause trouble for the homeland and its iron-fisted leader.

But he didn't suffer any illusions about his own level of importance. Working for a former KGB officer meant you understood your vulnerability in a system that honors loyalty but more so honors accomplishment. A plan had to go off without a hitch or just like Volkov's assistant who had not properly vetted Ralph

Sims, Volkov could also go missing or take a sip of tea some day that would be his last.

Putin valued men like Volkov, but only to a point. No one would be protected if they didn't do their job to the Kremlin's liking. No one.

Chapter Sixteen

Detective August Platonovich was restless. He valued tactical order and careful deployment of the Anchorage PD's limited resources. They only had so many bodies and being strategic for two large events in the city was stressful. It had to be right, especially for political gatherings. The tension around the pending decision from the 9th circuit on resource extraction versus protection was taking its toll on Alaskans and Alaska law enforcement. The bizarre death of the polarizing activist Marcus Peterson had added an element of hysteria from his supporters and Platonovich's long legal instincts told him to expect anything.

This day was likely to see trouble, which had the normally calm detective on edge. He couldn't sit waiting at his desk until the rallies started.

Instead, he got in his truck, drove toward Ruby's Café and called Ray.

"Hello Detective Platonovich. Are you giving statements to the press before today's twin events?" He was only half kidding.

"I trust you don't need my assurance that all will be fine today. APD has made thorough plans for officers to be in attendance at both the Park Strip and Kincaid Park."

"Are you trying to convince me or yourself August?" Ray quit talking like a reporter and so did August.

"Off the record? Perhaps. I am driving to your family's business now. I know that your mom, the Congresswoman is here and I wanted to check with her regarding her appearance today."

Ray was quiet for a beat. "Anything I should know or be concerned about?"

Now it was August's turn to be silent. Ray could hear chatter on August's police radio in the background. He waited.

August chose his words carefully.

"I think general concern is wise. There is a lot of emotion, much of it anger and frustration. Add to it a lack of good information, too much propaganda on both sides and that's a worrying combination."

"Hey, my mom will not spread propaganda." Ray was trying to lighten the mood. Not because he felt it, he felt sick to his stomach, but August wasn't helping him feel better. He was freaking him out.

The detective gave a quiet little laugh. "Yes, please forgive me. I did not mean to include your mother in that statement. Have you heard from Zilla?"

Ray wasn't sure how much August knew about Zilla's trip to the GDC compound. He knew Zilla and August had been cooling their heels and not seeing each other outside of work. Zilla had decided it was a bridge too far for an investigative reporter to date a detective. No matter how hard she worked to keep work and her private life separate, and she did, it still felt ethically shaky and she was a woman with unwavering ethics.

"Well, she's scheduled to be at the rally this afternoon so I expect to see her within the next two hours." Reporters are as good at not giving out information as they are at digging for it. This time August's laugh was a bit louder.

"Ok, thanks for at least letting me know I should assume she will be in the crowd today. Do you know that Jamie Lynn Carter is out of prison and scheduled to speak at the rally at Kincaid today?"

"Yes." Was Ray's quiet answer.

"I'll be there Ray. Many other officers will be too. We'll keep things orderly and safe."

"Keeping track of Zilla will be the big effort. She's going to want to be at both places."

"Yes, that sounds right. I'm at the café now. I'll speak with you later." Ray could hear August put the truck in park and pop the door open as he shut the engine off.

"Thanks for being on top of this August."

"Let's hope that I am."

##

The rallies planned in Anchorage would be a visible manifestation of the growing divide in the state and nation. Some Alaskans saw it as a continuation of a century old fight between resource development hawks and conservationists. But although there had been shouting and the occasional fist shake across the line when people had clashed over building the Trans Alaska Pipeline in the 70s or before that, the notion of testing nuclear weapons on Amchitka or the preposterous idea floated by bomb builders to use nukes to blow up a spot for a new harbor along the northern arctic coast, this fight was even more intense. More angry people were involved, the tone was ugly and the line was lethal.

There was no effort to understand the ideas of the other side. There was no seeing each other as Americans and Alaskans first. This was closer to physical battle than at any time since the Civil War.

And America's foes were gleefully feeding the disinformation network. Russia, China and North Korea released a steady stream of lies to the dark net, which oozed to the main flow online and out to the masses. Russia sent sophisticated 'scientific papers' claiming reconnaissance drones had collected air samples over Amchitka immediately after the blast, (that's how it was referred to in all foreign propaganda, never was the word earthquake used.) the write-ups contained spreadsheets of useless numbers that were sham air test results. These supposed 'tests' proved radioactive material had exploded from the island, the articles blared.

China pushed back directly, questioning how the United States could continue to threaten them over islands in the South China Sea when the Americans themselves were clearly doing the same thing! They were building up for war! Should China sit idly by and just helplessly wait to be blown up? No, the Chinese would not tolerate it.

North Korea sent out more pictures of Dear Leader, smiling and pointing at things that looked like ominous weapons, but could have been painted cardboard. Bold statements accompanied the photos and claimed that the American fools thought they were still the dominant power in the world, but were clearly, in Dear Leader's estimation, just delusional dogs.

Kim Jun insisted the rest of the world had moved on without them. If they so wanted to be isolationists, let them! They demand America First the rest of the world says America Out! The three countries were pumping a lot of money and technical resources into turning world sentiment against the separatist mutts in Washington DC. Let them twist in the wind.

And once they were able to declare war against the irresponsible leaders of the not so United States, once they could finally make their case in the international arena that the Americans were no longer to be trusted, it was over. When the world believed that America was now an unstable rogue state with far too many heavy weapons that could be captured by American anarchists and used against other countries, it would be too late.

The message was; the world must act together to rein in and control the war mongering crazies in Washington. It was the only thing that would save the planet from nuclear annihilation. Just as the world had to respond when Nazis swept through Europe in a toxic cloud of evil, now it was time for the world to step up and stop the Americans. It was sad and unfortunate to witness the country's fall from greatness, but it was now time to act.

There was even a rumor campaign started about the Statue of Liberty, complete with fake photos showing it being disassembled. It would be moved to Cook Inlet and stand between the mountain known as Sleeping Lady and the Port of Alaska right near the city of Anchorage.

Why this would happen was not part of the disinformation flood. It wasn't necessary to have a rationale explanation for these things. If you could convince people that a child abduction/sex trafficking and cannibalism ring was operating out of an east coast pizza shop, then the right headline font and doctored pictures would sell it. Yes sir. Facts were silly nonsense spread by hysterical liberal snowflakes in the fake news era.

Just ask the U.S. President.

Bernadette Carter still had nightmares about prison. She'd been terrified during her incarceration. Trying to maintain a facade of badass was exhausting. She had acted tough, tried to look fierce to protect herself, just as she had when she was a young girl fending off her stepfather and the drunken louts that hung around his dingy apartment.

The girls, Bernadette and her little sister Jamie Lynn had been their step dad's servants, running to the local store at all hours of the day or night, winter or summer and his dogs to kick when he was hung over or pissy drunk and in a foul mood. He stopped visiting Bernadette's bedroom when she was a teenager and pulled a knife on him late one night. But the psychological abuse continued and Bernadette unconsciously built a fleshy wall of armor around herself, putting on weight to protect from the leering eyes of her stepfather's cronies. She stalked the halls at her high school, holding her arms out a bit from her sides as she stared down anyone who looked at her, ready to fight at a moment's notice. Until she sought out counseling in lock up, she hadn't known how much she hated pretending to be mean. Bernadette Carter had fought against her very nature from the day her mother disappeared, leaving young Jamie Lynn and Bernadette with a man who had never loved them and barely tolerated them under his roof. If he hadn't made booze and cigarette money from letting the bums who frequented his place have access to Bernadette and Jamie Lynn, he would have thrown them out before Bernadette reached her 12th birthday.

Her life was completely different now. She was loved and respected by her wife Krystal. They lived in a modest but clean and safe home. They ran a counseling service for recently released felons who were trying to stay on a good path and she was a part time pastor of a small congregation.

She had the satisfaction of watching other former inmates pull themselves together with her counseling assistance. They stayed sober, got jobs, were regular attendees at her church, and they brought gifts of gratitude. Most of them lived hand to mouth, so they were only able to drop crumpled, small bills into the collection plate during services, but they were generous in other ways. They brought fish they'd smoked, or berries.

One woman who had spent 15 years in prison for murdering her abusive husband, made beautiful needlepoint designs of Alaska landscapes and gave them to Krystal and Bernadette to use as raffle gifts to raise funds. A new church member named George came from a tiny village on the Bering Sea. A decade earlier he'd fatally shot his brother-in-law when they were both in a crazed blackout from hours of drinking home made booze. He remembered nothing from that awful day and wore a perpetual expression of sorrow for a crime he could never undo.

George brought Bernadette a beautiful, hand carved staff that he had spent long hours creating. It featured a highly polished, gleaming main shaft of yellow cedar. Light but strong. The ends were meticulously carved walrus ivory spears, both detailed with arctic scenes that told picture stories of fearless, successful hunters tracking polar bears on sea ice. The sharp ends were covered with tight fitting, cedar caps that snugged tightly against the shaft. George told Bernadette that it symbolized his faith in her words and her ability to lead others. He said Bernadette's heart was as strong and true as the yellow cedar and even though she would always carry the burden of her past, she, just like the gift he had made for her, kept her psychological spears safely covered, hidden and contained away from the public. He said his gift symbolized something that could be used for saving others or used to cause harm, but he trusted her to use it only for good.

She was honored by his words and happy for the first time in her life. The inner work she'd done in prison had been transformative and she often laughed that she had to go to jail to find herself.

It was true.

Bernadette no longer walked with a menacing stare on her face. She could allow the softer nature that she had stuffed in a small box inside flow forward and envelope her in peace and love. She was content and excited for the future. It was still a little scary because it was so new, after only three years of seeing the world and her self differently. She didn't tell Krystal, but she was afraid it would evaporate and she would wake up and realize it was just a sweet dream and she was back in prison or worse than that, back in the filthy east Anchorage apartment on Muldoon Road, ducking the errant blows of her unpredictable stepdad and wondering if they would have any food at all that day.

She tried to keep the fear at bay by staying active in their work and her ministering to others. She was looking forward to the rally and all the families who would be in attendance. Bernadette knew she'd never be a parent, but she loved little kids and was in high anticipation of seeing a bunch of them at the Midnight Fun

Midnight Run event that afternoon. She was also honored that she would be the one introducing Congresswoman Ruby Walker.

Representative Walker had been to the women's prison several times when Bernadette was still in lock up and her words of encouragement had meant a lot. Ruby had told the women that being incarcerated didn't mean they were doomed. It meant they had work to do and after their debt to society had been paid, they had all the same rights and responsibilities of every other citizen. They could have success and they could live lawful and happy lives. It wouldn't be easy, but Ruby told them, they were clearly tough and if they would take advantage of the group sessions, the academic opportunities, the job training that was available to them while their sentences unwound, they could thrive outside of prison walls.

That had stuck with Bernadette and she had done exactly that. Now she was a happily married woman living a stable life and she was going to introduce the congresswoman at the rally. Bernadette carried sorrow from her attempt to murder Zilla Gillette. She knew it would always be there, like a stone tethered to her soul. She had accepted it as the price of bad decisions. She couldn't go back and change the past. She could only work to do good things in the future and help others avoid the pain and mistakes she'd made.

Mo Scott regretted few things. What was done was done. But she was currently wishing she had not decided it would be a good idea to hold community debates at Ruby's Café and Bar on Wednesday nights. When the enviros started advancing their fight through the court system, she thought it a good civic exercise to hold forums about the pros and cons of resource extraction versus holding some places in a special, esteemed status where absolutely no development would ever be allowed. She wanted to know what Alaskans thought and knew there was passion on both sides.

Part of it was self serving, since she could feed what she heard into her syndicated columns, which inspired even more debate online, part of it was trying to resolve her own feelings about it as an Athabascan woman with ties to this land that a lot of Alaskans could not claim.

Were conservationists correct in their assertions that some places had a right to exist without human interference, such as the ongoing Colorado River case? Should that be considered for other places? How would it affect those who wanted to extract oil, gas or coal from below the surface or those who wanted to cut timber, harvest rare plants or lay claim to fresh water supplies? And more importantly to an indigenous person who knew how many Native people depended on the gifts of the land and waters for sustenance, both physical and spiritual? Could granting something similar in rights to personhood for natural systems mean that no one, even the first people who had been on that land and water, could use it as they needed and had for thousands of years?

These were the questions she wanted to explore in the mid week debates, (tap beer, rail drinks and halibut burger specials were included!) and although it had started well enough, with thoughtful people trickling in to chow on bar food and weigh in with their ideas and positions, it started to change after a few weeks as the word got out about the evening gatherings.

The mood turned hostile as the parking lot began filling up with the vehicles of people who had not been regular customers of Ruby's. Big trucks with big name extraction company logos took up two parking spaces. Just as the trucks muscled in and demanded more room than needed, the owners elbowed in the door and didn't hesitate to loudly drag tables and chairs around into whatever configuration suited them. The not so subtle message was, *we run things and we won't ask before we decide to take over here or anywhere. Don't question us unless you want your head bulldozed.*

These characters wouldn't listen to any opposing viewpoint, they just shouted people down or booed loudly to drown them out. The respectful discourse evaporated by the third week and Mo found it was no longer a productive conversation, but closer to a bar brawl.

She didn't like the looks that a lot of the new patrons gave her boss's father in law either. He was a wonderful man, half father, half uncle and eventually when she and Ray the third married, he would be her delightful grandfather in law. The narrow eyed cold stares he was getting with more frequency bothered her terribly. She threw a few jerks out just for mean mugging Poppa Ray. She knew racists and wouldn't tolerate them for a second. Ruby's Cafe didn't need the dollars from tap beer that much.

Mo was dismayed that the evening events had become less about intelligent debate on complicated environment and resource development issues and more of the same type of boiled down jingoism that was part of the ever widening divide in the state and country. Difficult topics required thoughtful and respectful discussion, not shouting each other down or talking over someone until they give up. How will that ever help anyone see a different perspective or consider another way of defining rights? She was wiping the bar top, deep in these thoughts when she heard Poppa Ray's familiar chuckle.

"My, my, Miss Mo, you about to wear through the varnish wiping that same circle like that. Seems you're a thousand miles away young lady." He figured she was worried about the afternoon rally and speech by her soon to be mother in law Ruby, his much loved daughter in law. As was usually the case, the astute elder was spot on.

He had at one point in time hoped that Zilla would be the love in his grandson's life, but had come to realize that the two reporters were more like brother and sister than paramours and that wasn't going to change. When little Ray, as his granddad still thought of him, began courting Mo, he was happy. The first Ray Walker was glad that the third Ray Walker had found a life partner with plenty of intelligence, independence, a robust work ethic and above all, kindness. Mo was the real deal and Poppa Ray knew it.

Even after all the years that his wonderful wife had been gone, it was an unconscious effort of comparison. The long time widower had compared Ruby with his late wife Emma. He'd matched Zilla's qualities against her and he'd stacked Mo's personality against all that he'd valued in Emma too, and in every circumstance, none of the women had been lacking. Emma had been his queen and the mother of his son. Ruby, Zilla and Mo were also women of substance. He respected them all enormously.

Mo stopped swirling the bar towel and looked up with a smile, the lines of her worried concentration softened into pure affection. "Yeah, guess I could have started a friction fire...." for a distracted second or two, she resumed wiping, as if the momentum brought some small comfort and coaxed her arm to resume the task. She looked down at the bar as she tried to put her thoughts into words.

"I feel like the entire country is staring at the same horrible car wreck and instead of help, there are accusations about who is at fault and what needs to be done about it." She looked up at him; the turmoil in her eyes touched his heart. " I'm not even able to put it into words very well. Nothing makes sense. Instead of a collective shudder about how we got here and how we can help each other close whatever gate in hell opened up and spit out Donald Trump, we're arguing over whether it really IS a car crash or is it fake news? Is it a deep state lie? Is it a conspiracy ginned up by the hard Right? The hard Left? Are the crash victims only actors who are lying about it all?"

She tossed the towel in frustration. It landed and slid down the bar top. "How the hell do we counter that? I can write columns and Ray and Zilla can report hard facts till the last dog dies Poppa Ray and if people choose to simply deny the truth, what can we do? I'm really scared about our democracy and the intensity here is shocking. Alaskans are divided in a way I've never seen before and we've always had our scraps and squabbles. I thought holding the forums here would be a good way to bring people together but it was like plunging a knife into an old, infected wound. It laid open the raw pain, but did not help cleanse and heal. It's gone too far. The infection has reached the bone and maybe there's no saving the patient now."

She sighed and crossed her arms as if to prevent her hand from reaching for the towel again. "Guess I had more words than I thought, but talking about it doesn't give me any clarity. I'm so, so sad and so scared."

The elder Walker had to choose his words carefully. He could see how upset she was and Mo Scott was not a woman who was easily rattled. This deeply troubled person before him was the same one who had been beaten by a former abusive boyfriend but instead of cowering, she'd taken her power back. When he had driven straight at her, intent on running her over in the parking lot of Ruby's café, she'd pulled out the gun her uncles had taught her to shoot and killed his truck, then she'd bashed the hood with a ball bat and told him to stay the hell away from her. He did.

Ray Senior sighed, a slight frown of sorrow and long understanding of the ruthless nature of too many people on his face. He was a black man who had grown up in the segregated south; he knew what she was grappling with. A struggle that is never far from the surface for most people of color had spread like a wildfire in dry grass under the current President. It was a Get Out of Jail Free card for racists and they gleefully waved it around and accused everyone who didn't see things their way of being snowflakes, libtards or losers, their icon's favorite term for anyone who criticized him.

And on the other side was it any better? Some of the very people who espoused saving the planet and equal rights for all people were supporters of the late Marcus Peterson's attacks on Alaska Native hunters for harvesting the protein that had been an intrinsic part of their life for thousands of years. Some of what they thought of as 'helpful' was condescending and smothering rather than respecting the worldview and culture of the people they professed to want to help.

Poppa Ray longed for the right words of consolation. He wished there was an answer, but sadly, it would likely never really change. There would always be those who categorized by belief or skin color and some of those would hate, based on no more than that. How do you polish up that bit of awful and present it well? There was no non-bullshit way of doing it and trying to bullshit a savvy Athabascan woman was not only a fool's errand, it could get you in hot water. Besides, he loved and respected Mo; he would not try to paste a pretty veneer over an ugly national face.

"It is a troubling quandary dear Mo. Yes it is. But even as you and I both know there will never be a change in some hearts, there will be some ears that will never listen to reason, there will be some minds that will never believe the truth of a round earth and human equality......" he furrowed his brow and put his big, work gnarled hand over the top of hers on the bar, comforting Mo with the gentle warmth of the gesture, "We must not give up in despair. We must continue to believe that our adherence to the truth, to respect and dignity for all people and their beliefs, to our understanding that the only way change comes about is through listening to others, not shouting them down. To extend a hand in compassion to those who act out in crazy ways because they are afraid."

"Even when the bastards try to bite, cut or shoot your hand off Pops?"

"Yes. Even when the bastards do."

Mo put her other hand over the top of Poppa Ray's and gently squeezed it. She smiled for the first time and his heart was glad.

"Thanks for talking me off the cliff. It's all so overwhelming and frightening and hopeless. And I.....I'm damn worried about this afternoon. I just, just have a bad feeling. I hate saying that out loud."

"I know. I hate saying it too but I feel the same way. Would love to just cancel the whole shebang." He put his other hand over hers, all four stacked up together. "Ok. We got that out now let's focus on a good outcome rather than our fears. We're team Walker right? And there's a damn lot of power in that Mo!"

"Yeah! Go us!" They threw their hands up above their heads and smiled at each other, both hoping the other felt that team power.

They knew they were really going to need it later.

##

Jamie Lynn had become a fan of morbid humor.

As she prepared for the late afternoon event at Kincaid Park, she applied eyeliner, mascara and eye shadow to her one remaining eye. She was bitterly amused that applying 'eye' make up was now grammatically correct for her.

She liked her patch, felt it made her look even more badass than the hideous scars on her face and she carefully made up her one eye to remind men of how gorgeous she'd been. They were dogs, all thinking of one thing. They didn't care what you looked like as long as you had the right plumbing for them to use and exploit. What was that old expression about a bag over the head?

Yeah. That was men. But she didn't care. Never had. Didn't mind using her body to get what she wanted. It had served her well until she had to end it with General Alex and went to prison. That hadn't been terrific. It was harder to get heroin inside, but not that much harder and her habit along with the hunger of her demon, had only grown behind bars. She was not remorseful, she did not hope for redemption, a fresh start or respect. Fuck that. She wanted money. Money. Money.

And not a goddamn thing else.

Well, she thought with a smile as she blotted concealer along the deep purple scars on her face, she also wanted Zilla Gillette dead. Yes. That and a healthy pay day would make the years in jail and losing her sister to lesbian brain washing worth it.

Not that she cared about her big sister Bernadette anyway. If a sociopath doesn't feel anything for anyone, then Jamie Lynn Carter was the poster girl for that psychological disorder.

Her simple plan hadn't changed much since the days before prison and the death of General Burke. She would rip off Jerry Justice just as she'd planned to rip off the General. If that meant killing a few jerks along the way, even better. Jamie Lynn had her first kill when she was 12 years old and her body count was now three, nearly four after she'd beaten the daylights out of a former cellmate. She regretted that guards had tazed and stopped her efforts just as she was about to finish the unconscious woman off. Her face a bloody mash.

That had earned her extra time behind bars but it also upped her status among the other killers in lock up. Some of them had kept in contact and as they left prison, they got in touch, letting her know that if she needed their back up, they were there. It was the first time Jamie Lynn felt like she had her own posse and she relished giving them instructions to be at the Kincaid event. She didn't give details but made it clear that shit was going down and if they missed it, they'd be sorry. Even though most of them were on probation and would get tossed back in for just being at a gathering that was likely to turn violent.

They knew the risks and didn't give a damn. Just like Jamie, they didn't care about much of anything except kicking ass and burning shit down.

"Ok, that works." Jamie said to her reflection as she finished applying the cheap make-up that she'd bought from the local grocery store. Soon, she'd have the cash to buy good stuff and the cash to buy it in a completely different location. Jamie Lynn Carter was on probation for the next five years. After today, things would happen quickly and with a bit of luck, she figured she was due some, she should be out of the state and disappeared before her probation officer realized she'd broken the conditions of her release.

Staying away from Zilla Gillette was one of the first requirements that had been spelled out clearly to her. She smiled once more at herself as she fitted the black patch over her ruined eye. That condition was the one she was the most eager to break. "That nosy fucking reporter bitch is going down and no one is going to stop me this time." She nodded at her reflection as if sealing Zilla's fate. She gathered up her meager beauty products from the chipped, dirty sink in the tiny bathroom of the militia supporters who still adhered to the General's belief in taking the country back and saw Jamie Lynn as a martyr.

They respected that she'd gone to prison after the government had controlled the mind of the General and made him attack her, forcing her to fight for her life against the man she loved! Her sister had defended her and the General had unfortunately died because of it. His supporters were sad that he was gone, but determined to carry on his work and the fight to re-whiten the country. They believed Jamie Lynn would help lead them there.

She believed they were complete idiots, but as she stuffed her mascara and lipstick into the frayed purple Crown Royal bag that passed for her new makeup kit, she was fine with being in their midst. She could use them as she'd used the General and now that country ass hick Jerry Justice. They'd get left behind soon and Jamie Lynn was determined that nothing, not a goddamn cop, reporter or her stupid sister would stop her. Not this time. No way.

Chapter Seventeen

Zilla was guided to a plane. The herky-jerky, teeth rattling trip down the mountain was over and they were in a parking lot near an airstrip. The infuriating blindfold foiled her efforts to orient herself. She listened closely for sounds that may give her a clue as to their location but it was useless. They were not near a city, there was little to no traffic noise and the few cars she did hear were at a distance. Zilla figured they wouldn't traipse through O'Hare with her stumbling along, blindfolded and led by a couple of men. So, they were in the country someplace where being observed was not a concern.

"What time is it?" Zilla asked casually.

"It's about....." the younger of the two men paused, presumably to look at his watch

"Knock it off!" The usually silent driver said.

"Me?" The younger man asked.

"Both of you!" He barked at them. "YOU, his voice directed at Zilla, "Don't need to know what the hell time it is. You'll get back when we get you back. And YOU......Don't need to answer those kinds of questions. Use your damn head! She's trying to figure out how long we traveled. Don't give her any information about that."

"Ok, geez. Chill out dude. It's not like she can tell by sound what state we're in." The younger man was indignant.

"Just stop it. I'll calm down when you quit talking and we deliver her safely back to Anchorage. Let's get going."

Zilla stayed quiet after her coy attempt at finding out how long it had taken them to get down the mountain. She listened to their exchange and wondered if they were in fact out of the state. Canada? Many of the early members of Greenpeace were Canadians; maybe they were in the Yukon or the Northwest Territories.

At this point it didn't matter to Zilla as much as getting back to Anchorage and finding out what was happening. She was thrown off her normal axis to have been without any news for the last few days. The kind of media black out that a lot of people yearn for made Zilla feel like she had hives. She was itching for the latest headlines and wanted to get home and assess what was happening. The Midnight Fun Midnight Run event was happening on this day and uncertain of the time, she hoped feverishly that she hadn't missed it.

It struck her that wherever they had taken her, it must be Alaska or Canada since the daylight seemed endless as it is near the arctic in summertime. But that didn't really narrow it down. She focused on what she'd learned during three days at the compound and how she would write stories on it.

"Ok, we're going to the plane now. I'm going to take your arm." The younger man spoke quietly. Zilla appreciated the warning and wasn't alarmed when she felt his hand near her elbow.

As they started walking, Zilla scuffed one of her feet against the ground.

"Gravel airstrip?" She asked.

"Boy, you never quit do you? Yes. It's a damn gravel airstrip. There, you pried some information out of me. That should narrow it down to several thousand. We're almost to the plane, so get ready for the steps" The older man's voice was exasperated but held a bit of admiration for the astute reporter's efforts to learn something, anything about their whereabouts.

##

If only Murph wouldn't have gone back to the Silver Slipper. If he hadn't decided that after a few days of pondering, maybe now the bartender MC Ames would allow his simmering thoughts to come around to the idea that it might be best for him to talk about that package hand off to Jerry Justice.

Murph didn't have any new information, but when people felt scared of guilt by association, they had an overwhelming desire to talk and distance themselves from the perpetrators of crime.

Many times throughout Stuart Murphy's long and prolific journalism career, that had been the thing that cracked stories open. Someone would leave a late night message on his newsroom phone or he'd stop by to ask if they'd learned anything or changed their mind about talking to him and it would come out in a burst, as if holding it back was more awful than the consequences of speaking about it.

This was not the case with Ames. He may not have followed through with his terrible rampage if Murph hadn't poked the bear of his paranoia one more time. Murph couldn't know about MC's extreme fear that made him feel like he'd been swallowed whole, drowning in anxiety. MC hadn't been sleeping and was more agitated by the minute.

Murph did what good reporters engaged in due diligence do. He followed up and went back to the Silver Slipper to sweat MC for information.

He misread MC as he walked through the basement door of the Silver Slipper.

Murph caught a whiff of the chronic damp of the old building that exhaled moisture beneath a 70-year-old street. Decades of tectonic plate jostling, both large and small in the city that was perched on the seismically enthusiastic Ring of Fire, meant the earth moved a lot, every day, and small cracks and fractures allowed the moist scent of dank clay and seaweed from salty Cook Inlet to permeate everything. The basement walls of The Silver Slipper were no exception.

"Hello there Mr. Ames! How's the carry out business?" Murph smiled broadly at the younger man behind the bar.

"Whadda you want?" MC was in no mood to deal with a nosy reporter, he frowned and narrowed his eyes, glancing at Murphy and then looked down again at the open cooler behind the bar, carefully placing bottles of beer. MC had learned the hard way that stocking could be dangerous. Twice he had broken a bottle working in haste, both times cutting his hand when the bottle clanked against another and broke. He took his time now.

Murphy quit smiling and stepped up to the bar sliding into a high back, swivel bar stool. Everything about the Silver Slipper was authentically old or retro cool. "Has your friend, the southern cowboy been around to pick up any dinner orders lately?"

MC stood up straight, a long neck bottle of local brewed IPA with a raven label gripped in his right hand. Murph understood body language and knew the bartender would have loved to clobber him with that dark glass bottle. Murph didn't expect MC to be thrilled to see him after their last uncomfortable encounter, but he hadn't expected full on hostility. "Why do you keep coming in here asking questions and looking for trouble?" MC held the bottle waist high, the cooler stood open but he didn't move to lay the bottle in it.

"Easy now. I'm not looking for trouble, just a beer, although that IPA bottle you're choking right now isn't my bag. How about a Guinness or better yet, if you have a local dark beer, I'd try that." Murph had been a reporter for decades and he was a master at when to push and when to back off. He was trying to disarm the angry bartender.

MC didn't answer, but slowly lowered the bottle of IPA into the cooler, slid that door closed and opened another. He pulled a bottle, yanked the top, with a bottle opener, letting the cap fall to the floor, then poured the dark beer expertly into a tall glass, a creamy auburn colored head appeared and Murph smiled.

"You certainly know your craft. Have you been a bartender for a long time?" He knew the answer, having researched MC Ames to find out if the young bartender really was a crook or if he was over his head in what could be big trouble. Murph figured it was the latter. The kid didn't realize how dangerous the people he worked for were.

"Long enough to know how to pour a damn beer." MC set a coaster down, placed the glass of beer on it and turned around toward the back bar, never looking Murph in the eyes.

Murph was sure the shadowy Nakita Volkov was MC's real boss, even though ownership of the Silver Slipper had changed hands a number of times in the last several years, through a couple of half hearted restorations. An LLC called Baranof Holdings owned it. Murph was trying to sort out who owned the LLC. Licensed Limited Corporations are often small businesses, operated by one or a couple of people. The LLC protected them from customer lawsuits that could otherwise take the shirt off their back. An LLC meant someone could sue your business, not you, protecting your home and personal property.

Baranof Holdings belonged to another corporation and the legal layering had kept Murph from finding a local corporate officer name. He had not given up his efforts. It was part of his present call on MC at the Silver Slipper.

Digging.

"So kid." Murph spoke as he picked up the beer glass that MC had put in front of him. "Ah, that's a great tasting beer, why don't you talk to me about what's going on here? I have a feeling you're not part of it but being forced into doing some tasks that could land you in big trouble. Talk to me and maybe you'll help yourself out of this mess."

For a brief moment, Murph saw a look of hope cross MC's face, reflected in the mirrored wall of the back bar. It flickered across his eyes and he stood up a bit taller, but the wary look re-emerged and he turned to face Murph.

"I don't know what the hell you're talking about old man. There's nothing 'going on'".....he air quoted the words dramatically, "here, but maybe you're confused since you're not a cop or a lawyer and couldn't help me even if there was something 'going on'." Again with the air quotes.

Murph set the hook. "Well now, that's where you're wrong young man." Murph took another drink from his dark beer, his eyes on MC's face. "If there was...." he also employed air quotes, mimicking MC's actions, "something 'going on' here, you cooperating with the press and then if you so chose, the police, you'd be in front of the shit storm that will come, instead of right in the middle of it." He set his half empty glass on the bar. "That can mean the difference between a deal and a sentence."

MC laughed nervously, "Wow, you make a lot of assumptions. Thinking you know something when you don't know jack. Just because you 'think you saw something' when you were here before, doesn't make it so, and even if you did, that doesn't mean it was illegal."

Murph drained his glass and set it down, standing up from the stool, he laid a ten-dollar bill on the bar.

"Well, again, you're wrong. I did see a hand off and I know what that means and it ain't innocent kid. Now you can continue fucking around with these mobsters and end up taking the fall for them or simply disappeared which happens to most lackeys, but those are your only options. So think it through and call me when you come to your senses." Murph threw a business card on the bar and turned for the door.

MC was enraged. Paranoia and fear often presents an angry face. "Listen you old fuck! I'm a goddamned bartender, not a mobster! I don't know what the hell you're talking about but you better not come back in here."

Murph pushed. It was the final straw for MC. "Yeah, you do know what the hell I'm talking about and you're not a bartender, you're a Johnny come lately flight attendant who stupidly took a job from a gangster and now you're in over your head and already complicit. Good luck getting out of this dog pile." Murph headed up the stairs. His voice trailed behind him. "You should call me kid. Call me and then call the cops. There might still be time to save your ass from jail or a bullet. Better do it." The upper door to the street opened and MC felt a rush of warm air and heard traffic sounds before the door closed again, abruptly cutting off the breeze and street noise.

He stood shaking, not sure what to do but feeling trapped, scared and angry. The trifecta of bad feelings for people who get themselves into a mess they don't know how to get out of. A desperation that defies rational thinking and a reasonable resolution.

It's more likely to end in worse trouble as the compromised individual, in this case MC Ames, flails around, trying to end their woes through violence rather than taking responsibility and taking their legal hit. MC was terrified of prison and he was determined that no one would tie him to illegal activity. No one else had seen MC hand the bundle to Jerry Justice, only Murph. MC knew Justice was in much deeper than he was so he wasn't worried about him keeping his mouth shut, but the reporter was a different matter. The reporter, old as he was, would dog this story to the ground. MC couldn't let that happen.

They were on a small twin engine, prop driven Cessna. Zilla didn't need to see it to understand that. She climbed the narrow, steep aluminum steps to the aircraft door, a man's voice warned her to duck her head to avoid whacking it. She stepped in and felt a hand on her left elbow.

"Turn right and move forward. Just a few more feet, ok, your seat is on the left. Take it." The man's voice was not friendly but not aggressive. Zilla guessed he was the pilot.

"Are we leaving right away? When we get up, can I take off the damn blindfold?"

"No."

"Swell. I guess that was a blanket no? No, we're not leaving right away and no I can't take the blindfold off?"

"Stop bugging the pilot and strap in." She recognized the voice of the man who had driven her down the mountain from the GDC compound. "We'll leave when we leave and hell no you can't take the blindfold off."

"So you're coming along too? Planning to attend the rally?"

"Just put your seat belt on will ya?"

"Sure thing. It's nice how concerned you are about my safety. How long will we be in the air?" Zilla spoke in a rush, hoping to catch him off guard.

"For fuck's sake, give it a rest." As he was saying it, Zilla heard the door close and latch and the engines start. The small plane shuddered from the rotation of the props, as the engine warmed, the motion smoothed out. Someone outside shouted, "You're clear!" and the plane began to move.

"Ok. Sorry. I'll be quiet. Maybe try to get a nap in before we get to Anchorage." Zilla sounded contrite.

"I don't care. Just stop talking." His voice was more subdued, although louder to compete with the taxiing engine.

"Roger that. Going to sleep now." Zilla called out cheerfully.

But sleep was the last thing on her mind. As soon as the plane started moving, she started counting. Determined to do so until they landed. That would give her a rough estimate of how long they were in the air. More than seven thousand would be two hours, more than ten thousand was three. If she could stick with it, it would be helpful. A focus helped her stave off the growing anxiety about what was going on in Anchorage. She forced thoughts about August, about Ruby, about Ray and about Mo from her mind. She would have never considered that she should also be worried about Murph. She couldn't know how hard he'd just poked the hornet's nest that was swirling inside MC Ames tortured mind. Zilla shut down everything to focus on counting. She settled into the seat and silently ticked off the seconds.

##

Sergeant August Platonovich finished walking the perimeter of the stage area for the park strip rally on the edge of downtown Anchorage. He would drive to Kincaid Park next to check on security preparations for that rally next.

August stood for a few minutes watching municipal workers assemble risers for VIP seating, others ran red, white and blue ribbons through plastic rings atop portable guideposts, designating an area for a beer tent, (must be 21 to enter!) an area for the Congresswomen and her guests to be seated and a cordoned off walkway to the stage stairs.

This design August had insisted on. It was a long way from secure, but it cleared a four-foot wide pathway to the stage for the Congresswoman to navigate through the crowd. It was easier for the officers to see her as she made her way to the podium.

August's cell rang as he walked toward the southern edge of the park strip to his waiting truck. He reached for it, dropped his eyes for a second to look at the number. That brief break from his otherwise constant scanning of the area, meant he missed a figure that had emerged from a thick hedgerow near G Street, a block away from Zilla's H Street residence.

Jerry Justice strolled toward the busy preparations. He had aviator sunglasses and was dressed in a plaid shirt and khaki colored cargo shorts with bulging pockets. A camera hung by a wide strap around his neck and a Gilligan's Island hat sat on top of his head, cocked off to one side.

The quintessential dorky tourist. If August had noticed him, enthusiastically snapping photos, trying to look like another farmer from Iowa on his dream Alaska vacation, the seasoned cop would have caught that something was off about him.

But he answered his cell and Jerry Justice passed out of his line of sight.

"This is Sergeant Platonovich."

"Sir, are you on your way to Kincaid?"

"Yes officer Rand, I'm leaving the downtown area now. Will be there in 15 minutes."

"Good. Thank you Sergeant." The younger officer on the line sounded relieved.

"Something I should know?"

"I'll just feel better if you look over the plan here. I....I don't like this setting for a big rally that could have difficult individuals in the mix."

Officer Rand was a combat veteran from the Gulf wars. He wasn't a paranoid cop, he was very careful. It had kept him alive through some fierce battles and he had medals for saving others in two separate ambush attacks. "What bothers you the most about the Kincaid area?"

"It's the access sir. A two-lane road surrounded by dense forest. We can't secure the entire length of it and even if we could, we don't have enough assets to post officers all along that road and guard any entry from the coastline. This is a wide-open space. We can't secure the perimeter Sergeant."

August appreciated officer Joseph Rand's military jargon. The Sergeant had at one time worried that Rand was a bit off kilter. That maybe his war experience had traumatized him too much and if a police situation got dicey, August worried the veteran might have trouble with PTSD. What if he locked up right when his partner or a citizen needed him to take control or draw his weapon?

It was a concern Platonovich soon gave up. He had observed officer Rand on several occasions in suspect pursuits or returning fire during attempts to pin down a stolen vehicle with shooters in both the driver and passenger seats. Rand was laser focused, in command and brave but not foolhardy. He was an outstanding officer and August trusted him implicitly.

Officer Rand was worried about the perimeter of Kincaid Park and that ticked up August's anxiety another couple of notches.

"I'm on my way. I'll meet you at the chalet."

"Yes sir." The call ended and August got into his truck, checking his watch as he started the engine. 1:15 pm. The rally started at 4 pm. He wondered where Zilla was and if she was safe, but he put thoughts of her out of his mind as quickly as they had entered. He was in love with her, he had come to terms with that, even if she seemed to be putting more distance between them, he felt what he felt and he tried not to over analyze it. But he had a job to do and worrying about Zilla Gillette was a fool's errand. He'd never met a woman so well equipped to handle whatever came at her. He quit thinking about her and focused on the task at hand.

A U.S. Congresswoman was speaking at an open rally in Anchorage this afternoon and although Alaska's congressional delegation had always moved freely through thousands of Alaskans and tourists during the annual Iditarod ceremonial start on the snow covered streets of downtown, this was different.

The political tone had turned ugly in a way August would have not thought possible in this wonderful country that he had been proud to immigrate to and become a productive member of, protecting citizens through the rule of law that governed this nation. There was a terrible fraying of this iconic fabric of America, as if the flag itself had been rent into shreds by the tug of war over it as people tore the country apart. Both sides claiming they were the true Americans! Only they understood what the founders had meant when they wrote the Constitution and only they could bring the country back to greatness!

He was heartsick about the vicious tone and the selfish rhetoric, and the prospect of violence. He could feel it bubbling under the surface. It could blow up like a spewing volcano at any time and vitriol just like lava, indiscriminately burned everything in its path.

Jerry Justice was having a grand time. Playing undercover tourist was a hoot and he particularly enjoyed escaping the notice of Anchorage's top detective. Platonovich usually didn't miss a thing. Justice was tickled to death that he had boldly walked through the park strip, snapped photos of the set up, and slipped by Platonovich. He had to brag to someone.

"Hello darlin', I mean, sorry, shit. Woo ee, it's hard to remember that you don't like being reminded of what a sweet thing you are Jamie Lynn. Are you ready for me to pick you up?"

There was no noise on the other end and he wondered if the call had dropped, then..."I will be in twenty minutes or so. Where are you?" He heard her yawn.

Bitch has probably been up getting high all night. The irritating thought went through his head but he knew better than to ask her unless he wanted his eardrum ruptured.

"I'm on the park strip, checking out the scene. They're getting ready for the big doins', woo ee, yes they are. I gotta run home and change before I pick you up so twenty is fine."

"I won't ask what you're wearing or what you're changing in to because I'm sure both outfits are stupid. Just be here on time, fake ass cowboy."

He clenched his jaw, thinking how much he would enjoy beating the crap out of her and thinking about doing exactly that as soon as this shit show was over, but he held his anger; for now. "Why yes maam. I'll be sure to be right on time. Wouldn't want to keep the queen waiting."

"Fuck you Jerry. Just go pick up your broomstick hobbyhorse and get your ass over here. We got work to do."

Jamie Lynn had heard through the rag tag patriot's network that her older sister, the dyke preacher was going to be at the family race rally to introduce the bitch that had taken the U.S. House seat while Jamie Lynn was in prison.

For a brief moment she thought about calling Bernadette, warn her to stay the fuck away from the park strip, tell her that it might get out of hand, might be dangerous to be there and get caught up in the mess that Jerry Justice and his boys were planning to create, but the thought passed as quickly as it had come to her. She couldn't trust her sister. She'd gone to what Jamie Lynn considered the real dark side, she was religious now and would think turning the information over to the very cops that had cuffed her and dragged her off to prison would be the 'right' thing to do.

Bernadette was lost to her. Not that they'd ever had a warm and loving relationship, no one had taught them what that meant or what it would feel like to have such a thing. A nurturing, supportive family member was something neither had experienced as young girls, but they came as close as traumatized youth can to having a bond. Bernadette had covered for Jamie Lynn when she'd murdered a lecherous neighbor and they'd taken turns being a look out while the other stole food from the local quick stop gas station when they were desperate for something to eat. Their stepfather could always scrounge money for booze and cigarettes but rarely for food.

When he did provide some cellophane wrapped, microwave ready blob, it was their reward for putting up with the disgusting, drunken groping of his drinking buddies. Sometimes they would get a slice of pizza or a hot dog from the rotating heater at the same gas station they stole from on other days. Jamie Lynn shoving a pedophile down a flight of stairs and stomping him to death at 12 years old didn't seem so shocking when the reality of their young existence was unfolded. They had lived a life of trauma and constant abuse, being able to abuse others wasn't hard to fathom. What's common becomes normal. If you're constantly abused, it's normal to abuse others.

Or kill them.

Jamie Lynn knew there she couldn't warn her sister without tipping off law enforcement. There was already amped up security as it was, any hint of a potential for extreme violence would have the effect of shutting it all down. The Anchorage police would probably force the organizers to cancel the downtown event and that meant they couldn't take the Congresswoman. That meant Jamie Lynn would miss out on her big payday and there was no way in hell she was going to let that happen. Her sister had made her choices to become a lesbo hawking some god in a chair in the sky while sleeping with another woman. It all disgusted and enraged Jamie Lynn and she let go of the idea of ever seeing Bernadette again.

She thought she felt a slight flutter of pain where her heart should be, but decided it was probably just indigestion from the mix of drugs, booze and lack of sleep. She sat, impatient for the Arkansas cowboy to pick her up. The sooner this bullshit got underway, the faster she could get paid and get gone. That was all she needed to know.

##

It was hot on the plane and Zilla struggled to stay awake and keep counting. She made it to four thousand, a little more than an hour, when the whine of the plane engine combined with the stifling air in her less than first class accommodations, she got drowsy and her mind started to drift.   Thoughts of her father, gran and granddad were defaults for Zilla when her mind was tired or stressed or both. The soothing memories of the cattle pastures of her youth, traipsing along the well worn paths with a big stick to poke random stuff when she was young and riding farm horses out to bring in the cows for evening chores when she was a teen. Remembering her family offered comfort, even though they were all gone now. Her mother stolen from her in a robbery shooting when she was only three, her father and grandparents had also taken their leave of this existence.

She was alone in the world, but didn't feel lonely.

Most of the time.

She would be glad to see her friends and co-workers when she got back to Alaska's largest city. Their safety was a big concern since she wasn't sure what was happening in the powder keg situation in Anchorage. She took a few deep breaths to both calm down and wake up. There was a lot to think about. No time to nap.

The past four days of interviews and insight into the lives of the eco passionate had been eye opening, even though she was still blindfolded, in her mind's eye, there was a lot to review.

Many of the adherents of the off-the-grid mindset were young, college educated and deeply stressed about what they foresaw as a coming apocalypse of climate change induced chaos and destruction. Some of those she'd spoken to told stories of extreme weather events that had freaked them out and convinced them that action had to be taken. There was no other way to slow the collision course of fossil fuel Armageddon without aggressive action. These were not people who would have ever dreamed of going into a branch of the U.S. military without a draft, but they were willingly signing up for front lines of the battle for the environment. She went over some of the sentiments she'd heard expressed while recording and taking copious notes.

"My parents, grandparents and great grandparents all made their living from 200 acres of land. Raising chickens and rabbits to sell for meat and hay and corn for cash crops. The Texas drought killed the crops and killed my future."

"My brother committed suicide last year because our cattle couldn't graze on the burned out pastures and we had no hay. He shot the herd and then he shot himself."

"I watched the water creep closer to our neighborhood, every time there was a storm, all through high school. When I was in my junior year of college, the flooding started. Now my parents, grandma and little brother are living with my uncle in the middle of Louisiana, because our home on the coast is gone."

Story after story relayed drought devastation, horrific storm damage, lost food sources for both people and animals. The cycle of hard work and care for the land that in turn supported a modest life of enough to eat for the farm family plus crops or animals to sell for the cash that kept it all going was disappearing. Vanishing as fast as the water table, the forests and lakes, the fish and animals that were migrating north when they could, dying off when they could not.

Generations of people who had thrived by donning leather gloves to stack bales of hay, or plant arrow straight rows of corn and beans, men and women who knew how to pick good beef or dairy stock for breeding, or raised healthy piglets and chickens. People deeply connected to their land and their communities, who were honored to help feed their states and their nation. Those in coastal communities, the ranchers of the sea, hauling in troll lines, nets and pots filled with fish, shrimp and crab. All of them, people who raised their children to understand the joy and satisfaction of hard work, who could see their future and knew that if they put in the time, there would be enough to live on, to eat, to share.

Now it was hard to know what the next five years would bring, much less the next generation. Elders of all ethnicities were confounded by the rapid change that didn't square with all that they had come to know and understand about the natural world.

The fear of uncertainty was palpable throughout the interviews Zilla had conducted over the last few days and as the plane droned on through the sky, she felt the familiar weight of responsibility that comes from carrying the stories of others. This is the heavy side of a reporter's job. Carrying the pain and anguish of the human experience to distill it into a narrative that others would be able to absorb and learn from. To portray the collective plight so people would build understanding, compassion and motivation to make good choices in the ceaseless quest to help make the world a better place for everyone, not just the wealthy and powerful.

Comfort the afflicted and afflict the comfortable was at the core of Zilla's belief. She was not an advocate. She was a journalist who believed in truth and justice. The adage of affliction was one she adhered to because she knew that poking around at those who are the most comfortable meant doing the diligent work of discovery.

How did you get so comfortable? So powerful? Was it all your own hard work, in which case, congratulations, or was it because you stomped on the backs of those with no power, no money and no voice? If that's the answer, then Zilla and others like her will shine a light on that injustice and rat you out to the world. Afflict your illicit comfort in an effort to bring about the change that can lead to equality and fair treatment for a larger percentage of humanity.

Her drifting thoughts had caused her to lose focus on counting. She cursed under her breath, but realized that it had been a silly idea anyway. So what if she could determine whether it was one hour or three? Drawing a circle on a map with Anchorage at the center and out more than an hour's flight would include an impossible amount of wilderness. It would reveal nothing helpful for determining where the compound was located and even if the GDC had given her a framed map of the location, would it have mattered? She had agreed to not reveal their location to the public so knowing it added little to her reporting. She sat back and focused on how she would start her series of reports for the *Anchorage Daily Standard,* and worried about what might be happening in Anchorage right now. She tried to will the plane to fly faster. Zilla had a lot of great qualities but patience wasn't one of them.

##

After a quick trip to drop off her luggage at her lovely log home outside of Anchorage, Ruby and Ray pulled back into the parking lot at her namesake café. The wooden sign above the open porch that held tables and chairs for summer tourists who wanted to ogle the surrounding mountains while they chowed down grilled salmon fillets or halibut tacos, reminded Ruby of how much she missed the simple satisfaction of hard work in her own business. She was proud and honored to be the lone Congresswoman for Alaska and she worked hard in DC, but political work is much different from chopping onions for gumbo or sweeping the dance floor after a busy weekend. The subtle art of bartending meant engaging customers in lively conversation that avoided the landmines of politics, while refilling their beer glass or mixing a gin and tonic. When you worked as an elected official, your job was to take on constituent politics, much more exhausting and fraught with stress than unloading kegs of beer or managing a crowd of thirsty patrons.

Ruby knew she'd be back to her favorite perch on a stool at the end of the bar at some point. She had committed to two terms, four years, but would not agree to stay longer. She believed in public service but also believed in having the life she most wanted and that was in Anchorage, running her bar and café with her family.

They parked and walked in to find Mo and Poppa Ray scurrying around behind the bar preparing for the big evening rush that they knew would come after the kick off event on the park strip. The Midnight Fun Midnight Run would wind back to downtown and there would be multiple waves of hungry and thirsty walkers and runners flowing through the door to celebrate their fitness and fundraising at shared tables. Happy chatter about moose sightings along the coastal trail and selfies taken with runners dressed in outrageous costumes would drift over baskets of beer battered halibut and hand cut fries, pitchers of local brew and bowls of Ruby's famous gumbo. Mo was stocking the deep coolers that sat squat below the bar, the stainless door slid back to accept the bottles she was deftly stacking. The door would barely clear the top row when she was done. By closing time, bartenders would be reaching to the bottom, several layers down, to fish out bottles for last call.

Ruby had a brief flash of memory of countless similar preparations when her husband had still been alive and they would stock coolers and check supplies. Chop onions and peppers and okra. Marinate slabs of salmon and hand shape scores of burger patties, laying them in neat rows on big, flat stainless pans, layers separated by waxed paper, until they were nearly too heavy to lift and slide into the huge, boxy refrigerators in the kitchen.

For so many years it had been mostly just her and Ray, her always smiling, joking, hard working husband and little Ray, scooting around the dance floor on his trike. The lingering memories brought the usual mix of joy and pang of loss. As if he were having similar reflection, her son, the lanky six four journalist, no longer the silly kid who had delighted in hiding behind the swinging kitchen door to jump out with little curled hands and a childish squeal to try to scare his mom, slipped his arm around her waist and gave her a gentle squeeze.

Poppa Ray looked up from where he carefully counted stacks of bills, making marks on a note pad as he set up the tills for the evening sales. He peered over the top of his drugstore reading glasses; a huge smile lit his face. "Well, here we go! It looks like you're ready to go to work now. What a welcome sight you are Ruby girl!" He had dropped his pencil on the back bar near neat rows of ones, fives and tens and moved out from behind the bar to wrap his daughter in law in a warm embrace.

"Or I should say Representative Walker." He pulled back from their hug, his hands gently gripping her shoulders as he smiled, his eyes reflecting the real joy and intense pride he felt. "A member of Congress," he boasted, "now ain't that something?" He was so pleased to have her back in town that he acted as if they hadn't eaten breakfast together just an hour earlier.

Ruby laughed, her face reddening slightly. "Good to see you too, Pops. Good to be home." She turned her smile to Mo. "Great to see you too, honey." Ray had moved behind the bar while his grandfather scooped Ruby up in a hug and followed suit, wrapping his own arms around Mo, kissing her cheeks repeatedly, making her laugh and pretend to fend him off.

"Hi Ruby, I mean Congresswoman!" Mo was still giggling and Ray junior was still kissing her. "I can tell your son is extra happy to have his mom home too. I never get this treatment!"

Ray looked at her, his lips still pursed for more love pecks, but an exaggerated, wounded look in his eyes. "What? I'm Mr. Affection. All kinds of sweet, right? Tell mom how great I am Mo."

"I know you're great, dear." Ruby didn't wait for Mo to react. "But I also know my wonderful bar manager and your wonderful fiancée doesn't need to sing your praises for you. Your ego is plenty healthy." Granddad and Mo tipped their heads back and laughed. Ray pretended to look hurt, but the twinkle in his eye gave him away. "Now, what can I help with?"

Ruby slipped out of her father in law's embrace and stood with her hands on her hips, assessing the bar and imaging chores she could pitch in to finish.

"You sure you're all set for tonight, Ruby? Feeling ok about being here when things are so out of whack?" Poppa Ray's smile had faded as the sweet family reunion moment dissolved into the looming concern over the upcoming rallies as the tension between the pro-development and pro-environmental protection crowd had ratcheted up to fears of physical violence.

Ruby dropped her hands; her moment of thinking only as a business owner before a busy night suddenly disappeared. The thoughts that she'd worked hard to push out of her mind regarding the potential for serious conflict and armed clashes jumped up again. She was a member of Congress and public safety was an important consideration for her. Both as an elected official for the citizens she served, but also for herself. She was a target of the angst of those who wanted faster build up of extraction infrastructure. They hated her calls to evaluate projects through the long process of NEPA, the National Environmental Policy Act, rather than fast tracking permits to get projects underway in the hope that once they got started, it would be harder to derail if the dreaded Colorado River case brought the legal hammer down on extraction.

She was not a Polly Anna. She knew the country and the world still needed fossil fuel and it wasn't realistic to immediately halt projects that brought oil and gas to market. But she'd drawn a line with coal and fought diversion projects that wanted more water for golf courses and less for drinking water in poor communities.

Ruby's advocacy as a believer in climate change and the anthropologic causes for it, drew the ire of congressional global warming deniers from coal loving states and industry leaders who wanted less regulatory burden. She was a target of increasing vitriol as the old guard of oil and coal fought the rising voice and political demands of a younger demographic, insisting on a new deal for America that was green at its core.

Those who were supporters of this concept believed in it as a right for their future on the planet, as fully as those who believed that a hard hat wearing god had bestowed celestial rights on those with bulldozers, chainsaws and drill rigs to cut, kill, mine, drill whatever the hell they wanted. God and Donald Trump would help them Make America Great Again.

It was a vocal and angry divide. Security briefings in Washington were alarming characterizations of a country not drifting, but hurtling toward civil war. The far right dismissed the far left as 'libtards' or 'snowflakes', but minimized their opponents at their peril.

The protests and demands for immediate action on green energy development and the end of Big Oil were not led by peaceniks who used only the tools of op-ed outrage or sit ins to get their points across. They were not people who would melt at the first sign of conflict as the mocking nicknames suggested. They were freaked out believers that Armageddon was nigh and they were prepared to do anything to stop it.

Anything.

This wasn't the sixties. There was violence during those protests, but there had been a lot of symbolic efforts like daisies poked into the ends of gun barrels and people laying in front of police blockades then. New generations of young people weaned on wars and life after 9-11, created minds that were not so shocked at the prospect of mayhem and armed standoffs. Raised with entertainment that gave them an assassin's view behind an animated gun, shooting bad guys and gaining points while blood, gore and exploded body parts painted the video screens of their childhood.

Experts could argue till sundown about whether exposure to a constant diet of media violence actually made people more violent. But few denied that it de-sensitized minds to the shock and horror of war. It was a recipe for disaster as anger over who had the right message for America and indeed who was even considered a REAL American was polarizing and paralyzing the nation.

Ruby tipped her head and smiled with deep appreciation for the concern on her beloved father in law's face. The truth was she wasn't sure if she was ready, but accepting the responsibility of the oath of office meant she had to keep the fear she might feel off her face and step forward to lead, even when she doubted her ability to do so. Being a leader didn't mean you didn't have fear, it meant you led despite that fear.

"Yes." She said firmly. "I've polished up my speech and now I just want to help out here. Peel some potatoes or make roux. It will help the time go by faster and keep me calm." She laid her head briefly on Ray Senior's shoulder. "Besides, having a bit of non political time with my three favorite people in the world sounds great to me." She hugged Mo and Ray junior, wrapping her arms around them silently for a minute, then turned and walked through the swinging door that led into the kitchen, calling out to staff as she did. "Hello Jim! Hi Addy! So good to see you both."

The members of her family stood, listening to her happy chatter with employees who were busy prepping for the evening dinner rush, as if her warm embrace still locked them in place. They looked at each other, each trying to read the thoughts behind the eyes of the other, all of them guarding the mix of anxiety and helplessness they were feeling.

Whatever the next several hours brought, worry preceded it. Hard not to wish they could simply go back to the days of the main concern being empty kegs or at worst, breaking up a bar fight between a couple of over imbibing knuckleheads. Ray junior looked at his watch and wondered when Zilla was going to get back to Anchorage. Hoping she would be there before whatever was going to go down did.

He fished his phone out of his pocket and sent a quick- Hello, where are you? Text to Zilla and a-Have you heard from Zee? Text to Sergeant Platonovich. He stared at the screen for a few seconds, willing one of them to respond. Neither did and he reluctantly slipped the phone back into his pocket and turned to Mo. "At your service ma'am. Want me to wheel another round of cases out here for the coolers or should I grab more swizzle sticks?" He finished with a wink and full watt smile for his somber faced girlfriend. Her face slowly lit with a mischievous grin. "Hm, actually all those details have been handled. What we really need is for someone to swab out the bathrooms. Thanks for offering to help." She laughed and disappeared into the kitchen before he could protest.

Chapter Eighteen

Jerry Justice had one stop to make before he picked up his caustic cohort, Jamie Lynn.

"Hobbyhorse my ass." He mumbled under his breath as he idled into a 4th Avenue spot and jammed the stick shift into reverse, (real men don't drive automatics), a block away from The Silver Slipper. In about an hour people would start gathering downtown on the park strip for the family run event and in Kincaid Park for the D.A.D. resource rally, south several miles from downtown and hugging Cook Inlet.

He had to set a piece of the plan in motion before he picked up Her Highness and things really started to rock and roll. Jamie Lynn would have been surprised to learn of this since he had told no one, not the D.A.D. organizers who were likely already mustering at the Park, not Volkov and sure as hell not Jamie Lynn.

Jerry Justice trusted no one and always kept secret, certain elements of any scheme he was involved in. Information was power and Jerry Justice wanted it. Entrusting the full plan to no one but himself meant he had control. He didn't care if Volkov would disapprove, in fact he knew he would but it didn't matter. By the time the Russian money man found out what Jerry had orchestrated without permission, it would all be over but the shouting and Jerry Justice planned to be long gone from Alaska and the U.S., carting off the Russian money paid to grease the skids of local organizers to ensure enough thugs would show up to pull off the grab of a U.S. Congresswoman.

He had paid out only ten thousand of the thirty-five grand Volkov had funneled to him through the hapless bartender at the Slip. He still had twenty-three grand in cash after buying a plane ticket to San Diego. He'd access the larger payment, all seven figures of it, once he was in a beach bungalow in the Caymans. The money was in an account there. He had the account numbers and the pass code and had verified it himself, in fact, several times. Pulling up the offshore bank's website, plugging in the account and password to see the impressive line of zeros that followed the six was his favorite pass time since he'd gotten verification from Volkov that the funds were there and waiting for him.

Six million dollars. It didn't make him as rich as he knew he deserved to be, but it was all there, all free of tax or other liens and would let him live like the king he thought himself as for the rest of his life. He had stashed under the truck seat, a bundle of bills thick enough to strain the blue rubber band surrounding them. Ten thousand dollars to hand to Jamie Lynn when he picked her up in about 20 minutes. She'd scoff at the small amount, but only until he told her the plan. Use this cash to get to California; meet him in the bucolic surf town of Encinitas and he'd give her the location and account numbers for the rest. Jerry Justice had been working over women all his life for sex, for money, for favors. He was confident Jamie Lynn was like the rest. She was greedy. She'd take it.

But first he had to pay MC Ames a visit. He needed MC to handle a chore. It would both stop a bloodhound hot on their trail and cement MC's loyalty to silence about the overall operation. Division and chaos was at the heart of Nikita Volkov's plan to disrupt the infuriating unity of the U.S.

The current resource war blazing through the American court system was the perfect set up for violence in the streets regardless of the final decision. Volkov wanted anarchy. He wanted division. It was much easier to pick off opponents when they were fractured and the new tools of battle, Internet lies and doctored images were making his work almost too easy. People were quick to believe and react to negative information. So many were quick to swallow even the most outrageous and nonsensical lies, while being suspicious of basic truths. It was easier to run off a cliff into the abyss than do the work of research and fact checking.

That was boring. Busting heads was fun.

Volkov found Americans undisciplined and prone to irrational acts of violence. Any excuse to brandish weapons was a good day for many of them. They wouldn't last a day in Russia, but by American standards, these were held up as godly warrior icons.

Jerry Justice didn't give a shit one way or another. He didn't care about oil or coal or timber or god or shit on a shingle. He didn't care about a fucking thing, except lining his own pockets. MC and Jamie Lynn were pawns in his plan as many others before them had been pieces to move to get his win. He slammed the truck door, jammed his battered white cowboy hat tighter onto his head to guard against a strengthening wind and made a beeline down the sidewalk toward the street level door that led to the Slip. The faded elegant, cursive letters, hand painted on the chipped wooden door were a testament to the upper status the below ground club had once enjoyed. The Silver Slipper was no longer the hottest jazz club in town that also provided services to the crime bosses in the Last Frontier. It was no longer the best place for great music and celebrity spotting. Now it was merely a dreary, musty and damp shot and a beer joint, mainly used for money laundering and a drug delivery drop off for much of Alaska's underground.

It was three pm and MC had just opened the bar and was turning on the numerous in line switches of various beer themed lights hanging on the walls. Many of them were old enough to be real neon. That so many had survived bar brawls and chairs tossed across the main room was remarkable. MC loved the buzzing glow of the tube letters. This was his favorite part of opening up each day. Hearing Jerry Justice's voice coming down the stairwell brought an immediate wave of irritation that destroyed his brief moment of bartender bliss.

"Woo eee it stinks out here man!" Justice's voice pierced MC's mind as he hit the bottom step and shoved the door open. "Smells like piss and rats." He finished his sentence inside the door. His smile as big and friendly as the door knocking bible salesman he'd once been.

"What the hell do you want? Don't you have a rally of rednecks to organize?" MC shot him a disgusted look and wrinkled his nose as if the smell Justice had complained of was coming from the man himself.

"No need to be a dick, young man. The rally is going to go off just fine, thank you very much. But before it does, I've got a job for you."

MC had turned his back on his unwelcome visitor and was vigorously working a dust cloth over the seats and backs of the row of vintage leather covered bar stools.

"It's got to happen and you've got to do it." Justice's voice had lost any hint of his previous smile.

MC's arm faltered then continued scrubbing at the stools. "Who the hell are you to tell me what to do?" He boldly didn't turn around, but his voice belied his nervous tension. He felt the vise like claw of Justice's hand on his right arm, stopping the rag in mid swipe. He nearly pissed his pants in fear and surprise at how quickly this goofy looking cowboy clown had moved behind him and at the strength of his grip. "What the fuck? Let go of me goddamn it!" When he yanked, Jerry Justice let him go, but the desired effect was achieved. MC turned to face him, his face angry but afraid. Justice smiled.

"That's more like it. Look at me when I'm talking to you boy." He leaned in closer, moving an unlit slim cigar over to the other corner of his mouth, MC could smell stale tobacco and the scent of last night's booze wafting from his pores. Small flecks of tobacco outlined the corners of his mouth. "You listen close and get this right if you don't want to disappear." He narrowed his eyes at the younger man. "Got your attention now?" He stepped away and to MC's surprise, walked around behind the bar, the forbidden space for customers, grabbed the top shelf bourbon and poured two fingers into a water glass. He quickly downed it, raised the bottle to pour again, set it down and turned the glass upside down on the bar with a slam that made MC jump.

Jerry Justice wiped the back of his hand across his mouth, his eyes a cold, hard stare. "You're gonna call that fucking old reporter who came in here when you were handing over my money. You're gonna get him to come here and you're gonna get rid of him. Tell him you got hot information about where that money came from and why. Admit you were giving it to me. Cash, and lots of it because he's not going to be able to use that information anyway and it will get him here." Justice eyed the bourbon again with a drunkard's lust but decided, reluctantly, that he needed to wait for more drinks till after the day's mission was complete. Then he could swim in a river of the best whiskey there was. He walked out from behind the bar.

"Don't ask questions and don't think you have a choice." He pulled a black Beretta from an inside pocket of his corduroy jacket. "Tell him you'll take him to the Russian. Tell him the Russian wants to meet to talk about me. That will get that bastard to agree to get in a car with you. Drive him to some spot out of sight of others along the coast. I don't give a fuck where. Just make goddamn sure no one sees you shoot him. Leave him, don't touch anything and throw this in the Inlet when you're done."

MC opened his mouth to protest, but Jerry Justice pushed the gun into his hand and held his other hand up, palm flat toward MC's face. MC suppressed a shudder as Jerry Justice's wicked smile returned. "Shhh, don't say a fucking word," his voice was cold and lowered as if someone else might be listening. "Get this done or I'll be back to make sure you never make another shitty drink again. Woo eee, you better believe that sonny boy." He pushed MC's hand with the gun in it, into MC's chest, shoving him backward a few steps in the process, then turned and laughed all the way out the door and up the steps to the street.

MC stood in the silence. Shocked, furious and terrified. After a long few minutes, he walked behind the bar, wishing it was all a nightmare, but from the heft of the cold metal in his hand, knowing he was wide awake in a life that he'd lost control of the minute Nikita Volkov had entered it. He'd been a conceited fool to believe that his new career was on the up and up. Even though a small voice inside had warned him otherwise. Now that voice was screaming in his head that he better run and run fast. But another voice was louder. The laughing, mocking voice of Jerry Justice drowned out his own internal warning. *Woo eeee, too late to run boy. You gotta pay the price of admission kid. Now get to work or get dead. Your choice.*

Zilla was on the ground. The plane that had droned on endlessly was quiet, she could hear voices outside and was impatient to get out. She reached up to remove the blindfold and jumped at a voice immediately to her left.

"Don't touch that."

"Shit! You scared the crap out of me. Why can't I? We're on the ground."

"Only for a pick up stop. We'll be underway in a short while. Meantime, you hold tight, keep that blindfold on." The familiar voice of the driver was filled with a tension she hadn't heard before.

"Pick up stop? What are we picking up?"

"You ask way too many questions lady. We aren't picking up anything you need to know about."

Zilla considered her options. Yank off the blindfold, get off the plane and figure out what the hell was going on, or sit tight. Getting off the plane would mean she'd have to deal with the serious individual sitting near her. He might have a gun, although she somehow doubted it. They had been adamant about keeping their compound location secret, but she wasn't a hostage, she was willing to play along to get the story. Up to a point. But a stop on the way back hadn't been discussed and the tense tone, approaching fear in her guard's voice made her red flag warning jump up. What the hell was happening while she was sitting here like a lump?

"Look, no one said anything about an unscheduled stop and I have work to do. I need to get to Anchorage!"

"Your needs are not my concern. You'll just have to be patient. If you try anything, just know that I've got a gun pointed at you. I don't like it, but that's where this thing has escalated up to. We're all armed now."

"This thing? What thing are you talking about? You're starting to make me really uncomfortable. Especially with my eyes covered. What's happening that you suddenly feel a need to be armed? Especially as you're heading into the city." Zilla considered that he might be bluffing. He might not have a gun and be saying these things just to keep her under control.

But what if he wasn't bluffing? Zilla had been shot before and as she'd said to her reporter colleagues after she'd healed up, it was a real drag and I don't want a repeat. Still, this was more concerning by the minute. If the enviro crowd had decided to go militant in order to meet the other militants' head on, she could be caught up in illegal firearm use at the very least and possibly dodging bullets and crossfire, while blindfolded, on the other extreme.

She decided the risk was too big and reached up for the blindfold, at the same moment, she heard the rear cargo door squawk open. She pulled off the blindfold and heard her guard curse under his breath as she turned to look at the back of the small plane.

She'd been lucky and made the right gamble. He wasn't armed, but it was immediately clear that it wasn't from a lack of available firepower. Nothing had yet been loaded onto the plane, but in plain sight on the ground, two long wooden boxes on sturdy handcarts were being readied. One of them had a cover haphazardly lying across the opening, blocking the contents from view. But the other was open, the cover laying flat on the ground next to the box as two young men and two young women carefully laid more rifles and cartons of ammunition into it. There were at least 20 rifles and a number of large pistols in view. Zilla jumped up from her seat, crouching down to avoid bonking her head on the low ceiling. "Jesus. What the hell is going on here?"

"Damn it woman. Why the hell can't you take direction?" It would have been funny if the situation hadn't been so serious, like a schoolteacher exasperated by a recalcitrant child rather than someone who moments earlier had tried to sound like a menacing, potential killer. Clearly he was not.

"Never been my strong suit. Now either let me the hell off this plane if you're hauling illegal firearms, or tell me what's happening."

The young people were done loading one of the wooden boxes and were busy putting the top on, using small nails to tack the cover in place, belying the fact that this wasn't going to be a long shipment route before those guns were going to be free of the container and employed. Zilla peered out the small portside windows, trying to figure out where they were. It was useless, a small gravel airstrip surrounded by dense forest told her exactly nothing. There were countless similar spots all across Alaska.

Her guard, now resigned to giving her some information or possibly getting into a physical altercation, something he didn't care to consider, spoke in a quiet voice. He had a few days beard growth and spoke like the attorney Zilla suspected he was. "The guns are not illegal. They're all legally obtained and no one handling them has any felonies that would disallow them from carrying them." Zilla stared at him. He simply stared back.

"And?"

"And what?"

"Come on. What are you *doing* with them? Why did we stop to get them? What's going to happen when we get to Anchorage?"

He looked out at the kids, really that's what they were, twenty somethings, their young faces serious as they continued laying rifles, pistols and numerous boxes of ammunition in to the second wooden crate. He was sad about what was in the offing, but he believed as many in the Green Defiance Coalition did, that there was no longer a different viable option. It was going to come down to armed standoff and they had to be ready to display and fire these weapons.

"I hope we can merely make it known that we're not intimidated, that we also have and know how to use firearms. The old NRA saw that a good guy with a gun can stop a bad guy with a gun is one that we've sadly needed to take up now." He looked up at her, still standing, ready to pounce if she needed. "I don't like it. I vigorously opposed the idea but I was outvoted. I'm afraid Miss Gillette that when we get to Anchorage, there's a high likelihood that there will be a standoff and there could be bloodshed. It's starting to feel inevitable." He finished quietly. His voice trailing off.

"Nothing is inevitable, damn it! And you sitting here with your Sad Sammy expression while a bunch of young people with no idea what they're getting themselves into or what it could lead to is bullshit! You look like an intelligent man. Do something to stop this before someone gets killed!"

His eyes flashed and his previous sadness was instantly replaced by rage. "No idea what they're doing? I'm shocked that you're so naïve. None of these young people are doing this without knowing exactly what they're getting into. They've been training for this very event. Training for violence! Not because we want that. Not because we hope to have to fucking shoot anyone but because we might have to! We are being forced into violence by the rednecks on the other side and the rednecks in the Trump Whitehouse. We have no choice! Don't be an idiot. You can see what's happening. This is war."

"The only idiot is the person who thinks bloodshed will end this. I'm not naïve but I'm starting to think you and your group of green revolutionaries sure as hell are."

It was easier than he'd expected and as much as he hated to admit it, that Howdy Doody cowboy asshat had been right. The reporter who had been needling MC every chance he got, trying to pry information out of him was instantly willing to come to the Silver Slipper and get in a car with MC, allegedly to meet the Russian who would tell all to the scoop hungry Murph.

Reporters take risks all the time. Writing up their own accounts from the front lines of wars, or knocking on doors in neighborhoods where getting robbed, stabbed or beaten up is a regular occurrence. Hanging out with crazy, ruthless gang members, or showing up on the doorstep of people suspected of violent crimes, all in the name of witnessing first hand the actions of others. Not taking the word of others, but risking their lives to make sure they can verify and report the truth so others can also know it without risk.

It's part of the job and thousands of men and women do it quietly every day without bragging about how fearless they are because it's not about them, it's about getting at the truth, whatever it is. They do it because it's important for citizens to have good information so they can make good decisions that hopefully keep them and their families safe in the future.

Murph, just like his editor Ed Brooks, had reported from some of the scariest situations anyone without a flak jacket and a battalion behind them could imagine. Neither of them boasted about it, even in those moments when reporters are sharing pitchers of beer and anecdotes about their latest story. Murph had jumped into cars with heavily armed pimps and drug dealers. He'd followed anonymous tips and silently made his way into abandoned warehouses where chop shops were doing a thriving business or mostly nude workers were cutting large packages of cocaine into smaller parcels for street sales. If he'd been caught, he would have been killed and dumped in a ravine or the ocean.

But he never had. Not before today.

Maybe it was MC's simpleton personality, maybe it was his genuine nervousness, maybe it was simply the mistake of underestimating a frightened underling's ability for violence that threw off Murph's usually astute radar for trouble. Maybe he was too distracted by thinking too far ahead about how MC's admission about the money and connection to a Russian operative was going to make a big chunk of this puzzle come together. Whatever it was, it was a terrible mistake, only realized too late.

"How far away is this guy?" Murph looked at his watch as he jumped in the car with MC. "I have to be back to the park strip for interviews in no more than an hour. Can we get this done in that amount of time?"

"Yeah, sure, yeah. I mean, it's not far. I, uh, I gotta drive to, take you to, to...where he is." MC stammered and his hands shook as he struggled to put his seatbelt on. His palms were so sweaty and shaky that he had a hard time getting it buckled.

"You ok kid? Are these guys threatening you?" Murph seemed genuinely concerned, or at least interested and for a second, MC almost burst into tears and told all.

But then he remembered the stench of the fake cowboy with his painful grip on MC's arm and his menacing tone. The fear that welled up overtook his queasiness and he focused on remembering that this reporter wasn't his friend. He couldn't save him. He only wanted a story. Fuck him. MC wanted to live. This guy had to go.

He slammed the seat belt clasp together and let out a nervous laugh. "Threatening me? Oh hell no. Nobody threatened me. I just don't like nosy reporters in my car and the sooner I get this over with, the happier I'll be."

Murph studied the side of MC's face as the younger man backed up and maneuvered out onto the street. He knew MC was lying but he miscalculated why. Figuring the kid was in way over his head and now he was doing exactly what he was told because he was terrified to do anything else.

Murph had that part right he just didn't realize what it would result in. "Ok, whatever you say, just have me back here in an hour." MC sped off down 4th avenue, turning left and downhill toward the industrial warehouse area that hugged Ship Creek. "Yeah, right."

##

August Platonovich was rarely satisfied with security detail plans. Not because he didn't trust the Anchorage officers who worked under his supervision, he did, but he worried over all the ways that even the most thoroughly vetted plans could be foiled by those with bad intent. People motivated by fear, anger, paranoia or greed were unreasonable and unpredictable. A recipe that made planning for every security scenario contingency nearly impossible.

In the days leading up to now, the day of two big rallies. One planned for families, interested in a friendly outing with kids and neighbors before the Midnight Sun Midnight Run event at the park strip, kicked off with a speech by the popular Congresswoman Ruby Walker. Walkers and runners would follow markers through downtown and then wind along the beautiful Cook Inlet coastal trail before looping back to downtown for a barbecue and live music.

The other rally was the gathering that most concerned the seasoned lawman. There the crowd would feature angry development proponents who saw Alaska as a resource treasure chest that should adhere to their favorite and oft chanted- Cut Kill Mine Drill- mantra. How angry would they be on this day? How many that showed up would not be happy with only waving signs and screaming *NO way loser snowflakes!* at the caricatures of environmentalists that would be held up on the stage and later burned in a bonfire? Those individuals would certainly not be all of those in attendance, would not even be in the majority numbers, but the outliers worried Platonovich the most. They may be small in numbers but could negatively affect many.

August looked at his watch as he walked to his truck. He was leaving Kincaid Park after checking and re-checking the perimeter plans with his officers. They were nervous, facing the fairly impossible task of insuring safety in an area of hundreds of acres of trails crisscrossing through dense forest bordering the open coast. It was like trying to hold armfuls of sand. There was no way to guard against people slipping through. No way. They would do their level best but faced the sobering certainty that they didn't have enough officers to close a circle of security around the perimeter. They would position the majority of the officers in sight of the crowd. Visibility of armed officials is a big deterrent in itself, at least for most law-abiding citizens. They would also station numerous cops along trails leading in and out of the park. If things popped off and violence broke out, they wanted to be ready to catch any rats that tried to scurry away through the woods to escape arrest.

The homicide chief waved goodbye to the officers who were eagle eyeing the people walking from the parking lot, assembling on the lawn or walking into the Kincaid Chalet building. He answered his cell phone on the third ring, assuring the detective on the other end who was stationed in downtown, that he was on his way and would be there well before the start of the run rally. As he drove the winding road out of the park, he worked to stay focused on the day's security needs. But it was fruitless as his mind kept slipping to his worry over Zilla. Where she was and if she was ok. August knew that if anyone could take care of themselves, it was Zilla Gillette, but bad things could happen to even the most formidable person. He wasn't sure where he stood with the intrepid reporter. He knew he cared about her deeply and had tremendous respect for her intelligence, her ethics and her compassion. Regardless of what the future brought, whether they would slide back to being handshaking professionals or continue on a path of building a personal relationship, he wanted to know she was safe and putting the concern out of his mind was impossible.

Once they were back in the air, Zilla knew exactly where they were. She's refused to put the damn blindfold on, arguing she couldn't un-know what she'd seen and if they wanted to arm themselves, she couldn't talk them out of it, regardless of how foolish she thought it was. Ratcheting up the tension and potential for violence between paranoid, armed factions was a recipe for bad and Zilla knew it, but she couldn't reason with people who were acting crazy.

In all the years she'd reported on environmental rallies, the organizers had been careful to stay on a message of peaceful protest. Arms waving signs overhead was as wild as it got. This after the damage that had been done to the entire movement from the actions of a few who perpetrated violence through tree spiking, or monkey wrenching on infrastructure resulted in injury or death when activists broke locks and turned off pipeline valves. Workers searching for the source of alarms going off in the system were killed when high pressure blew up part of a pump station, driving pipeline shrapnel into their bodies. It was a gruesome event and support cooled for the causes the monkey wrenchers professed to be about.

Environmental and conservation organizations, to their credit, took a long hard look at their philosophy of advocating on behalf of the planet and natural systems that were being damaged but couldn't speak for themselves. They assessed their members, argued about whether it was just a few kooks who had been attracted to the idea of protest and the chance for acting out, or if they were being infiltrated by provocateurs who were trying to make them look bad to drive off their supporters and get people arrested. Leaders stressed a new way of bringing attention to the plight of endangered species and clean air and water. Briefcases and court filings took the place of street blockades and sit ins. Articulate talking points were flawlessly delivered to congressional committees by impeccably groomed people. Neatly trimmed, short beards and salon haircuts replaced dreadlocks and patched blue jeans.

Leaders denounced violence and championed civil discourse and respectful debate in the open, rather than the late night mischief that had caused injury and a turn off in the support network. That turn off meant reduced revenue from those who wanted to feel a part of a movement but didn't want to have to do more than write a check from the comfort of their recliner, to be involved.

For more than a decade, it had worked. There were always a few fringe jerks. Marcus Peterson had been a glaring example, but the new green revolutionaries knew how to walk the fine line between not expressing public glee that the insufferable narcissist Peterson had met his demise with a message that had a subtle undertone of disapproval for his actions and a self-righteous hint of, he got what he deserved.

It was hard to control every faction across the state and the nation though and it was also hard to get things done if you weren't pushing the boundaries as hard as the other side was. Zilla wondered if there was quiet acknowledgement and tacit approval of scenes like the one she'd just witnessed. She could practically hear their inner dialogue, working to justify it all. *'Yeah, we hate guns and violence, but they sure come in handy when you're dealing with angry rednecks.'*

"Let's fly over both locations. I want to see how many are gathering." The voice of the man who had argued with Zilla earlier brought her out of her pondering. They had flown to a private airstrip in the Matanuska Valley after leaving the secret compound. Zilla knew that now because she was able to see when they took off again. Where they'd been before this stop, she still had no idea, but now that they were up and flying west, she had her bearings. They were flying on the north side, parallel to the Glenn highway, heading in to Anchorage.

The pilot hadn't answered, but within a few minutes, they were nearing the downtown area of the state's largest city and flying over small groups of people, little clumps on the long stretch of green grass that was the park strip. There was still plenty of green between them, but more were walking up from every direction, parking was always a challenge for park strip events and parking blocks away in a neighborhood side street was common. Zilla's house was only two blocks away from park strip and she was familiar with vehicles wedged into every available spot along H Street whenever there was a concert or festival in the popular green space.

Still without a word, the pilot banked back around, flew over the park strip again and then turned south, flying toward Kincaid Park. There appeared to be around the same number of people as those gathering on the park strip, maybe 75, that were visible near the Chalet at Kincaid, but the parking lots were already completely filled up at Kincaid. It was going to be a big crowd.

"Please get me on the ground now." Zilla had worked hard to stay quiet while the pilot indulged the fly over request of her guard. Now she wanted out of the plane and was tired of waiting for them to stop controlling her. They had controlled, much to her annoyance, what she saw and didn't see while at their compound, but that was over now and she had stories to write and people to consult with. She wanted to get to work and even more urgent, was her need to make sure everyone in the newsroom and at Ruby's Café was ok. To her surprise, the older man who had been so rigid about her need to follow direction during her blindfolded travel now smiled at her, a first in all the days she'd been sheparded around by him. It was a low watt smile that radiated no warmth. "Ok, fair enough. We've successfully kept you from learning of the location of the GDC's main compound, so we can drop you off now."

"Main compound?" Zilla cocked her head and looked at him. "Are there others?"

Now he laughed, still with no warmth. "Always the inquisitor, Ms. Gillette. We'll have you on the ground in a few minutes. We're heading to Merrill Field now."

"You didn't answer my question."

He gave her a cold look, all trace of the brief smile now gone. "No, I didn't."

They stayed quiet for the remaining minutes in the air. Zilla grabbed her backpack as soon as the plane landed and taxied to a stop. She reached in and fished her cell phone from a side pocket and turned it on, waiting impatiently for it to boot up. She scooped up her gear and jacket, the phone pressed to her ear, Ray's number ringing on the other end.

##

Ruby, Ray Jr, Poppa Ray and Mo were walking to the park strip from the café. It was only four blocks away and even if they had wanted to drive, navigating the street closures and the growing streams of pedestrians, many with festive, colorful running outfits and kooky hats that were flowing toward the park strip, would have been a chore. It was much easier and considerably faster to simply walk. Besides, as soon as the rally was over, they would need to scoot back to the café to help bartend and deliver food to tables full of people who were the first wave of customers after this type of event, people who showed up but had no intention of running or walking the course.

They were content with just the outing on the park strip, then retiring to the closest watering hole for some beers and food. They would welcome the returning waves of participants and relinquish their tables to them, having finished their rounds of burgers, chowder, pizza and a couple of pitchers of beer. It was the kind of steady workday that kept everyone hopping behind the bar and behind the kitchen doors. There would be good tips to divide up at the end of the night and the tills would be happily stuffed with customer cash.   Ray answered his phone on the second ring. "Zee! Where the hell are you? We're on our way to the park strip now."

"I finally escaped." She shot a look at the man who had kept her so closely guarded for the last few days. She thought about tossing the blindfold in his direction, but decided to keep it as a souvenir of her bizarre reporting trip. "I'll meet you there in 15 minutes."

"Good. We've been worried about you and I can't wait to hear all about the Hole in the Wall Gang's hide out, but right now, I'd really like you here for another set of eyes to watch this crowd while mom, your congresswoman, is speaking on stage."

"Roger that sir. I want the same thing." She trotted across the parking lot, without another word to the people who were off loading the crates from the airplane. When she was a distance away, she spoke again, "Still there Ray?"

"Yes."

"This group has guns Ray. Lots of guns."

"They're bringing guns to the park strip?" Ray's voice raised up and Ruby and his grandfather looked at him, their steps faltering.

Mo was taking in the spectacle of a downtown party and didn't seem to hear him.

"Yes. They are quite serious about defending themselves and not backing down. They don't plan to start violence, but don't plan to shy away from it either."

"Damn." Ray looked at Ruby and shook his head. "Maybe I should just turn mom around now and have her cancel her speech today." Ruby, Ray Sr., and Mo had stopped and all three were staring at Ray jr. now, waiting.

"I'd say that would be wise, but I'd also be willing to bet that your mom, the fearless congresswoman, will not agree to do that."

Ray sighed as he locked eyes with his determined mother. "You'd no doubt win that bet. We'll see you soon Zee." He ended the call and faced his elders and his fiancée. "Zilla is back in Anchorage. She's on her way here but she told me the GDC members she's with just picked up a shitload of guns, a couple of crates of them. She says they plan to be armed at the rallies today. Mom? I would feel much better if you stayed away from this event. Zilla says they aren't planning to start any fights, but they aren't planning to run from any either."

"Honey, I can't do that. I have to be there today." Ruby's voice was quiet, like she was talking to a scared child. Her son was a grown man and no stranger to being around conflict as a reporter, but having his own mom at the center of it was not a regular event and one he was damned uncomfortable with.

"Why? Why do you have to be there? This could get out of hand and for your own safety, it would be good to have you out of sight. I can let them know there were too many security concerns and you had to cancel."

"Are you kidding me? Tell them I decided to hide out rather than face this head on? This is supposed to be a family event Ray! I should decline to be there but people with children will be? What kind of chicken shit message would that send?" Ruby had her hands on her hips now. Normally Ray loved it when she dug in, usually it was in face offs with tough or drunk customers, or city officials or other members of congress, but this was different. This could endanger her and he wanted help in making his case.

"Granddad! Tell her I'm right about this!"

Ray senior gave his grandson a weary, resigned look. "You are wasting your breath son. You know your momma is no way going to turn around and go cower in the kitchen at the bar. That ain't her way, never has been."

"I'm not suggesting she cower. Just be safe. Mo, am I wrong?"

"Don't drag me into this. Your mom doesn't need you to act like she can't assess a situation and make up her own mind. She's an adult and she's a member of the U.S. Congress for crying out loud. She one of the most courageous women I know. She can't just not show up, Ray. You know that. Quit trying to control something you can't."

Ray had known the answer before he'd raised the argument, but had to try. He pocketed his cell phone, shrugged his shoulders and walked toward the park strip again. The others kept pace with him. Another block and they left the sidewalk and joined the growing throngs of Anchorage citizens, gathering on the long green stretch of grass, that ran, arrow straight, east and west and divided the business district of downtown from the swanky neighborhood known as South Addition. The park strip was another great feature of a city that boasted miles of beautiful trails that hugged the coast and meandered throughout the city. Every year, multiple festivals, concerts, volley and baseball games and all manner of family outings took place on this public expanse of lawn. It was common to see huge, colorful kites flying overhead in the summer, making for fantastic photos with city buildings to the north and the majestic Chugach Mountains to the east.

Today was a fine example of residents taking advantage of free, fun events downtown. As they walked into the crowd and toward the stage, Ray hoped that was the way it stayed. Free was grand, but all he wanted was for the day to be fun.

And nothing more.

A low-key write up in the next day's *Anchorage Daily Standard* with photos of happy kids and silly costumes was his wish. A normal, peaceful city gathering with no shouting, stand offs or brandishing of weapons. Ray looked around for Zilla and August, knowing that seeing them would help him feel less anxious.

Boring would be nice, he thought, *a boring event would be perfect.*

Chapter Nineteen

Jay Cloudstone was lanky; some would say skinny, and only 21 years old when he was hired by the FBI to be eyes and ears in the D.A.D. meetings. Cloudstone was a perfect recruit. Attending the University of Alaska Anchorage Alaska Native Science and Engineering Program or ANSEP, he was focused on becoming an engineer to return home to his village, not far from Bethel in southwest Alaska. He longed to help build sturdy, sustainable housing, unlike the moldering HUD houses that slumped haphazardly along the main road in the community today.

He also had dreams of working on a massive mining project that he felt would bring much-needed jobs to the region. He was angry at the environmental groups from other places who wanted to tell his people how they should use and develop resources on the land that had been theirs for time immemorial. He understood and took seriously the concerns about contamination and toxic run off from gold and copper mining, but that was why he was determined to get a degree in engineering, so he could be there and keep a close eye on how it was built. He would make sure corners were not cut. If they were, he would blow the whistle on those who would take short cuts to profits.

He would have to explain to his elders why the water no longer sustained fish if things went bad. He was determined not to let that happen so he attended meetings on both sides of the development issue, looking for the perspective that seemed most honest. Was it developers who promised good paying jobs and infrastructure upgrades in the village and region or was it conservationists who promised healthy salmon, moose and berries for future generations? It was during this period of thoughtful study and right after he left a meeting, that he was first approached by an FBI agent.

Jay read a lot of detective novels when he was a kid, having grown up in a household where his Aunna, his grandmother, would not allow a television. Aunna Jenny was very religious and television meant only brainwashing by the devil, as far as she was concerned, so the siblings and cousins who swarmed around their house were free to play outside no matter the weather, or play board games with each other or read. Those were the options in his small village along the banks of the Kuskokwim River. In his books, Jay loved the far away worlds of dark city streets and clever criminals that were properly foiled by the hard boiled detectives he read about.

When he was 13, his uncle sent him a Tom Clancy novel. He marveled at the exotic, international characters, the fast paced action and the intense technical details. Reading about the integrity and bravery of Jack Ryan made Jay's decision to become an engineer a little harder. Being a spy sounded really cool. The fact that beautiful women always seemed to be close by wherever spies were found was a bonus.

He was more than surprised when he left a meeting at the home of a D.A.D. organizer one spring evening. Strolling down a south Anchorage neighborhood sidewalk and suddenly a man sidled up, walking alongside.

"Hello, Jay. My name is Don Wilson. Can I talk to you for a minute?"

"Wha..? Who are you and how do you know my name?" Jay wasn't sure if he should be afraid or just curious. Where the hell had the guy come from?

"Like I said, my name is Don Wilson," he opened his jacket far enough to show a very official looking badge clipped inside. "Special Agent Wilson. I work for the FBI Jay and I'd like to talk to you about the Defend American Development group. You were just at a meeting, yes?"

Jay felt like he was in one of the dog-eared novels he'd read 50 times over in his younger days. He thought the guy must have certainly been yanking his chain; it had to be a joke, yet the stranger knew his name and knew where he'd been. Knowing his name wouldn't be that big a deal, one of his college buddies might have put someone up to that gag, but no one knew about his attendance at the D.A.D. meetings.

He'd kept that to himself.

Not sure how anyone felt about the growing divide between the development enthusiasts and the protectionist crowd. He didn't want to debate the pros and cons, especially when he hadn't decided yet how he felt about it all, so he'd kept quiet about his visits to both side's events. He wasn't sure he wanted to talk to a complete stranger about it either, even if the guy did have an intimidating looking badge.

"Are you following me around? How do you think you know where I've been and why? I'm not doing anything wrong." Jay tried to be defiant, but his lifelong training to respect elders and people with badges, made that tough. His voice was more of a whisper than a declaration and he didn't like that.

"Look kid, no need to be upset or alarmed. Let me give you a ride back to your dorm. You won't need to pay for a cab or Uber that way and we can talk."

Jay figured the agent was letting him know just how closely he had been watched. This FBI agent knew Jay didn't have a car, used yellow cab or Uber to get around when he didn't use the city bus and still lived in the dorms.

It was clear that he had been watched for a while. He was partially terrified and partially ecstatic. If he wasn't in trouble, then what could this be about? He had to know. "Ok. I guess that would be alright. Can I see your badge again? I'd like to make sure I'm not getting into a car with a serial killer."

SA Wilson laughed quietly. "Smart thinking kid. Yes. I'll show you my badge and other id when we get to the car. I'd like to not draw attention right now. Let's keep walking. My car is two blocks from here."

Jerry Justice had spit shined his boots and oil polished his leather holster belt and bandolier. His pistol gleamed from the right holster and his oosik from the left. He had admired himself for a long time in front of the mirror. Waving the oosik around as he practiced his speech. He scowled and sneered at his reflection to look menacing, when in reality he looked exactly like what he was, a ridiculous middle-aged man waggling a petrified penis bone in front of his face. He pulled his pistol out a couple of times, squinting his eyes while he barked at his image in the mirror, pointing his gun at his reflection "You talking to ME? Huh? You think you can challenge ME, punk? Go for it then! You feeling froggy little man? Better jump then, boy!" He jabbed the pistol toward the mirror and grimaced.

Yeah, scary shit.

At least he thought so until he got to the crappy flophouse where Jamie Lynn was staying. When she opened the door, his ego shrank at her cruel laughter.

"Oh god! It's the Lone Ranger, come to save little ole me! Hahaha. You fucking joke! Get in here before you embarrass me more." She grabbed his arm, the fringe on his cowboy shirt swinging back and forth, and yanked him inside. "Just stand there while I grab my stuff. For Christ's sake Justice, did you actually LOOK at yourself before you left your apartment? You really thought this Wild West ensemble was the way to go?"

Remembering his playacting in front of the mirror, made him blush, which made him mad. "I don't need some jail rat telling me how to dress!" But as the words left his mouth, he realized how stupid they sounded. Jamie Lynn, whatever her many faults, was a woman who knew how to dress for the occasion. She had on a skintight pair of black leather pants, a black vest and a blood red, silk shirt. Her lips, nails and boots matched her shirt. She had a new eye patch with the D.A.D. logo on it.

She looked the part of the person tasked with pumping up the crowd. She was a sexy vision of resistance and Jerry Justice both lusted for her and hated her for showing him up. This bitch was unbeatable when it came to stealing the show. All of his pre-rally prep seemed pointless now. She would capture all the eyes and hearts and he would be the stooge standing behind her.

He felt like maybe now he understood why The General had tried to kill her a few years back. She was beautiful and deliciously dangerous but really fucking annoying.

##

Zilla leaped from the car without a word uttered, before it came to a full stop in the parking lot of the *Anchorage Daily Standard*. She'd had enough half conversations and non answers from Boston Ben as she'd started calling her driver and quasi guard during her visit to the G.D.C.'s secret wilderness compound. She had scooped up her backpack and jacket, even in summer it was unwise to travel into the Alaska backcountry without warm clothing, and had her hand on the door handle when they turned the corner toward the newspaper's offices.

She heard him yell something but didn't turn to acknowledge it. She was more than fed up with the game of hide the reporter, and more to the point, Zilla was angry that a man who was clearly in his 50s if not older, would allow and even encourage young people to take up arms to stand ready to fire at other fellow citizens. It was crazy, wrong and could result in death.

It pissed her off that an intelligent elder would take advantage of the ready passion and sometimes misguided righteousness of young people wanting to change the future for the better. That was admirable. Taking up firearms in the name of that change was folly. She wanted nothing but distance from such an unscrupulous man. Besides, it was go time. She had to get to the park strip and then to Kincaid. Straddling both events would require some coordination with Ray and two or three other reporters, plus at least two photographers. She figured Ray would want to cover the action close to his Congresswoman mom and she figured Murphy was probably already at Kincaid.

She sprinted to the small outbuilding on the edge of the parking lot. Ed, her short fused, brilliant editor let her park her Harley in it when she rode her bike to work rather than tooling around in her old Willys Jeep. Although he didn't say it, she knew Ed liked motorcycles and got a kick out of her skill in handling the heavy beast. Besides, everyone who liked motorcycles loved to hear a well-maintained Harley start up.

Zilla fished the keys from a zippered pocket on her backpack, unlocked the shed and rolled her 442 out. She put the kickstand down on the asphalt and settled the bike on the stand. Zilla grabbed her cell phone, hesitated for a split second, then called August. She felt a need to tell him about the armed Green Defiance Coalition members before she split for downtown.

August answered on the first half ring. "Zilla? Where are you?"

She smiled at the concern in his voice, and then felt an immediate stab of anxiety. Why couldn't the man be a Chiropractor or an electrician? Why had she fallen for the head of Anchorage homicide cops? Damn, fallen for. She'd just admitted it to herself. Then pushed it aside. No time for squishy feelings right now.

"August. Glad I reached you. I'm at the *Daily Standard* getting my bike. I'm heading to the park strip in a minute but you need to know about something I just witnessed."

"I'm glad you're ok and back in town. What is it?" He did sound relieved but concerned. Always on point.

"They're coming to the rallies armed to the teeth August. The G.D.C. members were loading crates of guns into the plane I just came into town on. They stopped somewhere in the Valley on our way back from the compound. I took the blindfold off, which they didn't appreciate, but I saw the guns August, rifles, pistols and a hell of a lot of ammunition."

The detective sighed on the other end. "I knew the resource development crowd would be armed, I expected that, but remained hopeful the conservationists wouldn't resort to weapons to make their point," he paused, "I should have realized how deep the resentment and anger has become on both sides."

"And how deep the pockets are of some of the supporters on both sides. There's a lot of money riding on swaying the country's sentiment in either direction. I'm heading to the park strip now August. I'll, uh, I'll see you there or at Kincaid. Be careful." Zilla didn't know what else to say.

"I would say the same thing to you Zilla. I know you'll be alert. Thanks for the information. Bye."

Zilla slipped her phone back into her jacket pocket, shoved the kick-start pedal out. The bike barked some cruising orders out of its chrome pipes after the third kick. She strapped on her helmet, settled her backpack and shot out of the parking lot.

The park strip rally spot was only six blocks away.

Ruby Walker was already on stage when Zilla walked up twelve minutes later. It had taken her longer to find a spot to park her bike than she's figured on and she briefly wished she'd just walked or jogged from the *Daily Standard's* office, but she'd soon need transportation to get the several miles to Kincaid Park and running back to get the bike then would add time she didn't want to spare.

Ray, Mo, Poppa Ray and a few regular customers of Ruby's Café were standing together by the left corner of the stage. People and kids milled around everywhere. Zilla saw a few familiar faces, some from around the city; some were the ardent supporters of the G.D.C., who had wasted no time in getting from Merrill Field to downtown. She saw guns too.

Ray gave her a silent hug, followed by Ray Senior and Mo, who gripped her tightly and held on for a long minute. Ruby was just getting started on stage and everyone was quiet as the popular Congresswoman spoke.

"Thank you for coming out today to take part in a fun and healthy family event. I'm Ruby Walker, proud to be here and proud to be your representative in Congress."

A cheer went up in the crowd, Zilla heard a few boos and faint scoffing catcalls on the edge of the growing audience. She knew Ray heard it too. He looked around intensely scanning the faces for hostility. He didn't have his notebook out, covering his mom was never part of his beat, but Zilla was writing in hers, noting the numbers assembled and the tone of overheard comments.

"I know you're getting ready to take off running, walking, pushing strollers and I see some wheelchairs in the crowd, which is terrific, but before you start off, let me remind you of another reason why we're gathered here today under this cloudless blue sky," more cheers went up, "during this glorious time of nearly endless daylight." Ruby paused, scanning the crowd in front of her, a bright yellow Cessna Super Cub flew over the park strip, lower than it should have, then lifted up and banked toward the Inlet, "we must work for more times when we can come together, like we are today, and stop ratcheting up the tension between those who profess to want good jobs and economic prosperity and those who profess to want good jobs and environmental prosperity. These things do not need to be, must not be, mutually exclusive. We can have all of this together, but we must work in unity to build it. I'm sure that everyone here today wants pretty much the same thing: financial security for your family along with a healthy, safe environment to live in. Shouting and division won't get us there. Let's put the angry rhetoric aside and work to build a strong future together."

The crowd didn't respond to what sounded like average political talking points. Then Ruby got serious.

"There's been too much pain around this issue. The deaths of the workers in the Amchitka earthquake. And yes, it was an earthquake! Regardless of the lies perpetrated on line by Russian and North Korean trolls, the tragedy at Amchitka was caused by a natural disaster, not underground military missile tests. The death of activist Marcus Peterson was another tragedy, but be clear, that's what it was. An accident. A tragedy. It was not a conspiracy to silence someone who celebrated the U.S. Supreme Court's decision to clean up Amchitka. The Defend American Development supporters didn't kill Mr. Peterson anymore than the Green Defiance Coalition killed the pentagon contractors who were lost in the earthquake. We may disagree on how much or where to develop resources, but we must start from a place of truth about the events that led to today, and I'm sure we all want........."

"You're a liar!" "You don't want the truth, you're covering it up!" the voices that interrupted Ruby came from the back of the crowd, as Zilla turned to try to locate them, she glanced at her watch, 3:20 pm. Immediately after, a strange sound, a deep thump, followed by an explosion and a huge flash of light bloomed near Cook Inlet to the west and north, a large cloud mushroomed up as the crowd gasped, a few screams were heard and all eyes turned to look past Ruby and the stage toward the expanse of salt water that was the serpentine body of the inlet. Chaos ensued as people realized that something enormous had just blown up. Parents grabbed children, gripped small hands and looked around with frightened, confused eyes, as if waiting for the next detonation. Ray yelled up to Ruby. "Mom! Get off the stage!"

Ruby held on to the mic, wondering what she could say to help calm the crowd, but realized she had no idea what the hell was happening and could offer no comfort in this moment. As she turned, slightly dazed, to put the mic back on the stand, Jerry Justice and Jamie Lynn emerged from the crowd and charged up the steps. Five men and three women with rifles stood at either end of the stage, pointing their guns at the faces of anyone standing near, including the congresswoman's family.

Jerry Justice snatched the microphone from Ruby, while Jamie Lynn grabbed her, pointing a pistol to her head, grinning like a banshee.

"Woo eee, that was a fucking loud explosion! Can I get an amen? No? oh well, never mind. We got what we came for, ain't that right darlin? I mean MISS Jamie Lynn Carter,' Justice grimaced playfully, a madman having fun. He turned to the terrified crowd, "She don't like that kind of talk. Me calling her darlin', but hey, she IS in my book. Jamie Lynn is a Patriot and an American hero. But this woman?" he jabbed a finger at Ruby, "this woman is a liar and part of the problem in the corrupt government. She can't talk about what and how to fix our problems because she's one of the mutts makin' em! Another corrupt deep state Democrat!"

Sirens wailed in the distance as emergency vehicles raced toward the inlet to the scene of whatever had just happened, the smoke cloud was large and drifting to the west, an acrid odor reached them. Zilla couldn't figure out what the scent was, but it reminded her of a strong cleaning compound and that was bad. Whatever had blown up, chemicals were involved.

Ray and his grandfather both started toward the stage, determined to get to Ruby and remove her from the maniacal woman who had her arm roughly locked around Ruby's neck, gleefully holding a large handgun to her temple. As they made the attempt, more armed men and women surrounded them.

Zilla had been worried about the G.D.C. young people bringing guns to the rally, now she almost wished a few of them would stand up to the multiple members of the D.A.D. crowd. Ruby was in extreme danger and she couldn't guess what the hell the crazy, lethal Jerry Justice and her nemesis Jamie Lynn were planning. Were they connected to whatever detonated?

Emergency personnel were siphoning off to respond to the mysterious explosion, leaving fewer officers to try to stop the stand off. Zilla looked up at Ruby, seeing more anger than fear in her eyes, she surveyed the crowd as average citizens backed away, wide eyed and afraid, as more people, all displaying guns, walked up to surround the stage. This was an orchestrated siege and she suspected the explosion had been timed to be part of it.

For a torturous minute she was unsure what to do. She couldn't rush the stage to get to

Ruby without being shot, probably several times. She couldn't rescue Poppa Ray and Ray Jr, for the same reason. She would have tried to take them all on if it had been hand to hand combat, that was her strong suit, but the difficult odds of facing off with a bunch of thugs became lethal odds when guns were involved. Getting shot again was something she'd just as soon avoid, thank you very much.

Zilla decided the best thing she could do in the moment was get away. If she got rounded up, they were all helpless. She slipped back, keeping her eyes on Jamie Lynn and Jerry Justice as they both muscled Ruby toward the steps leading off the stage.

"Hold em right there, boys. Woo eeee, we got em! Let's get this show on the road to Kincaid." Jerry was shouting as he pushed Ruby toward the right edge of the stage, grinning in the direction of Ray jr. and senior, the microphone was still in his hand. No one loved the stage more than Jerry Justice. Zilla took advantage of the momentary distraction as all eyes were on the scuffle on stage.

She slipped around and ducked down behind a man standing in confusion, unable to process what was happening. He wore a Midnight Fun Midnight Run race bib with the number 22 on the front. He had a hydration backpack with a tube that ran from his water bottle on his back to a clip on his shoulder, handy for sipping while moving along. He was still thinking about being in the first wave of runners and couldn't connect to the scene of panic unfolding in front of him.

Zilla sprinted off, veering left and right in an attempt to mix in to the rapidly dispersing groups of people.

Jamie Lynn yelled when she saw her. "Hey!" pointing a finger in Zilla's direction. "Don't let that bitch get away!" Three of the armed men who were keeping the two Walker men contained turned in the direction Jamie Lynn was pointing in. They started to turn but Jerry Justice intervened.

"Nah. Let her go. We got what we need." He leered at Ruby as they made their way off the stage. Armed supporters encircled them, turning out toward the few remaining citizens, pointing their guns at anyone who looked in their direction. They moved toward the row of parked vehicles along the south side of the park strip, moving Ruby and both Rays with them.

Mo, at Ray's urging, had slipped back and quietly escaped the loop of armed people who had closed around the Walkers. But she quickly changed her mind, decided she would stand with her family, threaded back through the armed thugs and much to Ray's dismay, was suddenly back at his side.

She was unknown by the D.A.D. crew who were nervous but euphoric about taking this stand. A stand for American development! A stand for American jobs! A stand to access the resources that God had provided and intended for man to use! They were sweaty and freaked out about breaking the law. They weren't sure what law but kidnapping a member of congress right off a public stage in front of dozens of witnesses was no doubt illegal as hell.

Shit had gotten real and there was no turning back now. They were committed and believed in Jerry Justice and Jamie Lynn. She was still spending the capital she'd made simply by being the young lover of the late, revered General Alex Burke. The General was dead, but Jamie Lynn was out of prison and helping lead the charge to take control of American resources. They hadn't been successful in seizing control of the government to take back the country, as the General had so ardently desired but by god they could win the resource extraction war!

Zilla was gone. She's sprinted across the park strip toward the dense neighborhood that stretches south, away from downtown. As soon as she got off the open expanse of grass, she bolted across 10th avenue, through a yard and into the alley. This was her neighborhood and she knew were there were fences and where there were open lawns. She wanted to get out of sight from anyone who might have pursued her. As soon as she got behind a garage, she paused to assess, peering cautiously around the corner. No one was after her so she ran on to her motorcycle, cursing the decision to park blocks away rather than wait out the traffic snarls to get her bike back to her own garage, a mere four blocks from the event on the strip.

She tried to call Platonovich as she ran but the call went straight to voicemail. Who knew what he was dealing with after the explosion near the inlet? Zilla could smell the chemical odor that she now recognized as ammonia. It was strong but residents of Alaska's largest city were in luck. The wind was blowing from northeast and was disbursing the now misshapen yellowish cloud out over the silty waters of Cook Inlet, away from the nostrils and eyes of people downtown.

Zilla was momentarily at a loss for what to do when she reached her bike. She straddled the Harley, strapped on her helmet and stood with her right foot resting on the kick-start pedal, thinking. Should she try to find the group that had Ruby and both Rays? Should she race to the scene of the explosion? Where would Jerry Justice and Jamie Lynn take Ruby and what did they plan to do with her? She tried Platonovich again, no luck. Then, wanting advice, she tried her editor, Ed Brooks. He didn't answer either, she left a message. *Ed, armed members of the D.A.D. grabbed the Walkers. All of them, including the Congresswoman. I don't know where they'll take them or why. Would like to talk through what to do next with you. What the hell was that explosion and where the hell are you?*

On a whim, she tried Murphy's cell phone next. It rang a few times before his slow, exact instructions for leaving a message came on.

Where were her elder news mentors?

It would be a few hours before she started to really worry about Murphy. By early evening, Brooks, Mo and even the Walkers would be in known locations, but not Murphy. No one heard from him all day and when multiple big stories were unfolding in Anchorage, it was perplexing that Stuart Murphy was not in the thick of it.

##

When they got to the east end of the warehouse and industrial area of 1st avenue, MC turned in to the parking lot of a former municipal utility storage building, a faded Commercial Property For Rent or Lease sign signaled that no one had parked here for their shift in a long time. Weeds poked through random cracks and holes in the asphalt like whiskers on a grizzled, unkempt face.   There was a metal latch and a formidably sized padlock on the steel door of the building, but even from the car, Murphy could see that it had been broken free of the doorframe. The lock was intact, but the hasp that was meant to secure it was pried loose. Murph looked around, not seeing another vehicle.

"So, where's your source kid? I need to get back within an hour, don't forget that." Murphy had silenced his cell, as was his custom when he was talking to deep background sources. He didn't need a paranoid individual getting jumpy and clamming up because his phone interrupted sensitive questioning. He knew this habit irritated the hell out of his younger co-workers who left their phones on 24/7 but he fretted that focusing on a single source of information was becoming a lesser skill of young reporters. Everyone now seemed to be able to track three things at once. Interviewing someone while monitoring twitter and text messages.

Murph wouldn't have it. Younger minds were more adapt at this new way of taking in multiple streams of information, but it was easy to miss subtle things, a word or nervous tone, a hesitation, if you were not completely focused on the task at hand. The world would keep spinning if he didn't answer a call immediately or read a tweet every 10 minutes. He zeroed in and read the face, voice and body language of those he posed questions to. It always paid off.

"Probably inside. Probably got dropped off."

"Probably?" Murph studied the younger man's profile. MC was staring at the peeling gray paint on the door of the warehouse as if willing someone to come to it and wave them in. Murph was uneasy, knew MC was frightened and was unsure what it meant for him but he had been in numerous other dicey situations throughout his career and was ready to get this going.

"Ok, let's go in." Murph grabbed his notebook, opened the car door and stepped out. MC sat, still staring at the door as if hypnotized. Murph leaned over and peered in at him. "Coming in kid or you planning to wait here?" MC nearly crumbled again, Murph's voice was calm, as if he knew MC was scared and like a kindly uncle, was letting him know it was ok if he wanted to sit this out.

MC had a stab of regret that he had ever taken the job that Volkov had offered. He'd been a fool to believe the too-good-to-be-true pay he was offered wouldn't have strings attached. Now he was in way too far and there was no way out to save his own hide without killing a guy who although irritating, didn't deserve to die. There was nothing to be done about it though. He knew he would be killed if he didn't follow through with shooting Stuart Murphy.

"No old man. I'm coming with." He stepped from the car and without another glance in Murphy's direction, walked toward the door, pushed it open and walked in.

Murph followed. When he stepped through the door, a faint breeze wafted out, carrying the smell of old oil and grease soaked gravel, the timeless perfume of abandoned warehouses. MC had his back to the door when Murph entered, when he turned, he was holding a gun.

"Whoa, easy kid. You don't have any worry from me, why the hardware? Your guy isn't even here."

"You brought this on yourself, old man. You should have kept your nose out of my business." MC's eyes were wide and he was breathing hard, Murph spoke quietly.

"Digging into other people's business is my job. Don't make this worse for yourself. Right now you'd maybe have some accomplice charges, but if you don't have a record, you'll be ok. Don't do something stupid kid."

"Stop calling me kid! I haven't done anything wrong! Only delivered a package my BOSS told me to! But you kept coming around and pissed off my boss. Now I have no choice but to put a bullet in you so I don't end up with one in me."

"No. That's not your only choice. Take some deep breaths, kid, sorry...MC. Just slow down and let's talk. I can help you." Murph was standing close to the doorway, having only made two steps in before he saw the gun in MC's hand. He was holding his arms at waist level, both hands were held up near his chest, he held his notebook in his left hand; his right was open palm, submissive, trying to both calm MC and let the nervous younger man know he wasn't a threat.

But it didn't matter. MC was scared, trapped and in way over his head. He'd never fired a gun before and screamed when it went off.

The bullet hit Murph in the gut. He made a strange noise, like someone had just punched him in the chest and knocked the wind out of him. MC shot again as Murph started to collapse to the floor. The second shot hit him in the neck. He fell over on the dusty concrete floor, half curled on his right side, his left hand clutched his ever present notebook, his right dropped to the floor, splayed above his head, his fingers reaching out as if trying to grab the crumpled forty ounce beer can and two discarded syringes that lay in the filth of past opportunistic parties.

MC stood frozen, his ears ringing in the heavy silence. His eyes locked on Murphy. He fully expected him to get up. Not believing that it was this easy to kill someone. Not believing that he had done exactly that.

It was an ignoble death for a noble newsman.

MC Ames, a flight attendant turned bartender turned punk murderer ended the life of a brilliant, fearless and masterful journalist. Stuart 'Murph' Murphy was 68 years old when he was shot. He would have likely worked, full steam, for another decade. Not because he needed the money, because he loved and believed deeply in the importance of solid reporting and its affect on the lives of all citizens who take the time to be well and widely read.

Stuart 'Murph' Murphy, astute, award winning, investigative reporter was dead.

MC froze for another two full minutes. He was unsure if he would be able to move. Terrified to try in case he really was locked in place or terrified that if he did move, somehow it would raise Murphy from the floor and that was even scarier. He kept waiting, for what he wasn't sure. He thought it would be more like movies he'd seen. There was no screaming, other than his own, no profound dying statements or accusations or tears from Murphy. Only a silence and stillness that was more unnerving than any outburst. He finally lowered his right arm, his hand aching from the fierce clamp on the gun.

When he moved, nothing happened. Murph didn't jump up and try to fight him. No one in uniform stepped through the door and ordered him to drop his weapon. There was no response from the living world. He slowly took steps. Skirting Murphy's body and backing toward the door, not taking his eyes off the dead reporter. Still not believing that he'd really killed him.

He stepped outside and exhaled, realizing he had been holding his breath. As he did, his stomach clenched, doubled him over and he threw up into the weeds that sprouted through a chain link fence along the edge of the parking lot. He stood up, looked around, whimpering as he swiped his mouth with his sleeve. He heard no traffic, saw no people. He climbed into his car, staring at the door, realizing he should have closed it, made it less likely that the body would be found right away. But he started the car and slowly drove away, glancing at the half open door in his rear view mirror, expected Murphy would be standing there, his face hovered in MC's mind. He could hear his voice so clearly that it was as if he was in the backseat. *"Whoa, easy kid. You don't have any worry from me. Why the hardware?"* *"Are they threatening you?"*

The voice was no longer concerned, now it was mocking. *"Easy kid, why the hardware?"* *"They threatening you?"* MC started to cry as he drove away from the warehouse and wound back up the steep street to downtown and his parking spot in front of The Silver Slipper. He hadn't been gone more than 23 minutes. He thought about Murphy's request to have him back in an hour. He was cold, as if his blood had turned to ice. His stomach churned again and he got out of the car, made his way down the steps and into the bar, feeling old and tired at 26. Something was gone inside of him. He didn't know what it was but he missed it and knew it wasn't coming back. He was a murderer and part of him had died along with Murphy. Whether he was eventually caught or not, MC Ames was a different man than he'd been in the morning. It was a difference he hated, but would not be able to change.

Both Ray Walker the elder and his grandson thought they would lose their mind from anger over the way Jerry Justice and Jamie Lynn were treating Ruby. Roughly shoving her toward the stairs from the stage, Jamie's arm clamped across her chest, her pistol barrel pushed into the flesh of Ruby's temple.

As the trio clumped down the stairs together, Jamie Lynn grabbed a handful of Ruby's hair, her pistol knocking against Ruby's skull. "Who wants to be part of the jury for this political bitch's trial?" Several cheers went up among the other gun holding supporters and Jamie Lynn grinned and shook Ruby's head, a small cry of pain escaped Ruby's mouth before she clamped her lips shut. They could take her, but they couldn't make her show fear.

The Walker men and Mo stood helpless, watching Justice, Carter and their beloved matriarch and congresswoman move away from the stage and toward a line of parked vehicles along the south side of the park strip. Their armed supporters had lost interest in Ray, Mo and Poppa Ray, and left them standing by the stage. The Congresswoman was the grand prize.

The jerks were getting away with Ruby and there was nothing to be done about it. The younger Walker looked around at the few people who were still on the park strip. Most had guns that had magically appeared from under jackets. The others were people with stunned expressions, frozen in confusion, fear and disbelief that they were witnessing the kidnapping of a member of the U.S. Congress. How could such a thing happen, in broad daylight no less, and in a crowd of people?

It happened because it was planned and orchestrated by Volkov and his American lackeys like MC Ames, Jerry Justice and indirectly, Jamie Lynn Carter. She'd never met Nikita Volkov but she was playing a role in his disinformation and chaos campaign. The Russian operative desired a fractured American psyche. A country where no one trusted their neighbor and being united meant against other Americans not against international foes.

President Donald Trump ran his campaign and now still espoused his supposed values and beliefs in his version of nationalism, America First- fuck the rest of the world.

The predictable results of fomenting suspicion and hatred for other countries meant that Americans were increasingly suspicious of each other and a divided America was precisely what Volkov's boss and his international thug club wanted.

The leaders of North Korea, China, Iran and smaller players like Syria and Cuba were all in for the Vlad Fan Club. If the former KGB agent now Russian President could dent and finally crack the steel wall that had represented the formidable nature of being united in the United States, they would cheer him on with any assistance they could muster. Fake social media accounts spreading disinformation were just the tip of the anti U.S. spear. Control of oil, food and fresh water supplies was the long-term plan and these countries were desperate to be on the winning team when it came to world dominance.

Similar disruptive events were taking place all across the nation. Not many were as sensational as kidnapping a member of the U.S. Congress, but the constant barrage of online lies, orchestrated violence and organized protests were taking a toll on the citizens of the greatest country on the planet.

Ruby's successful kidnapping was part of the fall out. Not that many years ago, any attempt by one American citizen to kidnap a member of congress would have been met with resistance from any other American, regardless of their politics. United States meant we would stand with each other against any foreign foe. It was simple to define. Now the lines were blurred and it was harder each day to know who was telling the truth and who was bullshitting the masses.

Foreign operatives had gotten adept at recruiting disenfranchised and paranoid Americans. The flood of powerful and illicit opioid drugs into America from China left a large percentage of Americans addicted and weak, and addicts are easy to control.

Ruby, grabbed and successfully taken away in a public venue was an indication of how fractured the culture of cohesiveness had become. Ray senior watched his daughter in law stumble as she was shoved into the back seat of a waiting car. Jamie Lynn held a gun on Ruby as she also got into the backseat. Jerry Justice jumped into the driver's seat and another one of his minions got in the passenger's seat. The man half turned so he could leer at Ruby. Ray senior's fists were clenched so tight he was leaving fingernail marks in his palms.

His grandson broke his spell of rigid rage. "Granddad! We've got to get out of here and follow them! I'll run to the café and get the car. Wait here for me."

Before his elder could reply, Ray shot off, sprinting across the grass toward the downtown skyline of tall buildings and in the direction of

Ruby's Café. Mo wasn't sure what to do, wanted to run, because she was terrified and hated feeling helpless, but staying with Poppa Ray made sense. She couldn't outrun Ray, who was already across the park strip and was now disappearing down an alley, so staying put was the only sensible option.

She put her hand on Poppa Ray's shoulder. He immediately turned to her and folded her into a hug, as if he too were resisting the urge to run but needed to do something. She fought tears. "Oh god, what will they do to her?"

"I don't know." He spoke in a small voice, unable to offer any words of comfort. He watched Jerry Justice pull away from the parking spot, the devil's grin on his face. Ruby's pale face and shocked, still expression burned into his mind's eye as he continued to hug Mo, to keep her from witnessing the departure that they were helpless to stop. Ray wouldn't be back before they were long gone. But Poppa Ray knew they'd take her to Kincaid for their charade trial. He had no idea how they'd get to her, but he fought the panic that wanted to overwhelm him. Clear thinking was crucial.

##

Zilla was waiting.

As soon as Justice pulled away from the parking spot, she followed. She knew the window would be small for a chance to intervene before the kidnappers made it to Kincaid park where countless other D.A.D. supporters with guns would be waiting. She desperately tried to think of a place where she could cut them off or force them from the road, but they had guns and Zilla longed for a good old-fashioned street fight. She'd gladly take on Justice and Carter and another of their gorillas to boot. She fought her temper and her desire to kick the shit out of them, recognizing she wanted to control something to quell the fear she had over Ruby's safety.

She couldn't do any of it. All she could do was follow at a distance, and think, think, think about how to stop them from getting to Kincaid, even though she knew that would be impossible. Where was August? And where the hell were Brooks and Murphy? Zilla was scared and confused about all that was going down. It was uncomfortable to be so close to an unfolding event, rather than the human fly on the wall that is a reporter's usual M. O. It made it hard for her to think clearly and her fear for Ruby's safety made her vulnerable. That was never good.

Getting through the angry crowd at Kincaid, or even up the curvy, wooded road that led into the park was an iffy prospect. She decided an element of surprise was her only chance. Zilla took the first left off the main road, abandoning her covert tailing of Justice. She dropped the big bike into a lower gear, twisted the throttle and sped off toward one of the neighborhoods that hugged the bluffs along the coastline as a plan to enter the park from a side trail came into her mind.

The acrid yellow chemical cloud had elongated into a hazy band that stretched north and south along the Inlet. Zilla had a better view of where the plume had originated. It appeared to be near Earthquake Park, at the end of the east/west runways for the International airport. What could have detonated in such a spectacular way and what was the chemical? She wondered if that's where Brooks and Murphy were. Perhaps, the two men were on scene there and wearing some protective gear to guard against inhaling fumes. *Maybe that's why they aren't calling back.* This hopeful thought evaporated as quickly as it formed. It didn't make sense that they would have magically obtained protective facemasks for chemicals they didn't have identified.

She was trying to rationalize their absence and that just wasted time. She had to get to Ruby. She had to think clearly. Now it was all about rescuing the woman who was beloved for more than the great chow her staff dished up at the café. She was the mom of Zilla's newsroom partner Ray and soon to be the mother in law of Zee's best friend, Mo Scott. Safety was front and center.   Reporting on the Green Defiance Coalition's hidden mountain compound and their surprising willingness to arm their supporters, a scoop that normally would have found the diligent journalist racing to the newsroom to report this startling information, was all shoved to the back corner of her mind. What she'd witnessed over the past few days revealed the Defend American Development organizers and the Green Defiance Coalition enthusiasts were arming for a resource war.

A war of physical violence rather than a war of words and litigation.

If Ruby had given a rousing speech to the assembled runners on the park strip and then went back to the café to help with the evening bar crowd and visit with locals, as planned, Zilla would be deep in the page at the Daily Standard right now, writing, researching and fact checking like a woman on fire. Instead she was leaning into curves, riding faster than she normally would, winding through residential streets, looking for one of the multiple coastal trail entry points that poked into neighborhoods throughout Anchorage.

Finally! Zilla saw the familiar trail marker posts and worn footpath that identified a trail entrance in between a duplex and another home. She dumped back on the throttle, the chrome pipes rumbling louder than she liked, never one to be a show off or loud, irritating rider, but the sense of urgency she had, quelled her usual respectful decorum when she quietly cruised side streets.   She braked hard, swerved to the curb, kicking the stand out before the heavy bike came to a full stop. Pulling the keys and stuffing them in her pocket, she yanked her helmet off, stepped off the bike and quickly hung it by its straps on the handlebars. It was possible her purple helmet, a respectful nod to Prince and the Revolution, would be missing when she got back, but right now, she wasn't concerned about possible theft. She had to get Ruby away from Jerry Justice and more critically, from the lethal grasp of Jamie Lynn Carter.

Zilla ran toward the wooded pathway that led to the coast, her helmet still swaying from its tether over the handlebars, and disappeared into the dense forest. She worked to tamp down her anger as she silently ran along the trail leading into the north end of Kincaid Park. She knew these trails well. She and Buck, her doggy side kick, had run nearly every mile of winding trails from one end of the city to the other. She knew where she could veer off the main trail and cut through brush, some of it unpleasantly choked with wild raspberry thorns or worse, Devil's Club stalks. Running in a leather motorcycle jacket meant she was immediately covered in sweat, but also protected from the brambles that tried to poke through her sleeves. There was no purchase for thorns on black leather.

As she got close to the large arteries of main trails crisscrossing Kincaid that led to the chalet and expansive lawn area of the park, she slowed to a walk, unzipped her heavy jacket to allow cooler air to circulate around her upper body. Thinking through how to approach the chalet, Zilla stopped to catch her breath and listen. She could hear people cheering, guns being fired into the air and sirens wailing from seemingly every direction as the sound bounced around her. She called Ray.

"Zilla! Where are you?"

"I'm at Kincaid." She spoke quietly, hunched over and turned slowly in a circle, peering into the trees.

"How the hell did you get in there? We tried to follow but got turned back by some of the armed goons taking orders from Justice and Carter. They've blocked the road Zee."

" I figured they would. I snuck in on a trail. Not far from the chalet now. I can hear a ruckus up the hill from where I am. Ray, I'll try to get to Ruby. Try to get her the hell out of here."

"I'm going to take your lead. Where did you go in?" Ray sounded desperate but eager to do something, anything to try to get to his mom.

"Went in off Raspberry Road, found a neighborhood with trail access and took off into the trees, off the trail system. Figured they would have people positioned on the main trails. It's lucky this park is so huge. They can't watch all of it. I'm close. Trying to figure out what to do next. No way I can describe where I am other than on the north side of the main parking lot in the trees. Try to get here Ray without getting shot at. I gotta go."

Zilla saw movement in the brush to her right and froze. She'd be able to disarm someone if she maintained the element of surprise, but if the person with a gun saw her first, she'd be caught or shot.

She held her breath, waiting. The racket of hollering people and the frequent shots being fired aloft made it hard to hear rustling close by, but she did. The smell of ammonia was stronger. The wind must have changed direction as she got a whiff of it. Again, leaves and brush being crushed underfoot sent raspy noise her way.

Then, a sound that raised goose bumps on her sweaty skin; the weird, distinctive noise of a bear popping its jaws.

Shit. What's worse? She thought. *An angry gun toting Jerry Justice supporter or a grizzly bear irritated at having afternoon snack time interrupted?*

##

Ruby Walker was smart enough to be scared but tough enough to be damn mad at the smart ass cowboy and vicious, patch-eyed woman who kept one hand wrapped tightly in Ruby's hair and the other wrapped tightly around the grip of the pistol she held against Ruby's head.

They were at the Kincaid Chalet and there was an enormous crowd of D.A.D. supporters spread out on the sloping lawn in front of the Chalet, at least 200 by Ruby's quick estimate. Jerry Justice and Jamie Lynn shoved Ruby toward the concrete slab sporting a dozen picnic tables in front of the building. Ruby made eye contact with people as she was pushed past them. A few looked away, uncomfortable at her defiant glare, but most stared right back with a malice that nipped at her resolve to not show fear. It was unsettling to see so many people in an ugly mood and directing that anger at her.

Ruby tried to stay calm to keep her thinking clear, but it was difficult in the face of so much naked hatred. She could smell it in the crowd.

Why is there so much anger and division in the state and country? Her thoughts raced. *When did we go from the nation that boasted about being 'united' to the suspicious, deeply divided collection of factions that the U.S. had devolved into?*

There wasn't a single or easy answer. This resentment had been building for a long time, going back decades. Defined by declining jobs and wages, irrational fear of people with brown skin, epidemic rates of opioid and heroin addiction, rising healthcare and housing costs, disinformation campaigns online. The list went on and on and the fallout was devastating.

Ruby tried to understand the desperation that drove people to take extreme and illegal measures in a Hail Mary attempt to drive change, but she couldn't. Hurting people, taking someone, anyone, much less a member of Congress against their will would never result in positive change.

Ruby saw this as the heart of the current stand off. People who feel they are being forced to accept things they fear or dislike. A feeling that the government no longer represents them or what they need. Certain that dangerous terrorists and cartel criminals are flooding across the border to sell drugs, kidnap and rape girls. Shooting anyone who gets in their way.

In Alaska, the vitriol was concentrated, focused on the fight over resource development versus conservation. The fight had been going on since before Alaska was a state, but it had amplified in an alarming way. It was as if the growing anger in the country had become a magnet for all the shrapnel of destroyed hopes and dreams and drawn it together into a jagged, lethal mass; A mass that couldn't fit together but couldn't go back to its original shape either. The pain was deep and the rationale for the fix misinformed and wrong but gained momentum daily.

Jerry Justice made sure Jamie Lynn had a tight grip on Ruby's arm, not that she could have gotten away if she'd tried to run anyway. There was no shortage of angry people who would jump at the chance to tackle a politician, woman or not. He strutted to the edge of the patio in front of the Chalet and jumped up on a picnic table, raising his gun over his head and shooting as he danced around in a circle.

"Woo eee! We got her! We got her! And now we can hold a proper trial! A trial BY the people, FOR the people! A trial to find out if this enemy, this traitor should be released or not. What should we do folks? What's the verdict?"

People screamed an immediate bulge eyed, spit flinging response. *Hang her! Hang her high! Drain the swamp! Fuck all libtards and weak ass snowflakes!*

Jamie Lynn grinned and pumped her right fist in the air. The left cruelly clenched Ruby's hair. "Yeah! Let's kill this bitch!" She yelled into Ruby's face. Ruby didn't blink.

"Whoa, whoa now. Settle down folks. Woo eeee, ya'all got yourselves so riled up now." Justice holstered his pistol and stood, legs spread wide, facing the crowd. He held his hands up to get silence, crossed them high across his chest, facing the crowd. He poked his face out toward the crowd, stretching his neck like a turtle.

"Just take it back down a notch or two, good people. We want to make sure we have a legitimate process here. We are Americans!" A cheer went up in the crowd, "And that means we make sure justice is served." He was in his element, hamming it up for the crowd, grinning like the devil he was. "So," he raised his hands again, the right one once more gripping his pistol, then let both arms drop, "What's it gonna be?" He raised his voice and adopted his best evangelist tone. He turned to point his gun at Ruby, standing in front of the picnic table, right where Jamie Lynn had shoved her.

"Do we have enough evidence to show this is one of the corrupt, greedy swamp monsters that is destroying our way of life? Do we know with certainty that she would vote to take away our jobs? That she would push to let animals run carefree so we can't hunt them? So we can't develop the land because we gotta make sure we don't hurt the critter's environment? It just circles around and around folks" He started mincing back and forth, waving his pistol dramatically. "Woooo eeee, you can't eat a steak cuz you're supposed to live on gluten free lettuce and turn all the cattle loose so they can be happy and run around because they have rights. Well then you can't develop the resources that GOD put here for that very reason, for us to develop because the wild cows have to have plenty of land to range on. And you better not step on that grass! You better not! That's habitat people! And you can't disturb the wild cow habitat." He stopped his sashaying around and faced the crowd, his hands on his hips. "Does any of this make any sense to ya'all?"

"Hell no! It's bullshit! We need jobs! Fuck cows and greenies!" the crowd was wild. More than half held guns above their heads, rifles were at risk of clanging into each other so many were aloft.

"No, it don't make no sense. Not a damn bit of it and it's time it stopped." He pointed at Ruby again. "It's time it stopped and it seems the only way to drain the swamp is to take them DOWN," Now he started yelling, "It's time to lead America to prosperity again! To say no to these arbitrary laws set up by rich cats in Washington that help them but cut us off at the knees! It's time that we get the say in how the future looks." He raised his arms above his head. "IS SHE GUILTY?"

"Yes! Yes! Yes! Hang her! Hang her! Drain the fucking swamp!"

"Woo eee, that was swift justice ladies and gents! We had our trial, the verdict is in and it didn't take us but about 10 minutes. See? We don't need lawyers dragging things through five layers of courts for millions of dollars. Swift justice. This is how it should be! My name is Jerry Justice and I believe in law by the people and for the people! Not for the politicians! It starts today. Right now! We carry out this sentence and then get to work. Do you hear me?" he was shouting again, "It's time for our rule of law! It's time for us to say how it goes! It's time for Cut, Kill, Mine, Drill!"

He pointed to the edge of the stage. "Now we don't have a traditional set up for a proper public hanging on account of the rapid nature of this here trial," he paused to laugh, "but trees have been the time honored deliverers of quick justice for centuries and one of them right over there will do just fine!"

A hate filled, ugly roar went up in the crowd. Guns were pumped up and down above shouting red faces. Jerry Justice leaned in to the vitriol.

"First we'll have us a good old fashioned public hanging and then we'll go after the rest of the traitors that would stop God's plan for us. The fake news liars who spend all day, every day just working to make up vicious lies about us for money. Our courageous President Trump is right. We should take them to court and punish them for their treason! OUR court! OUR justice! OUR resources!"

He was fairly screaming into the mic and Jamie Lynn, caught up in the fever, punched

Ruby, knocking her to her knees on the stage then dragged her back to her feet by her hair. Blood trickled from Ruby's mouth. The crowd screamed approval and shots were fired into the sky. The yellow chemical cloud stretched out along the western edge of the park like an atmospheric disease.

Zilla caught the attention and the eyes of the bear she'd seen and came up with a crazy, on the fly, plan. It would either work or get both her and Ruby killed, but she knew she couldn't wait for back up. The bear was agitated, swaying back and forth, sniffing the air, deciding if it should run or charge. The D.A.D. crowd had closed off the single road leading into Kincaid Park. APD officers were waiting on SWAT back up before considering a shoot out. They were thin in numbers as the majority of those deployed for today's multiple security details were scrambling to get to and identify the source of the explosion.

There was no time left. If she didn't do something, Ruby was going to die. She took a deep breath, picked up a broken, but solid branch from a downed tree and jumped toward the bear.

"Sorry about this dude." She whispered toward it. The big animal started to rise up on his back legs, to get a better look at this crazy human. Before it was fully upright, Zilla swung the branch and whacked it, as hard as she could, right across the face. The bear roared and swatted before dropping down to give chase.

But Zilla was already running. Discarding the branch, she made a beeline right toward the center of the hollering crowd. All of them were staring intently at the stage, blood lust in their eyes. None of them saw her zooming up the trail, the pissed off bear close behind and getting closer. As soon as she reached the edge of the group, she veered toward the stage, running as fast as she could, in the hope that she could sweep past everyone and get to Ruby and Jamie Lynn before someone grabbed her. The bear stopped, bewildered and uncertain in its anger, about tangling with so many humans. It stood and as if on cue, roared again. Zilla jumped up the steps two at a time as screams and shouts behind her made clear the bear was the new center of attention.

"What the fuck is...." Jerry Justice couldn't finish his statement because a foot to his throat cut the words off and sent him flying backward, choking and gagging as he landed with a loud thud on his back. Zilla spun around and landed a second kick alongside Jamie Lynn's head. Her adrenaline driven effort sent both Jamie Lynn and Ruby sprawling. Zilla was sorry she'd knocked Ruby for a loop along with her captor, but if it worked and Zilla was able to rescue Ruby, it was ok. Getting knocked down was a lot better than a hanging.

The angry crowd was now the scrambling, bear focused crowd. Eyes had turned from the stage toward the aloft bear, it was just enough time, before multiple shots rang out as people fired in the air to stop the bear's advance or shot directly at it. The bear dropped down, still roaring its anger and now fear and turned to flee before faltering and falling as a hail of gunfire brought it down. Zilla would feel terrible about that later, but right now she was wrestling Jamie Lynn for her gun and yelling at Ruby at the same time. "Run Ruby! Get out of here!"

But Ruby was focused on Jerry Justice, still laying on the stage, choking and gagging, unable to draw a proper breath through his damaged windpipe. She was on her hands and knees and scurried toward him instead of off the back of the stage as Zilla had hoped. She grabbed Justice's revolver from where he'd dropped it, pulled the trigger back and pointed it at his face. She rose to her feet slowly, the punch mark on her right cheek a bright angry red. A lump on her forehead was visible from the fall to the stage. She kept a bead on Jerry Justice.

Zilla had kicked Jamie Lynn's gun away from her hand and was rolling toward the back of the stage, locked in battle with a woman she'd never met but was her years long nemesis, stretching back to Jamie Lynn's militia recruiting days before she went to prison, largely due to Zilla and Ray's reporting.

Zilla's fight training focused on never being in her current position. On the ground was bad.

Hard to use personal combat skills when you're on your back, especially when you're fighting someone in a full-blown rage. Jamie Lynn was screaming an inch from Zilla's face. It was the scream of a lunatic and would have fear paralyzed a lesser foe, but Zilla was fighting for her life and she was glad Jamie Lynn was wasting a bunch of energy by screaming. It would only tire her faster.

##

When the explosion and ball of fire erupted near the western edge of Anchorage, it took August about 15 seconds to call the troopers. He studied the growing cloud of mysterious yellow in the sky, tamping down the fear over its toxicity as he held his phone, waiting through only one ring.

"Hello, Sergeant Platonovich. This is Mark Kennedy. What's the latest?" Caller i.d. was a time saver in emergencies. Platonovich was glad he could cut to the chase.

"Trooper Kennedy we need a helo right away. How quickly can you get one up and over the inlet?" He desperately wanted to be on board but thought it better to get eyes on the source of the explosion, as fast as possible and to pick him up added time they couldn't afford.

"Already on it sir. They've fired one up and are doing final checks right now." Kennedy had been in law enforcement for a couple of decades. Longevity in law enforcement in Alaska was rare and officers like Kennedy were high value individuals. Even in a full on and confusing crisis, his voice was calm.

"There are two other emergencies that need immediate attention Sergeant. A mob of armed D.A.D. supporters barred access to Kincaid Park where Congresswoman Walker has been taken as a hostage. Her life is in extreme danger Sergeant." His tone relayed the shocking information that an American lawmaker was being held at gunpoint by other Americans, but didn't vary from a measured cadence.

"I'm well aware of the plight of Ms. Walker. I've got officers working to get into sniper positions now. We're hoping to resolve this without killing some of them, but it's likely violence will be unavoidable and that's putting the Congresswoman in more danger."

"Yes, sir." Kennedy's quiet response.

"You mentioned two things trooper. I'm driving past the Point Woronzof parking lot right now, trying to pinpoint the source of the explosion. What was the second emergency?" The detective alternated between watching the gravel road he was hurtling down, kicking dust and stones up behind his truck, and scanning the sky, focused on the source of the noxious cloud. He was more confident by the second that the location was at or near the Anchorage sewage treatment facility. A knot tightened in his stomach. He knew there was anhydrous ammonia at the wastewater plant. A lot of it.

"It's the other side, August," rare for Kennedy to use a colleague's first name rather than official title. Never knew who was listening or when a call might end up as part of a future legal proceeding. The change in his tone made Platonovich grip his cell phone harder.

"Other side?"

"The enviros. Green Defiance Coalition people. They're armed. Never saw anything like it. Instead of banners and laying in front of bulldozers, these Green Revolution guys want to go to war, just like the crowd backing up that crazy mutt from Arkansas."

"Where are they?" The detective could now see the shimmer of heat waves above the tree line, mixed in with the billowing clouds of yellow tinged smoke. The smell intensified.

"They showed up at the park strip right after Justice and his crew nabbed Congresswoman Walker. Half of his crowd wrapped around him to protect them on the way to Kincaid Park. The other half were still milling around when this other bunch showed up. Some of em are convinced Justice's mob had something to do with Marcus Peterson's death, the others look like a lot of their opponents. Just want to fight. They're squaring off. No shots fired yet, but it's going to pop off any minute and we're damn low on extra officers to deploy right now to back up your people."

August rounded the last corner and hit the brakes, the pickup slid in the gravel, back end fishtailing under the hard stop. Before him was the scene he had dreaded. The Cessna was nose first, tail pointed skyward, stuck through the roof of the main building that housed the treatment facility where solids were filtered out of the raw sewage. The explosion had likely come from something on board the aircraft that detonated on impact, but had missed what he suspected the real target was, dozens of pressurized metal containers filled with anhydrous ammonia. That explosion would have been much larger and more lethal.

August felt no relief. The fire was spreading quickly toward the building where the bottles, locked by gates and other physical security measures, were not shielded from the heat. A mega blast would be imminent if firefighters didn't respond immediately. The pilot had missed the main target or been unaware of its location. August figured the ammonia tanks were certainly the aim. A random crazy flying a plane into a sewage plant for shitty kicks seemed highly unlikely. This was part of someone's plan. He was sure of it. Who was behind it was the puzzle. The D.A.D.? The G.D.C.? What the hell was the purpose? Purely a distraction?

Now, as road dust wafted around his truck from the sliding stop of a few seconds ago, he felt a surge of despair. Several miles away, Alaska's lone U.S. Congresswoman was in the clutches of vicious kidnappers and may already be dead. In the opposite direction near the heart of downtown, clans of angry oppositional believers were ratcheting up long simmering resentment about who had the right to decide the future for the planet. They could already be firing shots at each other and he was staring at what would be a devastating second explosion if the fire were not put out very soon. Even in it's blessedly remote location on the far edge of the city along the beach of Cook Inlet, the detonation of the vast amount of anhydrous ammonia stored there would make Timothy McVeigh's horrific 1995 Oklahoma City bombing look like firecrackers in a soda can.

Three disasters were crash converging in his city and he felt helpless to stop any of it. But that feeling lasted only an instant, then determination and his lifelong faith in the power of good over evil propelled him to action. He yelled into his phone and threw his truck into reverse to get away from the fire.

"Kennedy! Get the forest service now! See if they can get a plane up with fire retardant to dump on the wastewater sewage plant immediately."

"What the hell are you...." Kennedy's voice held his bewilderment. *The wastewater treatment plant? What?*

"It's on fire! The plane crashed here and there's going to be an even bigger fireball if it's not out soon. It's too dangerous for fire department trucks to tackle. It either gets put out from the air before it reaches the building filled with anhydrous or city residents are going to be hurt in big numbers."

"Calling now." Kennedy hung up without asking for more details, even though Platonovich knew he was confused, but he trusted the detective's sense of urgency. There was no time to talk it over. If a plane couldn't get up quick enough to douse the flames, there was the potential for more casualties than their Congresswoman and members of the two sides of the resource wars.

As if that wasn't bad enough.

August spun his truck around and gunned it back down the gravel road to where it joined blacktop on the edge of the Woronzof parking lot. He decided a second later to take the right turn that threaded between a patch of swampy lowland and the enormous hangers of Fed Ex, UPS and other cargo plane companies spread along the back road, west of the international airport. His tires squealed in protest as he slammed his brakes and turned hard to make it onto what would be a straighter run then the snaky road that hugged and ran parallel to the edge of the coast. As his speed quickly climbed to 90, he felt confidence growing. Not because any of the trifecta of disasters were closer to resolution but at least he was giving directives and he was moving. Toward what he wasn't sure, but being in motion helped him think. He knew it was fruitless to drive toward the road into Kincaid Park, he could only hope the snipers would be able to get into position, but the where was difficult. The chalet at Kincaid was one of the higher spots in what was otherwise dense forest and heavy vegetation.

He barked into his cell phone, commanding the voice activated assistant to call APD dispatch while he sped past runways and hangers. He would marshal as many officers as he could for the park strip to try to defuse before there was gunfire, unless it had already happened, there was constant chatter on his radio as officers, troopers, emergency responders and dispatchers all tried to assess and stop the simultaneous tragedies unfolding in Anchorage.

##

MC Ames was falling apart. When he drove away from the moribund warehouse that contained his new secret, the body of Stuart Murphy, he felt a moment's relief. He'd gotten away with it! No one saw him! It was going to be ok. Nobody could tie him to Murph's death.

His relief was short lived. Doubt started to creep in a block away, his car pointed up the curvy street that led from the industrial/railroad district back up to the heart of downtown. Had he left fingerprints? Had anyone seen Murphy get in his car and drive away? He'd been right downtown. In broad daylight! Anyone could have seen them! What the hell was he thinking, getting in a car with Murphy in the middle of the day?

Sweaty and shaking, he pulled up in front of the Silver Slipper and scurried down the steps to the dank basement lounge. Hoping for comfort from the now familiar surroundings, he instead felt claustrophobic and freaked out by the quiet. The bravado that had enabled him to pull the trigger and kill a man he didn't really know was long gone. The adrenaline that had dumped into his system had dissipated and he was a stinking mess of fear and paranoia. He was going to get caught. He was sure of it. He was going to get caught and he was going to prison where enormous muscle bound murderers were going to pound his ass until he broke in two.

Tears rolled down his face as he pummeled his fists on the bar top. The echoing sound freaked him out and his mind raced with terror. It was over. He'd completely fucked his future. All was lost. He dropped his head to the wooden bar and sobbed loudly. Self-pity racked him and he screamed through his sobs, snot and tears dribbling into pitiful pools on the bar top. He kicked over a stool in his rage, then another and another, until all were prone and more than a couple were broken.

But it helped. MC took a deep breath and scrubbed his sleeve across his face, wiping away his shame, replacing it with anger, outrage and an idea.

If he was going to prison, he was going to take out the guy who was responsible for sending him there. Now that he was a killer, the idea of shooting that reprehensible cowboy slime ball Jerry Justice was more than appealing. It felt necessary. A new voice in his head demanded it be done.

The voice sounded like that damn dead reporter Stuart Murphy. He was relentless! MC couldn't escape him and his prying, insistent voice even after shooting him dead.

Hey kid. You know you're going down for this. What a dumb move. Taking me to a spot where the city has CCTV cameras on streetlights to monitor one of the worst crime areas in Anchorage. The cops are coming for you kid. I could have helped you, but you fucking killed me instead. Bad idea kid. Bad idea.

Murphy's voice was a whisper that seemed to come from behind him, when he whirled around it was to his left, then his right. It surrounded him and wouldn't stop.

You better hit the road kid. Better scoot outta town right now or get ready to be Bubba's prison fish boyfriend. Hahahaha. HAHAHHAHAHAHAH!

Murphy's laughter echoed through his brain, loud and mocking.

"Stop it!" He slammed his hands over his ears and jumped left and right, shaking his head like it was on fire. "Shut up, SHUT UP! It's not my fault! I didn't have any choice! I had to kill you or I'd get killed! Stop it!!" MC grabbed his car keys off the bar, his left hand still cupped and switching madly back and forth between his ears, trying to shut out the voice that was in his head. He ran up the steps, two at a time, didn't lock the door. Ran to his car. Grabbed the gun from the glove compartment and threw it on the passenger seat.

Later, he wouldn't remember any of what transpired over the next two hours. He was in a panic blackout and his body was on autopilot, putting the car in drive, pulling away from the curb and heading to the park strip. He focused on killing Jerry Justice before the cops found him and ripped his life away.

MC made it only two blocks before police cars with flashers rolling blue and red off the corporate buildings on the north side of 9th avenue blocked the intersection. For a second he was blinded by a white light of fear, certain they were there to nab him, but he heard gunshots and looked from the squad cars to the park strip, where an enormous crowd was separated by a line of too few officers.

The families who had been there earlier to celebrate a family fun event scrammed from the ugly scene as soon as the horror of their U.S. Congresswoman kidnapped at gunpoint had ended.

Now it was the D.A.D. heavily armed, red faced and hollering, squaring off with the G.D.C. The only reason there wasn't a full on clash already was because the G.D.C. group was also heavily armed, something the D.A.D. leaders hadn't figured on. They were surprised and uncertain if it was just a show by a bunch of snowflakes with fake or unloaded guns or if these wimpy looking granola crunchers were crazy enough to start shooting.

That uncertainty was the only thing that had kept a full on gun battle from erupting. It was eroding fast. Both sides were loud, angry and getting closer to the other. MC got out of his car like a man in a dream. He left it sitting in the intersection, the driver's door open, the engine running. The gun hung loosely from his hand as he made his way toward the mob that any other rationale person would be running away from.

MC was not rational. He was a killer now and an insane grin spread across his face as he moved toward the park strip. He slowly pulled the handgun up and squinted one eye, drawing a bead on the first officer in the soon to be overrun line. Then he moved the gun and pointed it at a D.A.D. supporter who was screaming in the cop's face and waving his rifle above his head. Then he pointed it at one of the G.D.C. members. A young woman with a bandana over her wavy curls. She was shouting but looked too sweet to be a threat.

He pulled the trigger and kept walking. His arm straight in front of him, elbow locked. He pulled the trigger again. The curly haired young woman fell and the crowd roared and slammed together, bowling over the officers, who disappeared under the crush. Shots and screams rang out. Chaos replaced the shaky stand off that had kept death at bay as the handful of officers barked orders and worked to keep the peace until MC shot and first one then another and another person fell. At first G.D.C. members dropped to the ground as the D.A.D. crowd employed their guns, but when the third environmentalist went down, their friends screamed and pulled up their own firearms. Now it was a full-blown gun battle and MC kept walking forward, a crazed zombie, pulling the trigger, over and over until it was empty, still aiming and pulling the trigger, unaware he was out of bullets. He didn't seem to notice the first shot that hit him in the left arm, even as it jerked backward with the velocity. The second shot hit his right hip and he dropped like a sack of stones. Being out of the main line of cross fire, likely saved his rotten life. He lost consciousness and no longer smelled gunpowder or heard the shots or screams of rage and pain.

MC would wake up in a hospital bed, handcuffed to the rail, bewildered about how he'd gotten there or what had happened. But hopeful that his memory lapse meant he'd killed Jerry Justice and that was why he was shot up in the hospital. When he found out the truth, he began to plan his suicide.

##

"Code silver! Shots fired! Shots fired! Officers need immediate assistance on 10th avenue and A Street intersection! Any and all units in the vicinity, get there pronto! Code Silver! Crowd riot! Gun battle! Multiple people down!

August was roaring down International road, his truck topping 95 as he slid his magnetized police light onto the roof of his black

Chevy, siren blaring. He clenched the steering wheel fiercely, willing himself to get downtown faster, silently praying no citizen would blow through a stoplight and T-bone him or get T boned by him. The detective had a fleeting thought about Zilla, wondering where she was and if she was safe but it was gone in an instant as the call for back up on his radio continued, the dispatcher voice more urgent, edged with alarm and approaching panic. Something seldom heard in the voice of people trained to be calm and clear headed.

August knew the scene downtown was bad. A bloodbath. The near hysterical voice on the radio confirmed it. He nearly rolled his truck taking the turn onto C Street way too fast. But he made it and floored the accelerator, the big eight-cylinder engine screamed as it jumped over 110 miles an hour. August knew how reckless this kind of driving was in the middle of a city, but he kept his foot jammed to the floor as he made his way toward downtown and the fight that was raging there.

For the millionth time in his long career he wished he could beam himself to the crisis. And also to Kincaid Park where he feared a similar battle was happening. Unsure where Ruby Walker, Alaska's lone member of the U.S. House, was or if she was alive. He tried to keep that and the thought that Zilla may be in similar trouble, from locking his mind up. He couldn't take control, guide officers effectively and hope to resolve the multitude of violence in the city if he was seized by fear and panic.

August was one block south of the park strip when he saw SWAT vehicles in a line across C Street, blocking all four north and south lanes. He took his foot off the gas pedal and watched officers rapidly directing traffic onto side streets leading west. They were funneling people away from the hotspot on the strip, to minimize the number of civilians in harm's way. August pulled his truck over to the far lane, jamming hard on the brakes. He let the one flasher on top of his cab continue washing red and blue light in a circular sweep to warn travelers that they were coming up on a hard stop in the form of a formidable line of battle hardened vehicles designed for blocking or ramming.

August reached for extra ammunition clips, listening to the cross chatter on the radio as he prepared to exit his truck.

"We need help out here! The fire's spreading toward the main tank storage! Where the hell is that plane!

"More shots fired at Kincaid! Snipers can't get a clear elevated spot, we're going in through the trails!"

"Officers down! Officers down! No control of the riot on the park strip! Need back up now!"

It was rare to hear panic in an officer or dispatcher's voice. To hear it in three voices at once made August sick to his stomach. He jumped from the cab, pistol in hand and approached the line of officers advancing on the park strip.

Chapter Twenty

Alaskans may as well live on an island; the state is so removed and remote from the 48 contiguous states to the south. It was built into the local language. Non-Alaskans were from 'Outside', a place that had for decades been far away and out of immediate contact except by marginal phone connections. Satellites, fiber optic cables and streaming technology had changed that. Immediacy was at the fingertips of Alaskans in the same way it was for New Yorkers.

Live video was flooding the Internet from multiple observers across the city. Viewers in the lower 48 and across the world were catching feeds through Facebook, Twitter, Snapchat, Whatsapp, Instagram and hundreds of individual alerts, like a new age version of the antiquated phone tree system for spreading important news. This only took seconds to reach millions, rather than hours to reach a few dozen.

President Trump was briefed that a U.S. Congresswoman had been kidnapped at gunpoint and was being held hostage while armed battles raged in Alaska's largest city and a fiery plane crash meant a chemical explosion threatened even more of the citizenry.

Supporters of both the Defend American Development organization and Green Defiance Coalition were gathering in growing knots of protests in cities and towns across the U.S., all screaming for justice for both sides. The dramatic live stream feeds of violence, shots ringing out, tear gas canisters, drawing smoky trails zoomed overhead toward the protests and captured the attention of the world.

The President suggested he might need to declare a national emergency, (his personal preference) or martial law to allow the military to take over in Anchorage. He liked the idea of wielding power to crush the rioting in Alaska and other parts of the country if needed. Trump characteristically took to his favorite method of dictator decrees, his Twitter feed.

What the hell is going on in Alaska? Everything was going great after I created incredible new jobs cleaning up their island. Great pay. Great work being done. World Class jobs. They get an earthquake that kills a lot of fine workers and the state goes crazy? Everyone says I'm the toughest President in the history of the world. They better settle down today or I'll send in my military. Believe me.

Nakita Volkov could not have been happier.

Only slightly more than one hour had passed since the initial disruption on the park strip led to a cascade of confusion and terror. Every single resident of Anchorage that wasn't asleep or offline, was locked to their respective devices, watching in horror as the city descended into chaos. Anchorage is a violent place, one of the most dangerous cities in America, but even for people accustomed to daily stories of mayhem here, this was a new level of fear. Radio, television, streaming on phones and other portable devices all picked up various versions of the danger unfolding and the urgent alerts by APD to lock down, shelter in place and stay indoors.

Volkov was in the air, safely away from Anchorage and sipping his second martini, a rare indulgence when he was working. The Russian operative was quietly celebrating the success of his dark efforts to spread the kind of disinformation, fear and paranoia that would sew division and foment wide spread fighting. He was well aware of Trump's online threats spewing about letting the military control Anchorage and possibly other cities in the U.S. He would allow himself a third chilled vodka if he received confirmation that the kidnapped congresswoman was dead. This would insure a civil war in a country that was stressed out, addicted to rage and teetering on the brink of collapse. He closed his eyes as he conjured the thought. He had little confidence in the southern cowboy tough guy he'd enlisted, and overpaid, to carry off the high profile killing, but it wasn't hard to pull a trigger.

It irritated him to leave before he could confirm all details were dispatched with. He was not a man who left loose ends. But he had to time his departure to just before the Cessna took its kamikaze dive, spearing into the thousands of pressurized pounds of anhydrous ammonia, because all flights would be grounded after such a massive explosion.

If he'd had any indication that the terrorist pilot, committed to killing himself in the name of service to his version of god, Putin, would fuck up the actual execution and miss his intended target by a few dozen feet, killing himself but no one else, Volkov would not have boarded an early afternoon flight to San Diego. He would have stayed to try to revise the plan that was now without the benefit of a massive cloud of toxic gas blanketing the city as he had hoped. It was 90 minutes into the flight before he found out about the failure. It took several minutes of intense personal struggle for him to control his rage. He fought the powerful urge to crush the martini glass and drive a shard into the throat of the cloyingly sweet but clearly disinterested flight attendant.

But he did. Nikita Volkov enjoyed violence as an outlet for his anger and the desire to hurt the efficient but indifferent young woman was strong in those few moments after he'd gotten word about the plane's near miss. She'd stopped to ask if he needed anything at the worst possible time. Volkov sliced his hand in front of her face to silence and drive her off before he acted on his powerful impulse to slash her. She recoiled at his rudeness, not realizing how close she'd come to a blood gushing death. Volkov reined in his fury. He was a highly disciplined, well-trained member of the former KGB, just like his boss and he would not lose control of his emotions. It was a weakness he detested.

He would calm himself, finish his drink and plan for his version of damage control. When there wasn't as much damage as he'd hoped and planned for, it meant a revised plan of new violence to leverage an increase in Kremlin control of the ignorant masses of weak-minded Americans. He sat back, relaxed his breathing and forgave his momentary lapse in displaying anger in front of the flight attendant.

He smiled to himself in realization that this was a minor set back in the Kremlin's long running plan. America was so fractured now, like a million tiny cracks in a glass tabletop. Growing mistrust of, within and between the two major U.S. political parties, suspicion of anyone with brown skin by anyone with white skin and going the other way, contempt of law enforcement and the judicial system all the way to the previously adored U.S. Supreme Court and most pleasing of all, the dissolving faith in the American election system. The American conservatives freak out over liberal support for their so-called Green Deal that sought to choke the fossil fuel industry to death with solar panels, wind farms and carbon neutral jobs.

All it would take was one small acid filled glass, set in the center and the Democratic table would implode into millions of hopeless pieces, flinging toxins in the eyes of the country, blinding them so they could no longer find each other and rebuild their infuriating wall of unity. Their flailing hands would only reach their new Commander. They would find Vladimir Putin and his top henchman Nakita Volkov and in their blindness, they would be helpless to do anything but bow to his demands.

Poppa Ray was a long way from his feisty, Air Force days when he'd been a young hothead and relished the chance to bruise his knuckles on a Saturday night. Most Anchorage regulars to Ruby's Café knew him only as the mellow old dude who filled the air with great jazz notes on his saxophone every Tuesday night. They wouldn't have recognized the angry man focused intently on the road as his grandson maneuvered them down a side street in the same neighborhood Zilla had slipped into. The elder Walker gripped the dash with his left hand to avoid sliding when Ray junior took a curve too fast. He didn't comment on the speed, he wanted to go faster, but even in their fear and panic, both men knew reckless driving through a small neighborhood could be a disaster of a different kind. Kids were everywhere.

Ray senior wished he'd had a chance to get to his own weapons, but there'd been no time and now he was struggling with the thought of how they would be able to help Ruby when they were the only ones who would be unarmed. He squeezed his eyes shut for a moment. *Think, think, damn it!*

Ray junior rounded another corner in the windy area and saw Zilla's Harley on the side of the road, casually leaned onto its kickstand.

"Here's where we'll go in Granddad." He pulled over but before he could put the car in park, his grandfather yelled and pointed.

"No! See that mini mart up there? Go to it! Hurry!" He was loud and animated in his excitement.

"Granddad, what the hell are you talking about? We don't have time to go to the damn store!" Ray was bewildered and alarmed, wondering if the stress of the day had addled his grandfather's mind.

"We need something son. We can't go in there empty-handed and expect to get Ruby out. I got an idea."

Ray junior reluctantly jammed his foot back on the gas. "I hope the hell you know what you're doing." His fear funneled into anger.

"Me too." His answer made Ray junior angrier but before he could say anything, they'd pulled up in front of the small convenience store and Poppa Ray was unbuckled and out the door before the car was fully stopped, leaving the passenger door splayed open. He ran into the store, his quickness a surprise to his grandson who had never seen his grandfather move in anything but a slow, liquid ease that made him seem younger than he was. His leap to the sidewalk and sprint into the store was further confirmation that Poppa Ray was a long way from being a feeble old man. He was back in less than 90 seconds, carrying two plastic bags.

"Let's go." He said, slamming the door and arranging the bags between his legs. Ray junior could see the white tops of plastic soda bottles.

"You need some damn pop right now?" Ray's accusing tone was brittle with rage. He pulled the car next to Zilla's bike and threw it in park, reaching for the door handle at the same time. He was too furious to stay in the vehicle another minute with his clearly confused grandfather. He decided he would leave him here, in the car, like the daffy old man he apparently was. Then Poppa Ray spoke.

"I told you we need something. We're gonna make grenades."

Ray junior looked over as the elder Walker grabbed the sacks of his strange supplies and jumped out. Ray had no way to determine whether his grandfather was completely off his mental rails or knew what he was talking about. There was no time to argue. They had to try something and one thing Ray junior knew about his namesake, Poppa Ray was a capable man who still had secrets up his sleeve. He grabbed one of the bags without a word from his grandfather and they took off down the trail.

"I've ridden every inch of these trails through the years. If no one is stationed on the west fork of this one, I have an idea for a short cut that will get us really close."

"Throwing distance close?" Ray senior asked.

"I, I guess. I think so. Yes." The younger Ray wasn't sure if he was encouraging crazy thinking, *(we're going to throw 7-up bombs?)* but it didn't matter right now. All he could think about was getting to his mom and getting her to safety.

Ed Brooks, *Anchorage Daily Standard* editor was on the west end of the fight on the park strip. He was trying to get photos of a historic day of tragedy and conflict in Anchorage. He had tried his lead reporter's cell phones several times, fearing what may have happened to Zilla and Ray and bewildered by the lack of response from Murphy. Brooks feared his most veteran newsman had lost his phone or was in trouble. His news antennae signaled the latter.

He kept making pictures, hearing shots, screams, shouts and sirens. Focusing to keep his mind off memories of the brutal work of his war correspondent days or the concern that Stuart Murphy might need help.

##

Zilla was in trouble.

Jamie Lynn straddled her chest, her knees pinned Zilla's arms to the stage, two beefy men, admiring stragglers left over from Jamie Lynn's militia days when she'd been General Alex Burke's lover and top recruiter, had jumped up the steps and were now holding Zilla's legs down with crushing weight. Both men pressed heavy engineer booted feet onto her shins.

Jamie Lynn was strangling Zilla, screaming as she thought of how she'd almost died this very same way when the General had tried to kill her. Choking her with hate filled eyes, until her sister Bernadette, planted an axe in his head.

This finally, was Jamie Lynn's revenge. At long last, after years in prison and her bitterness over the financial loss that seemed again to be imminent, she could at least have the satisfaction of killing the self righteous, goody two shoes, cunty bitch that just wouldn't mind her own fucking business. Jamie Lynn clenched her teeth as she squeezed, knowing she'd go to prison again but finding the thought well worth it if Zilla Gillette was dead.

"Get the hell off her or I'll shoot him in the eye!" Ruby's voice was loud, angry and confident.

It made Jamie Lynn and her two goons, turn to look. Zilla drew a coughing breath while her captors took in the scene. Ruby was shaking, but whether it was fear, rage or both wasn't clear. Apparent was her position of advantage. She held the gun hammer fully cocked back, pointed inches from Jerry Justice's face.

"Settle down there now gal. Woo eeee, you don't gotta kill nobody." Jerry Justice employed his quieting a mad dog voice. Looking down the dark barrel of his own gun.

"Ha! Go ahead and kill that smug, oosik toting, idiot cowboy son of a bitch. Do me a favor. One less chore for later." Jamie Lynn was laughing, mocking Ruby, her hands still around Zilla's neck.

"I'll shoot you next." Ruby said, never taking her eyes off Jerry Justice.

"Not before 23 people shoot you, dumb ass." Jamie Lynn cracked.

"Ok, ok, stop all this now before it gets out of hand." Jerry Justice was smiling at Ruby, trying to play nice. His life experience had convinced him that all women were simpletons that could be easily swayed or ordered to bend to his will. Ruby wasn't having it.

"Ok. But he's dying with me." She raised her voice. "Is this what you want? You want your leader dead with me?"

For a few breathless seconds, everything seemed to stop. Some of the assembled rabble rousers were like the men helping Jamie Lynn by pinning Zilla to the stage, holdovers from the General's heady days of militia angst, when he and Jamie Lynn promised to lead the way back to American greatness. But the majority of the group was loyal to Jerry Justice. They'd heard of Jamie Lynn's patriotic 'honor' but she was a latecomer to their group and most of them were D.A.D. loyalists.

Their hesitation gave the Walker men time to get in place.

From the blessed cover of the thick willow patch that bordered the edge of the opening and had served as prior cover for the black bear, now sprawled on its side, shot riddled, Ray senior was crouched down, unscrewing soda bottle tops as he whispered the plan to his grandson.

"Shake, run, throw. Shake, run, throw. That's what you got to do little Ray." He hadn't referred to his grandson in such a way for many years. It revealed his fear that his plan might be whack. "You'll only get a few off before they start to blow. You gotta keep moving or you'll get shot son." He had dumped out half the soda and was pouring blue and white crystals from a plastic jug of toilet bowl cleaner into the bottles, quickly screwing the lids back on and handing them to his grandson. "You only have a few minutes now, head to the back, throw into the middle of the crowd. I'll go the other way and do the same."

Ray junior suddenly realized what they were doing. His granddad was a genius and he had a little glimmer of hope. Grabbing the six bottles, tucking them under his arm, he could feel the expansion stretching the plastic. It was going to be fast.

As he turned, he saw what was in the other bag. Granddad had bought 3 pints of 100 Proof Everclear. Oh beautiful, booze obsessed Anchorage! The liquor store in the back of the little convenience mart had contained exactly what the old man had hoped for. Paper napkins, likely yanked from near the spinning hotdog cooker, the other hallmark of city quickstops, were twisted into long wicks and sticking out of the pint bottles. Ray took off as silently as he could through the brush without another word. After only a few steps, he followed his elder's instructions.

Shake, throw, run. The first bottle disappeared nearly exactly into the center of the crowd. He'd pitched the second and then the third before Granddad lobbed one of the mini Molotov cocktails into the crowd. His timing was impeccable. The first soda bottle exploded and the flaming booze ignited a chemical gas flash fire. He was already throwing the second one and running with the final bottle as Ray junior delivered the last two soda bottles to the mob. The final one exploding mid air above the crowd, barely far enough away from Ray to avoid injury. Chaos and screaming replaced the momentary uncertainty of the assembled group.

My eyes! My eyes! My lungs are burning! Help me! God, help me, I can't breathe!

Granddad lit and threw the final pint and three people were splashed with liquid fire as others started shooting into the brush toward the two directions of the incoming IEDs.

Both Walkers zigzagged into the forest then circled to the back of the stage. Ruby was still holding the gun close to Jerry Justice's head, steadfast in her commitment to kill him if Jamie Lynn didn't release Zilla.

Jamie Lynn eyed the mayhem in the crowd and looked incredibly irritated, rolling her eyes and looking up at the goons as she started choking Zilla in earnest again. She spoke through clenched teeth. "Just kill that bitch while I finish this one off." True to her word, she didn't care if her order meant the death of Jerry Justice. Good riddance to him, the elected twat holding the gun and Gillette. Three irritating problems taken care of at once was the trifecta of terrific in Jamie Lynn's book. Prison or no, this shit was great.

"Jamie Lynn? It's time to stop. It's over. It's time to go home now honey." The woman's voice behind her was calm, but strong, resolute.

Jamie Lynn froze. Her body stiffened as she straightened bolt upright, a chill shuddered her body. *Had she just heard her mom's voice?*

Behind her, in full pastoral regalia, holding her ornately carved staff like a lesbian Moses was Bernadette, Jamie Lynn's reborn sister. Former self described protector of her evil little sister. The woman who had tried to shield a young Jamie Lynn from the abuse of their stepfather, who had covered for her when Jamie Lynn claimed her first victim at 12 by killing a leachy old neighbor, who had taken out the General when he was trying to strangle Jamie Lynn, who had for years, obeyed the horrible directives of her sociopathic younger sister and who had gone to prison for trying to kill Zilla Gillette for her.

Bernadette stood, both hands wrapped around the staff, held in front of her. The religious iconography on her flowing garments was like a Holy flak jacket. She was completely protected from the assembled crowd. They were bloodthirsty and some were crazy, but they all feared anything that smacked of godliness. The people in excruciating toilet cleaner splatter pain from caustic residue on skin, eyes, lungs and those putting out alcohol flames on their clothing were in no shape to challenge her, even if they had an inclination.

Jamie Lynn, realized it was her older sister, shot a sarcastic look over her shoulder eager to get back to killing Zilla, although choking and releasing and choking again had been a macabre, pleasurable game.

"It's you? What the hell are you doing here? I'm a little busy right now, in case you didn't notice. Don't you have a dyke preacher conference to attend or something?"

It was a surreal scene. Screaming people were writhing on the grass, being attended to by others, a dead bear lay on bloody soil nearby. Ruby still held a steady grip on the pistol she had trained on Jerry Justice's head, Zilla was drawing ragged, coughing breaths, the goons still crushing her shins and Jamie Lynn sat on her chest like a schoolyard bully. And now her formerly cowering and insecure sister, stood at attention like the solider for god she aspired to. She slid one hand up the cedar staff as she spoke.

"I'm sorry that our mom abandoned us Jamie Lynn. I'm sorry that......'

"Who gives a shit about your fucking sorrow....." Jamie Lynn tried to interrupt but Bernadette shouted her down. Her voice amplified by the strength of her decision.

"NO! YOU must listen now! I'm sorry for the pain we had to deal with as children and I'm sorry that I couldn't help bring you to the light willingly Jamie Lynn. But you must go now to atone for your sins little sister. And I must also go to atone for mine."

Jamie Lynn started to laugh. "What the fuck ever." She turned back to stare down at Zilla, cocking her patched eye toward her intended victim and closed her hands around her throat again. "What's over is this meddling, enemy of the people, nosy ass bitch's life. Ya hear me, ya stupid fake news hac......." Jamie Lynn's one eye opened wide as her voice faltered. Ray saw it happen from the backside of the stage where he and granddad were standing, trying to figure out how to help end the standoff on the stage. They were fresh out of soda pop bombs.

Later he would tell Zilla the story. How Bernadette had raised her left foot, while she slid her right hand up. In one motion it seemed, she pushed down with her foot and up with her hand. The top fell away from the staff, revealing the carved, walrus ivory tip, as she raised it off the ground, her foot knocked the end cover off, revealing an identical ivory spear. And in one fluid motion, she brought the spear forward, parallel with the ground and plunged it into her sister's back. "God forgive us." Her final words as she grabbed the other spear tip, aimed it at her bare throat above her flowing garments and thrust herself toward Jamie Lynn, driving the spear through them both. Jamie Lynn opened her mouth, once, twice, like a fish on land, gulping for air, she coughed, spit blood into Zilla's face, then slumped and toppled over as Bernadette dropped, pulling them in tandem to their left.

The Carter sisters were dead.

The weaponized shepherd's staff that Bernadette had taken them both out with, bonked the stage with a wooden *thunk* as the women fell. There was a second of shock as Zilla stared, gasping for breath but now free of Jamie Lynn and the goons, who jumped in surprise at the swift, violent murder suicide and lost their foothold on Zilla's shins. Ruby, stock still, miraculously kept the gun trained on Jerry Justice, the need for leverage to escape the mob hadn't abated. The Walker men stared, frozen in momentary shock.

Before anyone moved, a second explosion blasted into the air. The Anchorage firefighters and helicopter pilot, who had tried mightily to douse the flames at the wastewater treatment plant, had evacuated from the site just as Bernadette was approaching the stage. They hadn't been able to contain the fire away from the tank storage building and getting out before it blew was their only option to survive. The fire trucks were lumbering away, down the gravel road toward Earthquake Park, not nearly far enough away, when the detonation occurred. Four of six AFD firefighters died in the initial blast, two others died later that day of severe chemical inhalation burns to their lungs.

If the sewage treatment plant had been closer to the heart of downtown, scores of others would have died. As it was, the caustic release sickened hundreds of area residents, providing terrible, but effective crowd control throughout the city. Like a water hose on a dog fight, the second blast quelled the last of those engaged in a gun battle on the park strip and the crowd at Kincaid, many of them covered in burns from Poppa Ray's IEDs and flaming pints of Everclear. Eye witnesses to the harpoon killing of one of their leaders, had lost their will to fight.

Both the Defend American Development adherents and the Green Defiance Coalition believers, collectively and silently decided to stand down.

There would be more casualties and arrests, hospitalizations and the philosophical differences that had created the divide remained for fights in the future. Violence and death didn't change the worldview of either those seeking to exploit and develop or those seeking to protect and create a green revolution. But for today, the fight was over.

In following weeks, some said it was the Devil himself, gleeful over his two scores, others said it was God expressing rage and reigning down punishment. Still others argued it was the militant greenies, targeting a long detested source of ocean pollution that was the sewage treatment plant for Alaska's largest city.

The true responsible party, calmly finishing his airline vodka, would never be tried for his crimes and the mystery suicide pilot that had flown the plane into the treatment plant would remain a mystery as the second explosion of this harrowing day thoroughly incinerated the body.

Zilla had reclaimed her breath. She jumped to her feet; the pinching pain in her shins fueled her anger at the two men staring at Jamie Lynn, hypnotized by her expanding pool of blood that soaked the stage beneath her.

Their momentary hesitation was their loss and Zilla's gain. Gritting her teeth, knowing her scraped shins were not going to love it, she swept the legs out from under the first man, immediately delivered two blows to the second, one to the side of his head, one to his throat, both hit the stage on their backs at the same time. Zilla grabbed their guns and threw them off the back of the stage. Ray and Poppa Ray had shaken off their shock and grabbed the two rifles from the lawn. It hardly seemed necessary now, but they raised them up to ensure that any remaining plans by either side to ramp back up would not materialize.

Like tear gas disbursing a crowd, the toxic fumes from the second explosion sent those who could still walk toward the parking lot and their cars, some limped along, supported between or carried by others. All hoped to escape arrest. The strength of their previous convictions evaporated.

Poppa Ray quietly walked up onto the stage and took the gun out of Ruby's hands. He kept it trained on Jerry Justice and slipped his other arm around his daughter in law.

"It's over Ruby. This cracker is going to jail." He squeezed her shoulders and she laid her head on his chest and started to cry for the first time since Jamie Lynn and Jerry Justice had snatched her from the downtown rally. It had seemed like days but had been less than two hours.

For the first time in his life, Jerry Justice, former child star of Arkansas public access television, former evangelist and sexual predator, current criminal in a world of trouble, was silent. He tried to open his mouth to speak but no words flowed with that easy oratory magic that had been his bread and butter for decades. Nothing. Not a croak of a sound. He sat on the stage, his legs splayed in front of him, oosik leaning out of the holster, cowboy hat knocked askance. He wondered if God had taken his voice forever.

August Platonovich watched in horror as the second explosion told him the efforts by the fire department had been too late.

But once again, the city was fortunate. The only thing that had gone in Anchorage's favor during this day of death and destruction was the wind.   Thousands of residents would suffer mild to severe irritation from the residue that made its way into the ductwork of Anchorage air system infrastructure, but the vast majority of the deadly cloud floated off toward Denali, North America's highest peak. A snow and ice covered legendary badass of mystic stone that had swallowed more than a few climbers who dared to attempt the summit. Denali took its human payment when it wanted and cared not about the foolishness of humans or their destructive creations.

##

August pulled his phone from his pocket and quietly answered like a man in a dream.

"Platonovich." Staring at the disintegrating cloud to the west, his eyes fatigued and fixated. "Yes?"

"Sir? It's Kennedy. I'm afraid I've got more bad news."

August nearly burst into hysterical laughter. Bad news? Had Kennedy cracked up in the madness of this day? What the hell else could have possibly happened? He barked his response. "Out with it Lieutenant! What are you talking about?"

"One of the shooter suspects sir. His name is MC Ames. He was taken down by officers after advancing and shooting at the park strip crowd."

"And? Kennedy, we've got casualties all over the damn city."

"Ames is still alive sir. But he confessed in the hospital to killing one of the reporters for the *Anchorage Daily Standard.* It's uh…"

August heard paper shuffling and in the seconds it took for officer Kennedy to say the name, he thought he would have a stroke. He felt the cold horror of certainty that Zilla's name would come next.

"Uh, Stuart Murphy. Yeah. Long time reporter for the Standard. Been seeing his byline for years," More paper shuffling could be heard as August closed his eyes and listened.

Kennedy continued. "Ames said Murphy was, quote, "'threatening to expose him,'" unquote, as part of a money laundering scheme that Murphy accused him of running out of the Silver Slipper. No surprise that Ames denies that.

Although he also said the guy who hired him to work at the bar, a Russian who spread a lot of money around, may have been involved in some illegal activity, but Ames claims he doesn't know what it was and wasn't part of it. Says he was just hired to run the bar."

August kept his eyes closed as he spoke. "Were you able to confirm? Has Murphy's body been recovered?"

"Yes. The M.E. has it. Billfold on the body had i.d. It's him."

"Thank you officer. I'll drive over to the morgue now." August ended the call and walked slowly to his black Chevy pickup. He hated the cold transition of reducing a full, productive life to 'the body,' but he understood the necessity for officers to quickly separate and compartmentalize their feelings. A cop couldn't let emotion cloud their thinking.

He drove the few miles to Martin Luther King Jr Avenue, parked in the huge lot and sat staring at the Chugach Mountains. Deep shades of green undulated in the massive rolling foothills, leading vertically to the rocky brown granite peaks. The lush, green base of the range looked soft and inviting from such a distance, while the upper range loomed dry, hard and barren, capturing the yin/yang between flourishing life and the certainty of change. From constant replenishing to the inevitability of withering death. Regardless of how mighty, tall and seemingly impermeable these ancient peaks appear, soon enough they will erode to flatness and dust.

August stared, bone tired, for a few more minutes. Now that the city had calmed down and arrests were made, it was unpleasant tasks like this one that remained. Gathering information from the medical examiner about the death to deliver to family and friends. The lean detective slowly climbed out of the cab, feeling much older than his 52 years. How many hundreds of times had he performed this particular duty and never was it easy or routine.

Shot, stabbed, bludgeoned, strangled, burned, poisoned, blown up. August had investigated and arrested suspects in every category. But after that satisfaction, came the grim task of informing the family. First, a debrief with the M.E., jotting down the grisly details of someone's last experience on earth. Thinking through as he wrote, how he'd verbally sand the worst of the jagged edges off the details before relying them to a sobbing mother, grandfather, sister or co-worker.

That was August's task at the end of this horrible day, find Zilla, Walker and Brooks to give them the answer to a question they all had. Where was the hardest working reporter in Anchorage on the day of the biggest story in the state's history?

The homicide chief suspected he knew where they would be, as he drove slowly toward downtown, the streets empty of the usual weekend traffic. He confirmed his hunch a few short minutes later when he pulled into the parking lot of the *Anchorage Daily Standard* and saw Zilla's Harley and Brooks' old Datsun in the parking lot.

He took his time walking up the worn plank steps and stood at the top for a long minute, scanning the mountains to draw strength from reaffirming what he'd so recently acknowledged. That no matter how out of whack everything seems in the middle of a tragedy, no matter how humans try to orchestrate and mandate, there is no control and everything is under control. The mountains never change and they are always changing. Life and death. Right and wrong. Love and fear. Happiness and sorrow. All flowed apart and together.

August exhaled a weary puff, walked in the door and gave the reporters, editors and photographers gathered quietly around desks in the newsroom, the news they didn't want to hear. Their colleague, friend, mentor, legendary hothead, tireless advocate for the importance of journalistic truth and damn fine human Stuart Murphy, was dead.

Chapter Twenty-one

They worked through most of the night. Stunned, heartbroken but propelled by the need to help others understand what happened. Even though there was no understanding it. The newsroom crew did what they do best, focused on their work and put their own emotions on the shelf to address the needs of a grieving public.

Zilla left at 4:00, the early morning sky was rosy and too optimistic for her sad spirit. She drove straight home. Too much coffee and just before 4 am, after they'd finished writing and were at the staring into space stage, she'd had two fingers of scotch from the stash in Ed's office. He had gone home at midnight. Someone had to catch a few hours of sleep to come back at 5 to edit, proof headlines and get it online.

No one drank while they worked. That was unethical and unwise. Writing about senseless violent behavior, while swilling down a few drinks could rip off the sarcasm filter, and that would be bad for a reporter.

The bottle of scotch came out after they were done. There was nothing left to do but struggle with the sadness, fight the anger and dull the edge of the blade that cut them all, with a little good scotch. That's exactly what it was there for. Brooks said the scotch and bourbon was for after writing about tragedies, the tequila and vodka, for when they won a Pulitzer.

They'd won two and both times Brooks had fetched the vodka and tequila. He offered shot glasses for the tequila and ice and orange juice from the modest kitchen in the lunch area to mix screwdrivers. What Brooks lacked in bartender chops he more than made up for in efficient simplicity.

In the early hours of a day that would hurt like staring at the sun, they'd had scotch, talked quietly about what they would do later that same morning, who would contact APD for updates, who would post, after they had gone home for a few hours. Sleep for three, shower, grab a sandwich and head back in, that is if you could sleep at all.

Zilla got home with an empty and unhappy stomach but she couldn't face her kitchen, thinking of the dinner party she'd had just a few weeks earlier. Murphy had been there, Mo, Ray and a few other reporters and copy editors. It had been a grand time of her great cooking, Ray's great bartending and Murph's great stories. Her kitchen was usually a sanctuary and a place to unwind tension after a tough day. Not this morning.

She climbed her stairs but couldn't imagine getting in bed. No Buck to nose her hand and snuffle up the scent of her day. The quiet stillness piled on more sorrow.

She pulled off her clothes as she crossed her room, dropping shirt, jeans, bra, as she walked. Grabbing her work out clothes, Zilla stepped into the bathroom, pulled on her running sweats, drank some water out of the faucet, straightened up to look in the mirror. Fatigue and sadness reflected back. She looked pale and pinched. She wiped her mouth, went down the stairs and out the back door.

Zilla jogged to the back of her yard, went through the gate, pausing long enough to lock it, then bolted down the alley, running like she had as a kid, reckless, too fast, heedless to the risk of injury from a fall.

Trying to make the burn in her lungs dull the burn of her heartache. But it wasn't to be, and after a mile, she slowed, falling into a reasonable gait.   4:40 in the morning is an interesting time to be out. The late night drug, booze and sex zombies are still faltering around, bumping into things and half-heartedly looking to score.

For a few moments, Zilla envied their addled oblivion and pondered who was worse off. Those caught in the cycle of always seeking the next drink or fix, suffering the ravages of addiction, or those who were substance sober but hooked on their different versions of manifest destiny, moral outrage and lethal self righteousness.

She shook the thought off, her mind too overwrought and fatigued to examine the existential mess that was humanity. She hadn't felt so alone and lonely for a long time. Running without the sound of the clicking nails and huffing pants of her long time running companion still hurt her heart. Buck had died five months earlier, at the very start of spring, and the thought of him still stung as much as the day he'd left. She missed his constant exuberance and eternal puppy personality. His ecstatic, leaping joy at seeing her every, single, time she walked in, regardless if she'd been gone for 10 minutes or 10 days.

Ray and Mo had made several suggestions about where to find a new pup, but Zilla couldn't stand the thought. It was still too fresh for her. She couldn't just swap him out for a new one, like tossing a pair of old shoes. Buck had been family and she mourned him as such.

It had taken her more than a month before she was able to don her running gear and hit the trails. Every time she tried, the silence that met her when she pulled her sweats and jacket off the hook would lock her up. Unable to change and take off without the doggy joy of impatient and thunderous scrambling back and forth, excited whining, leaping and twirling, panting like he'd already ran 10 miles before they ever hit the door. After nearly 5 weeks of failed attempts followed by extra long sessions of practicing form, she forced herself to dress, leave the house and run.

Zilla cried for the entire 4 miles, tears streamed in horizontal lines across her cheeks, seeped into her ears. But she made it. It still wasn't fun, but it was important and she restarted a running routine. Now it was more like part of the work day than the fun adventure her buddy had made it with his nose seemingly magnetized to the ground as he flew along, ecstatically sniffing up the chem trails of other dogs, humans, moose and mice.

Rounding a curve only a mile from home, Zilla decided to sprint up one last hill, challenging her lungs to work hard enough to shut down the flow of painful thoughts. When she first saw a figure, sitting motionless on the ground and slumped back against a young birch tree, she hoped it was someone sleeping off the previous evening's party, but her gut told her that wasn't the case and she stopped, bent over, putting her hands on her knees, breathing hard and staring harder. Was he asleep? Passed out? She stayed back several feet, watching for movement. Nothing.

"Sir? Sir? SIR! Can you hear me?" She walked closer as she called out, her voice getting louder as did her dismay. Now only a few feet away, she realized his tongue was purple and pushed out between his lips. He was young, Alaska Native and dead. She grabbed her cell phone and called 911, directing the officers to the patch of woods she'd been running through.

While she waited for the patrol car, the dispatcher asked if she could perform CPR till the officers got there, but Zilla told her that it was clear he was dead and that even though he had a bootlace around his neck, tied to the tree behind him, Zilla thought she shouldn't touch him. Something about the scene did not say suicide to her. It made no sense that he could have died that way, simply sitting on the ground with one of his bootlaces around his neck.   She carefully crouched down to get a closer look. There was no sign that he had struggled against a loss of air that would lead to death. The ground was undisturbed near his boots, no scuffs of loose soil.

His right hand was bloody as if he'd been fighting or punched something. But other than a small brush of blood on his pant leg, there was only the confounding scene of a young man, sitting on the ground, leaned against and tethered loosely to a tree.

It looked suspicious to her but when the APD officer arrived, he looked more bored than concerned. Another dead Native kid. Ho hum. Another statistic to add to the column of young Alaska Native men who took their own lives in staggering numbers, five times the rate of suicide in the rest of the country.

Zilla went from sorrow and shock at the terrible discovery, piled on to the previous Armageddon she'd just survived, to red hot anger that this officer was willing to write this up in short form rather than do the careful work to ensure this wasn't a murder scene made to look like a suicide. How easy would it be to kill someone then haul them out to a secluded spot and arrange them in a way that suggested they'd taken their own life? Easy answers are welcome to those who hate hard work and filing out reports. She fired questions at the officer about how this would be investigated and memorized his nametag so she could follow up.

Two days later when the young man was identified as Jay Cloudstone, the FBI was suddenly interested in the details of his death. An agent contacted Zilla to ask what she'd seen when she'd first arrived.

Nakita Volkov had been a very busy man before he left Alaska. First he'd figured out that the serious young man, who showed up at rallies, was working with federal law enforcement as an informant. He then followed Cloudstone with one of his recently purchased lackeys, not letting the other man know what they were up to. Volkov knew violent surprises were effective for messaging. He killed Cloudstone, made his horrified helper carry the body to the patch of urban trees and set him up to look like a suicide. Having established his ruthlessness, Volkov told his underling that he would be his pilot of no return to blow up the treatment plant or his entire family would die a torturous and slow death. It was why the plane was close but not on the target. The terrified and reluctant kamikaze flyer had tried to pull up and avoid the crash. It was too late but took him just far enough off course to lessen the explosive destruction.

Jay Cloudstone, young, smart and passionate about his education and professional plans had become a statistic, not of suicide, but rather of his sense of duty. The medical examiner, putting in lots of overtime this week, had found evidence of poison in his blood. Volkov, like his boss, liked poison. It was easy to carry, administer and almost always effective.

Cloudstone died after agonizing seizures. His right fist bloodied from repeated thrashing against the rough concrete walls of the lackey's basement. Volkov had been out of the room when it happened and was plenty angry about it. Yelling at the frightened man that a suicide by hanging wouldn't bloody someone's knuckles and if it raised suspicion, more of his family members would suffer. Now it didn't matter. The young FBI informant was dead. The pilot who was forced to assist with that death was also dead, nothing but ashes in an exploded and burned out storage building.

And Nakita Volkov was long gone. He would have a few days off before reporting for his next duty. He'd been instructed to continue his counterintelligence work in the U.S. Spreading mistrust and division among the lemmings of America. So easy to fool it was child's play.

He was awaiting word on where his next post would be. Perhaps Idaho, or maybe Michigan. The Kremlin would soon decide if Trump would be supported or if another, more destructive force would emerge and offer a new menu of delicious distraction to confuse ill educated Americans. The work would be the same.

Divide. Conquer.

Chapter Twenty-two

The President's tweet attack and threats of a national emergency combined with the swift actions of several governors who sent National Guard members to restore order at D.A.D and G.D.C support rallies in Chicago, Boise, Los Angeles, Dallas, Detroit and Madison, worked. Overwrought Americans disbursed and returned to their homes to simmer and plan.

For the moment, Guard members had pushed both sides back from the cliff of civil war, but it was not a resolution of peace, more an uneasy pause in a long-standing rift. There was most definitely a wall being built, but it wasn't on the southern border, it was being constructed right through the heart of America. Nakita's boss supplied the bricks and mortar.

##

Ruby had become a national hero to some and another symbol of government overreach to others. If she had been undecided before, the horror of the events in Anchorage had settled it. She was not a quitter. She would finish the final year of her term but not run for re-election. She regretted the disappointment of so many Alaskans who implored her to stay in, but she would return to Anchorage, run her business and be ready for grandkids when Ray jr. and Mo got hitched.

She didn't vocalize it, but she believed the U.S. Government was dangerously dysfunctional and she couldn't work with people who wrapped themselves in the Constitution but continually undermined it by putting politics, homophobia, racism, sexism and a host of other isms, above the rule of law.

Those who saw the future of America through the lens of manifest destiny and those who saw it through the lens of the green revolution were equally resolute in their insistence that compromise meant failure and the loss of the American dream. There could be fossil energy dominance or a denouncement of it to slow the ravages of climate change. There could not be both.

Ruby was grateful that congress was on summer break so she could stay in Anchorage for a couple of weeks. She'd almost closed the café for a few days but figured the city needed as much normalcy as possible, so instead she pitched in with Mo, Poppa Ray, her son, when he was off deadline, and the rest of the staff in cleaning, stocking and cooking. She held fundraisers at the café for families who had funeral or medical expenses resulting from the rallies turned riots. She did what she'd always done. Stayed busy and helped the community.

##

"Hey chief, wanna grab a beer?" Zilla was standing in the doorway of Ed Brooks's office. Four days after the riots stopped, Zilla had filed the last of her stories on the G.D.C.'s leadership, their compound and their determination to protect earth's natural systems. By any means necessary. They were no longer so easily dismissed as hippy greenies or snowflakes. They saw the fight for the future just as dire as the other side that still employed the mantra of exploitation. Cut. Kill. Mine. Drill. In a weird way, it had secretly raised their credibility with the D.A.D. Anyone willing to fight with real weapons rather than legal briefs was a worthy adversary and the next time there was a clash, it was on.

It was this analysis that Ed was pondering now, deep in thought as he stared at a digital page he'd edited and then edited again.

"Boss? Hello? It's after 6, which feels early after the last couple of weeks, but I could use a frosty one. How bout you?"

Brooks looked up, his eyes owly round and serious behind his glasses. Whisker stubble salt and peppered his chin. He absently rubbed the ever-present gold earring in his wrinkled lobe. "Uh....ok." He looked around at the piles of papers and books and then smiled, like a man in a maze who discovered the right way out. "Yes. I could use a cold beer too. Heading to Ruby's, I assume?" But she surprised him.

"Nope. Let's take a ride to Darwin's. Ruby's has been non-stop packed and I want to talk to you about something that's rolling around in my head."

"Hm. Ok, I'm intrigued." Without another word, he grabbed his keys and they walked through the newsroom and out the door. Zilla ran her hand along the edge of Murphy' desk as she walked by it, a new habit for her. As if the old wooden desk had soaked up enough Murphy essence to get her through this time of adjusting to his absence.

They jumped in Ed's old Datsun pickup and motored downtown, to park in front of Zilla's favorite coffee spot in Anchorage, Side Street Espresso, next to her second favorite watering hole in Anchorage, Darwin's Theory.

Darwin, the decades long owner was a savvy businessman who ran a bar that specialized in smart women bartenders that didn't put up with stupid behavior by people who couldn't handle their booze. Whether you were a life long resident or a 10-minute tourist, you were always welcome at Darwin's as long as you minded your damn manners.

The tiny bar could be wild on St Patrick's Day. Zilla had a distinct memory of Darwin, standing on the customer side of the bar in a leprechaun outfit, his long legs sticking out of green silk short shorts and a tipsy woman customer gleefully rubbed her hand in slow circles on his butt. During Fur Rondy and Iditarod, the bartenders dressed up in old time dance hall outfits that would have made Miss Kitty proud.

They squeezed in, past the bar and to the back where they grabbed a small table next to the popcorn machine. After their beers came, Zilla started talking.

"Ed, I've really enjoyed working with you." She locked eyes with him.

"Oh hell. I already don't like this conversation. Brooks took a long pull from his beer and leaned back on the barstool, holding Zilla's gaze.

"I'm not quitting. But I do want to leave."

"How's that?"

"I need a break boss. It's not the work, I love reporting. It's everything else. I can't get clear about August. Should I forget about it or go for it. I think he's having the same struggle."

Brooks winced. Relationship talk was scarier than any city under siege he'd reported on from conflict front lines across the world.

Zilla knew the signs and held her palm up to indicate she wasn't planning to go on. "And it's other stuff too. I just need to take off for a while."

"So, what's your plan? Do you have one?"

"Sort of. I bought a horse a few months ago. Boarding it out on Elmore Road. Did you know that?" he shrugged, she continued, "I'm going to ride toward the Brooks Range and spend some time in the backcountry. No phones, no television, no human noise other than my own."

"You're riding off into the sunset alone?"

"Well, I probably won't leave at sundown. Who really does that anyway? Why would you start a trip on horseback when it's getting dark? Stupid. And I'm not sure if I'll go alone. I just want to go for a few weeks. If I don't go now, I'll have to wait till spring. I'd rather not. Can you agree to this? To let me do this?"

Brooks drained his beer and signaled to the smiling bartender to bring two more. "Well, you do have a ton of vacation time stacked up Gillette and I understand the need to break free from time to time. Hell, if I was younger, and knew how to ride a damn horse, I'd go with you. Sounds like a worthy adventure. So go do it." He smiled and nodded. Classic Ed. Don't waste time navel gazing. Make a damn decision and execute it.

Zilla was relieved. She was happy this part was done, but the more difficult task of August, seeing August, not seeing August, not knowing what to do about August remained. That was next.

Jerry Justice was terrified of prison. Without the benefit of his props, cowboy hat, bandolier, leather holster with its shiny pistol and oosik, tall boots and of course a stage and microphone, he was just a small man with a balding head who would run nothing on the inside.

The scams that brought him riches and women outside of prison would get his ass beat inside those cells. He was somewhat relieved when the only charges that stuck were kidnapping, endangering the life of a member of the U.S. Congress and inciting mob violence. These were not shoplifting charges, but because MC Ames was successful in his suicide effort, there was no way to tie Murphy's murder to Justice.

He'd slimed his way out of it and the conservative judges he'd been brought in front of gave him some hand slaps in the form of 8 years with 5 suspended. He'd likely have a rough go of it in lock up, but he was a master finagler and he'd probably get out in 18 months for being a model prisoner.

##

"So, you're really taking off Gillette?" It was Friday night and word of Zilla's impending departure had filtered out through the newsroom and was the bar topic at Ruby's, where Ray, Zilla, Poppa Ray and a few other reporters were holding court and shooting pool. They felt the hole Murph left and set a chair at the end of the table with a glass full of beer from the pitcher they were sharing. Murph's spot.

Ray asked the question and all eyes turned toward her, which, she hated.

"Yes. And it's your shot." She pushed the pool cue she was holding forward, pointing it toward the table where she was winning. "Quit trying to throw off my game dude."

"I'm not. I just don't get it. The mosquitoes are gonna carry you away and drop you on a grizzly's dinner table. A month from now your horse will come wandering back to Anchorage and maybe a hiker will find your bones in a decade or two." Ray grinned broadly and comically leaned over the table and shot. There was no way he could win now so he was clowning.

"Charming Mr. Walker. Your imagination is weird and makes me worried for Mo and your future kids." She sunk the eight ball, won the game, stuck the pool stick back in the wall rack and sat down. The other reporters went back to shuffleboard and teasing each other.

Ray's smile softened and he got serious. "I know you'll get mad at me for saying this because it sounds sexist, but I wish you weren't going alone. A lot can happen out on the country Zee. To anyone. Will you at least take a satellite phone or a beacon transmitter? AND a gun?"

Now it was Zilla's turn to smile. "Yes, brother Ray. And I won't be alone I'll be on a damn fine palomino named Sunray. I'll take a sat phone, a rifle and my other new friend Jade." Zilla hadn't been able bring herself to get a dog, but she had a new trail companion and although her new pal didn't run, didn't bark and didn't jump around in circles, she was smart, attentive and increasingly friendly to Zilla.

Jade was a falcon and Zilla loved having her overhead on the trail rides she'd been taking to prepare for the long trip into the backcountry.

"Great. My best friend and work partner is relying on a guard with feathers to keep her safe."

"Not safe. I'll keep myself safe. Jade is a companion and a great hunter. We'll probably eat a lot of rabbits. I'm hoping to avoid mice for lunch, and she will alert me to a bear or moose long before I see it. That's all I ask for."

"What about August Zee? Are you gonna leave the poor dude hanging on forever or are you going to cut him loose?"

"He's a grown man Ray. He can decide whatever he wants for his life."

"But he wants you in it."

"I know."

"And you?"

"I asked him to fly to Anaktuvuk Pass in two weeks to meet me on the trail."

"You dog!" Ray laughed, jumped up and leaned over to hug her. Ruby sat at the end of the bar, talking with a patron. Mo made drinks, four ice filled glasses sat in front of her as she held two bottles of booze and poured with both hands, talking and laughing with customers all the while. Poppa Ray was checking on orders for gumbo and halibut tacos and for a few hours, everything felt normal, as if the terrible loss of the week before had only been a bad dream and the state and the country was still a place of unity, respect and service to each other.

Ray walked up to the bar and hugged his mom for the umpteenth time of the evening and Zilla said a little prayer for them all. Believing, as she always had that good would still prevail and democracy, with all of its loud messiness would remain strong.

Her homeland would stay united in the foundations of freedom, equality and respect. The triumph of justice, of love over fear and compassion over greed would grow stronger each day until this terrible time of division and near collapse of the country was a historical lesson in what not to do when you have the freedom to do anything.

THE END

Made in the USA
Monee, IL
08 August 2020